QUEEN

Queen of the Night

Rebecca Ambrose

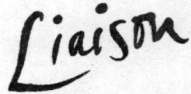

First published in 1997 by
HEADLINE BOOK PUBLISHING

A HEADLINE LIAISON paperback

10 9 8 7 6 5 4 3 2 1

ISBN 0 7472 5719 1

Typeset by Avon Dataset Ltd, Bidford-on-Avon, Warks

Printed and bound in Great Britain by
Mackays of Chatham plc, Chatham, Kent

HEADLINE BOOK PUBLISHING
A division of Hodder Headline PLC
338 Euston Road
London NW1 3BH

Queen of the Night

Chapter One

Justin Walker sat amidst the baroque splendour of the *Sala Caruso* in a state of utter terror. He had come to the summer school longing to meet the great Italian *diva,* Bella Conti, but now that the wonderful event was about to occur he was scared witless. The stifling heat of a Rome afternoon in mid-July didn't help either. Although the French windows leading to the upper balcony were half open there wasn't a hint of a breeze and his shirt was sticking to his chest and armpits.

Nervously he glanced around the room at his fellow students. There were about twenty of them but he only knew a few by name. One of those, Marina Stewart, gave him a wry grin as their eyes met across the rows of chairs. He'd chatted to her last night, after their first communal meal, confessing that he was a big fan of *La Bellissima,* often travelling to opera houses all around the world just to hear her magnificent voice in action.

Now he wished he hadn't said so much. Marina gave him a conspiratorial wink that was meant to be encouraging but only made him feel more apprehensive. It wasn't her fault, but Justin felt resentment grow in him. This was to be his special moment, a chance to get near to his idol, but Marina was already sharing it with him. Her blue eyes sparkled at him from across the room, bright and seductive against the pale gold of her skin and hair. Briefly he speculated about her. She was a sexy girl, no doubt about that, but did she have a voice?

There was an excited rustle in the room and Justin's eyes swivelled back to the door where Bella had already made her entrance. Silently cursing Marina for distracting him, Justin took a deep breath and concentrated his whole being on the

1

object of his devotion. This was what he'd been dreaming of for months, ever since he first saw the course advertised in *The Sunday Times*. Now the opera star was in the room with him, radiating glamour and charisma, and all he could do was stare in open-mouthed wonder.

Bella Conti seemed smaller in real life than on stage but that was inevitable. Without the magnificent costumes her figure was still impressive, the jutting bosom and slender waist giving her something of an hourglass shape, but she seemed shorter, more compact and her cotton top and jeans gave her an informal look that Justin found quite startling.

Eagerly his eyes took in every detail of the Italian woman's face. Her hair was dark and voluminous, curling around features that were more feline than he'd expected, with eyes that were nearer green than brown. If she was wearing make-up it was only the merest hint, for even her full lips were pale and natural-looking. Although not a classic beauty, Bella had the kind of looks that drew men's eyes and her voluptuous figure and proud carriage only emphasised the hint of sexual promise in her eyes. Justin thought she was the most exciting woman on earth.

'Good afternoon, everyone,' she began with a smile, her eyes scanning the small crowd. When her gaze lighted on Justin for a couple of seconds he felt as if he'd been given a benediction.

'It's so nice to see you all here,' she continued. 'As you know, this is the first summer school that Signor Postoni has held at the *Accademia del Voce* and I'm sure it's going to be a great success. Luigi is an old friend of mine, a man to whom I owe a great deal, so I am delighted to be able to give this master class for his students.'

The room now seemed filled with a different kind of warmth. Bella's soft, Latin tones had soothed everyone into a state of comfortable relaxation, Justin included. She went on to explain that she would be dealing with the topic of *coloratura* that afternoon, giving a demonstration of how the simplest melody could be turned into an elaborate show-piece of ornamentation, taxing even the most experienced singer and displaying their virtuosity.

2

'But I need a gentleman volunteer,' she smiled.

Justin felt his heart leap in his chest and a prickling sensation began at the nape of his neck before travelling throughout his body. Despite the adrenalin rush his balls felt heavy and his cock stirred a little. He wiped the trickle of sweat from his brow with the back of his hand.

'Don't worry,' she continued, her wry smile showing she understood the daunting nature of the prospect. 'All he will have to do is sing an *arpeggio continuo* while I elaborate upon it. I'm sure any one of you gentleman could perform the task perfectly. Who will . . . ?'

Justin felt his arm shoot up of its own accord, even though his eyes were blinded by the afternoon sun and his breathing was ragged. He sensed, rather than saw, those greenish eyes flit from one to the other of the eight males in the room.

A mocking voice in his head told him he hadn't a chance. Why should she choose him rather than anyone else? But he knew she was facing in his direction and then her voice came, low and insistent. 'The gentleman near the window, in the striped shirt – your name?'

Somehow Justin staggered to his feet, the backs of his knees pushing back the tubular steel chair. He stammered his name and she gave him a radiant smile. 'Justin,' she repeated. 'Would you come out here, please?'

As he made his way to the front he saw Marina out of the corner of his eye, grinning broadly, and felt a surge of irritation. That girl knew how much this meant to him, and she was just waiting for him to cock it up. Bitch!

Bella reached out and took hold of his upper arm, guiding him near to her. Justin was trembling all over, and not just because he'd been chosen to sing. It was all happening so quickly – too quickly! Just to be in the same room as this woman was an overwhelming experience, but now that she'd made physical contact with him it was devastating. He felt his knees sinking dangerously and swallowed hard. How the hell could she expect him to sing a note now that she'd actually touched him?

'Don't be nervous,' she said, hand still on his shoulder. 'You came here to sing, didn't you?' He nodded, but his throat was dry as dust. 'What are you? Tenor?' He nodded. 'Then we'll start with middle C. Take your stance, Justin. Will the girl near the piano give us the note, please?'

Although his mind was almost blank, Justin struggled to recall everything he'd learnt about singing. He could hear his tutor telling him to raise his rib-cage, push back his shoulders, plant his feet comfortably apart, but his body seemed incapable of following instructions. Frozen to the spot, he was only aware of the rich, exotic perfume that the *diva* wore, a perfume that was confusing him with its subtle assault on his senses.

'Come, Justin, you must stand well,' he heard her say, her tone verging on the severe. Jolted out of his temporary paralysis, he did his best to correct his posture and took several deep breaths.

'That's better. Now you look more like a singer.' She turned from him to address the others. 'Remember that before you utter a note you must look the part. I mean, the part of an opera singer. For you are playing that rôle first and foremost, over and above any other part you are going to play. Your audience must have confidence in you, and the way you move and stand is vital in establishing that at the start. Now, Justin, please give me your note.'

She nodded to the girl at the piano and then he did his best to imitate the sound that rang out into the silent room. His first effort was cracked, truncated, but Bella gave a sympathetic nod. 'Once again!'

His second note was stronger, longer, but still his usual richness of tone evaded him. Bella said, businesslike, 'Now continue with the descending arpeggio: doh, soh, mi, doh.' He performed it slowly. 'And up again, a little faster.'

Justin was in a strange state, in which his voice was performing of its own accord. The rest of him seemed to be in a kind of suspended animation. He couldn't bring himself to look at anything other than the back wall, with its framed opera posters against white plaster. The thought that everyone in the room was just waiting for him to screw up was so horrendous that he felt as if he were, literally, singing to save his life.

Then, out of the blue, came a sudden clear note that made all his anguish worthwhile. Bella was singing, and the room rang with sweetness. It was obvious that she was singing *mezza voce*. If she didn't moderate that magnificent voice she'd probably break the windows, Justin thought. She began her ornamentation, adding brilliant little trills that made his spine tingle. His own voice wavered a little as he began to lose himself in the beauty of her performance, and she gave him a split-second frown which was enough to put him off his stroke even further. He lost the rhythm of the arpeggio and they became out of sync. She stopped in mid-flight and his singing faltered to a halt.

'You should never let a woman put you off,' she told him, eliciting relieved laughs from the audience. Justin caught sight of Marina, who was grinning sympathetically, and scowled.

'I'm sorry. It's just that you were so . . .'

'Never mind, we'll try again. You know what they say, Justin – once more, with feeling!' He began the descending notes with new determination, but his tone was too breathy. Nevertheless he persevered and soon Bella's bosom began to swell beneath her loose cotton top as she inhaled deeply. Again the sound that came forth was sweet and sure, running agile rings around every note he uttered, making him feel like an incompetent fool. If only he hadn't volunteered for this torture! But it was too late. Here he was making a prize prat of himself in front of the assembled students on the first afternoon of the course and there was the rest of the month to go. Would he ever live this down?

Like a bird caught up in a powerful thermal Bella's voice soared its way to high C, performing elaborate aerobatics that held the whole room under her spell. Justin knew she was singing well within her range. She was famous for her high *tessitura*. Although she was spilling the notes out at top speed each one was crystal clear and perfectly pitched, turning the routine exercise into a dazzling display of vocal pyrotechnics. When she finally laid the last of her cadenzas to rest the room exploded into hysterical applause.

Smiling she bowed, first at her audience and then at

Justin, who was flushed with a mixture of shame and excitement. Her expression was part sympathy, part contempt. It was the sort of look that Don José might have received from Carmen after she'd tired of him.

Then, before the clapping died away, Bella began speaking to him, *sotto voce*. 'I said, "with feeling", dear. You sang like a metronome, though not as exact. You are English, yes?'

As he nodded, speechless with embarrassment, Justin realised that the room had gone quiet. Everyone heard her next remark. 'I thought so. Ah, you Englishmen, you are so cold, so lacking in passion. How can you ever make great singers? You sing with the head, not with the heart. I hope you do not make love the same way!'

A titter went round the room and Justin wished he could sink through the floor. How dare she make such outspoken judgements when she didn't know him? Marina was grinning openly at him from the second row. She, above all, must know how complete his humiliation was.

And yet he was amazed to find that a part of him revelled in Bella's criticism, craved it even. He wanted her to tell him how presumptuous he was to dream of singing with the *diva*, how inevitable it was that he should sound like a croaking frog beside her exquisite performance. He longed to throw himself at her feet and tell her he was not worthy to be in her presence, let alone to sing along with her in that travesty of a duet.

Instead, he shuffled back to his seat with scarlet cheeks, hoping no-one would stare at him. Fortunately Bella soon went on to describe her performance as Queen of the Night in *The Magic Flute*, a part of which she was the acknowledged mistress, and everyone listened with rapt attention while she played some recordings and gave them a commentary.

The rest of the afternoon passed quickly, but Justin's mind scarcely registered a word or a note. He was too involved in his own fantasies. Time and again he imagined himself playing opposite *La Bellissima* as her fans called her, his voice more than equal to the task. He would play Pinkerton to her Butterfly, Alfredo to her Violetta, Rodolfo to her Mimi. He would . . .

'So thank you all, so much, for giving me your time and attention this afternoon . . .'

Justin was jolted back to reality by her closing words. He rose with the rest of the class to give her the customary standing ovation. She smiled graciously and slipped out through the door, leaving a flutter and buzz behind her. With a shock, Justin realised that she was not scheduled to make another appearance until she presented the awards in the end-of-course festival. He felt bereft. He alone of all the students had been singled out for glory, and he had failed abysmally. How could he face any of them again?

Although he did his best to avoid it, a confrontation with Marina seemed inevitable. She caught up with him in the corridor when all the others were streaming off to the café downstairs. 'Justin – how do you feel, after singing with a goddess?'

He turned on her with a black scowl, but she laughed in his face and within a few seconds he found himself laughing with her. It really was absurd, after all. He was taking himself far too seriously. And there was something enormously appealing about those bright blue eyes and full, pink lips. She was twisting a strand of her fair hair around her forefinger, coquettishly, and Justin felt a healthy pang of uncomplicated lust for her.

'Crap!' he grinned. 'I was utter crap, and please don't insult me by pretending I wasn't.'

'Oh, you were crap all right,' she cheerfully agreed, linking her arm through his. 'Come on, I'll treat you to a *caffè correto*. You look like you need it.'

'*Correto?*'

'Yeah. It's what the Italians call coffee with *grappa*. Corrected. Their idea of a joke.' Once they were seated in the bar with a small table and two fragrant cups of coffee between them, Justin felt more relaxed. It was a relief to confide in Marina, to tell her how he was now dreading the rest of the course.

'Don't be daft, everyone will have forgotten about your performance by tomorrow,' she assured him.

'Do you really think so?'

Her clear blue eyes held his for a moment. 'Look, any one of us would have felt the same if we'd been picked to sing with her. Talk about putting you on the spot! I thought you did brilliantly, in the circumstances. Okay, so you didn't give the performance of your life, but you kept in tune and kept going, which was all that was required of you. Don't kid yourself, Justin, she only wanted your voice as a foil for her own. She's just a big show-off!'

Justin grinned. He was warming to Marina. Maybe the rest of the month wouldn't be such an ordeal after all.

They chatted about themselves for a while and he discovered that she lived in Reading with two other students. Suddenly she asked if he had a regular girlfriend. He shook his head and her eyes sparkled wickedly at him.

'So you're out of practice in the passion department, just like Bella said. Well, if you need any private tuition, I was complimented on my Carmen in the Tilehurst Operatic Association's annual gala last spring!'

She was teasing him, he was sure. Yet as their eyes met Justin saw a hint of desire lurking there and suddenly realised that she fancied him. A tingle of electricity took him unawares, but then reality took hold. He wasn't here to fool around, only to learn as much as he could.

Even so, his eyes dropped automatically to the attractive swell of her breasts beneath the lemon cotton top she was wearing, a colour that set off her light tan to perfection. There was no doubt about it, Marina was a very attractive girl. He felt flattered by her interest in him, but that was as far as it would go.

'Carmen – that must be a marvellous part to play,' he said, neatly side-stepping the insinuation she'd made.

But she wouldn't let him off the hook that easily. 'Passion, Justin, that's what it's all about. As far as I'm concerned that sums up all opera. You have to really feel it to make it work, just like love-making. Don't you agree?' Again she was challenging him with those naughty eyes.

'I've always wondered about Bella,' he said. 'Everyone knows she's not married, but does she have lovers? She described Luigi Postoni as an old friend, but is he more than that?'

'It's none of our business, is it'

Marina sounded surprisingly frosty. Justin shrugged. 'Course not, I just wondered what drives that voice of hers. Sometimes it sounds like it's powered by sheer lust.'

'Hm. Well, I must get going. There's the director's reception tonight and I want to have a bit of a siesta beforehand.'

'See you later, then.'

He watched her walk away, the trim behind swaying just a little in the tight jeans. Maybe he'd take her up on her offer later in the course, when he felt more confident. Right now the idea of screwing anyone seemed impossible. He felt . . . emasculated, was that the word? Being put down like that in front of everyone had been a dreadful ordeal. And yet, because it was Bella who had done it, he couldn't deny that there was a certain perverse satisfaction in it. That magnificent look of contempt she'd thrown at him, those scathing tones. For a few intense seconds he'd felt ready to grovel at her feet, to thank her for his public humiliation. He'd never had such feelings before and it was all very strange, abnormal. But then *La Bellissima* was far from being a normal woman. Being enclosed in her aura had been like entering a rarefied atmosphere and he was still reeling from the after-effects.

The students were dispersing, returning to their rooms in nearby hotels, and Justin felt the need to be alone. He'd begun to wonder whether Bella would be putting in an appearance at the reception that evening. If so, he wasn't sure how he would face her. It might be better not to risk it, say he'd had a bit of a tummy upset or something. The way he felt right now that mightn't be far from the truth.

The single room where he was staying was hot and noisy, being situated on the first floor with chaotic Rome traffic honking away outside. Even so, it seemed a welcome haven. Justin showered then lay down on the bed wrapped only in a towel. He still felt shell-shocked. Over and over again he was replaying the scene as he would like to have played it, with himself as hero. Instead of the humiliating lack of conviction in his singing he would have risen to the occasion, stunning everyone with the magnificence of his voice.

He sighed, imagining the surprised smile on Bella's face as she realised that she had picked a winner at random from the motley crowd. His mellow tenor voice would perfectly complement her exquisite soprano one. Together they would make music to send shudders down every spine, earning him the eternal envy of his fellow students. At the end she would bow to him with a slightly ironic smile, her bosom heaving with emotion.

'Thank you,' she would say, with deep sincerity in her dark eyes. Justin would return her smile with just the right degree of irony, enjoying her pleasure in the discovery of his voice.

Afterwards she would ask him to stay behind, tell him she just had to try out some parts with him. Her excitement would be evident, her cheeks flushed, her eyes piercingly bright. Justin would play it cool, of course, casually agreeing to meet her later in one of the practice rooms at the academy. They would be alone, without even a *répétiteur* to play for them. Excitedly she would put him through his paces, their voices blending perfectly in duet after duet. Then she would ask him to dine with her at her sumptuous apartment near the Via Veneto. She would tell him how she was going to make him a star. They would drink lots of top quality wine and then . . .

Justin's hand crept below the towel to his growing erection. It was some time since he'd had a wank, but now he felt the urge quite strongly. A vision of Bella in the costume she wore as Desdemona at Covent Garden suddenly came back to him, the diaphanous golden dress with the low neck in which her breasts swung like bells when Otello pushed her to the ground. His cock swelled up to its throbbing maximum, thick and meaty in his hand, and he felt a surge of restored pride.

Imagining it was Bella's palm that enclosed his shaft, picturing the expression of passionate longing that possessed her features, he began to rub himself gently. The tinglings in his glans intensified and he had a vision of passing between sturdy open thighs. The huge breasts were on display in his mind's eye, firmer and more delectable than he would have expected, and his mouth fastened on each dark nipple in turn, eliciting delightful squeals of pleasure from his mistress. His cock nudged at the damp crevice beneath the curly dark hairs and at last found its way in.

His palm sticky with juice, Justin imagined the unutterable bliss of that moment when he mastered the woman who had long ago conquered him. Fiercely he would ride her, making her submit to him with elaborate cadenzas of ecstasy and trilling cries of bliss. He would make her sing all right, longer and louder than any man had done before him. The long, horny note of her coming would be unearthly, shattering, and would trigger him . . . oh yes! . . . trigger him so that he joined her in the ultimate expression of harmony.

Justin gasped and shuddered as his orgasm set his whole body afire, spurting over the towel. It was a long time since he'd climaxed so intensely and after he'd wiped himself he lay there in a daze, marvelling at the power of fantasy. Yet it was *she* who had done that to him. Bella was truly a love goddess, a star who gave to opera what Monroe had given to cinema, the ultimate image of female sexual power. And the thought that he had sung with her, that she had touched him, paid attention to him, was still terrifying. If she looked at him with scorn in her eyes once more, he would die.

'I can't go to that party tonight,' he told himself 'I just can't face her again.'

Four hours later, Justin was standing in the reception room of the academy with a glass of Asti Spumante in his hand. The room was imposing, with its baroque plaster ceiling, chandeliers and gilt mirrors. It reminded all who entered it that the greatest voices in the world had given recitals there. Despite the imposing décor and nervous fluttering in his stomach, Justin knew he'd been right to come after all. It would have looked really bad if he'd stayed away after that afternoon's fiasco.

Besides, people were actually being nice to him. Three of the students had come up to tell him how brave he'd been to

11

take up the challenge of singing with *La Bellissima* and had made him feel perhaps he hadn't made quite such a hash of it after all. One of the men had even said that to expect him to sing with feeling had been asking too much: it was a marvel that he'd been able to sing at all. So he was feeling much better about himself by the time he caught Marina's eye.

She was looking absolutely stunning in a pink mini-dress with a low V-neck, showing plenty of plump cleavage. Her blonde hair was fluffed out around her shoulders and glinted fetchingly in the light from the chandeliers. Her legs were lean and tanned in their minimal gold sandals and she was balanced on the tiny heels with perfect confidence. When she smiled at him his earlier arousal returned with a vengeance and he found himself wondering whether her invitation to explore their mutual passion was still open. Then he saw who she was talking to, and his spirits sank. What hope did he have of attracting her to his side when Luigi Postoni himself was giving her his full attention?

The director of the academy was an incredibly good-looking Italian with just the sort of world-weary good looks that women fell for. A Marcello Mastroianni type with liquid brown eyes, his flowing dark locks were tinged with just enough grey at the temples and his tall frame was in obvious good shape. From the way he was looking at Marina she could be in with a chance, too. Lucky bastard! Justin could almost taste envy in his mouth, turning the sweetish fizz sour.

But then something happened in the room. Although he was facing away from the door, Justin felt his spine prickle as everyone's head seemed to turn towards the entrance. It had to be *her*. Sporadic applause broke out to confirm it, but he still couldn't bring himself to turn around and face her. All his fake confidence was oozing out of him, like spunk in a wet dream.

'Thank you, everyone! *Salute*!' he heard her say, a laugh in her throat as she acknowledged the ovation. There was a clink of glasses as she proposed a toast: 'To the eternal beauty of the Opera, its aspiring singers and its devoted fans!'

At last he turned and saw her, resplendent in a tight-fitting dress of iridescent green. The light bounced off the sequinned material, dazzling him, and her face was made up with dramatic emphasis as if for the stage. Her coral lips were full and sensual, reminding him of his self-indulgent fantasy about her, and he felt a flush creep about his ears. God, why did she make him feel like a dirty little schoolboy whenever he was in the same room with her?

Two girls came up and engaged him in conversation, for which he was grateful. They were nice enough, but their earnest talk about various artists and performances soon bored him. His eyes kept straying to the two women who interested him more. They made quite a contrast with each other, Marina being young and horny in a carefree, casual style and Bella being the sophisticated *femme fatale* type, for how could she be anything else? They seemed to represent two opposite poles of female sexuality, and now that they were both caught up in conversation with the director their juxtaposition fascinated him.

'Justin, I don't think you've been listening to a word I've been saying!' one of the girls grumbled.

'No . . . sorry. Actually I'm dying to go to the loo. Not too good for the concentration, I'm afraid. Be back soon.'

It wasn't really a lie. Justin's bladder always called when he was nervous and now he felt in dire need of a leak. He sidled through the crowd and out into the corridor, welcoming the quietness and solitude. After his earlier fantasising, seeing Bella in the flesh was just too much. Unlike the way she'd appeared earlier in the day she was now looking more like her stage persona, radiating glamour and charisma. He didn't think he could stand being too close to her for too long.

But the minute he re-entered the room she seemed to make a beeline for him. He averted his eyes but she was on him at once, touching his arm to gain his attention and sending hot spirals of panic through his system. 'Justin – don't run away. I wanted to give you my apology.'

'Apology?' He stared into her dark eyes. They seemed full of genuine contrition.

'Yes, for being such a cow this afternoon. First I put you on the spot, then I criticise not just your performance but your very personality. It was unforgivable.'

'No, you were right. My singing did lack passion.'

Bella smiled, her eyes twinkling at him. 'Dear boy, you are young. True passion is like the bouquet of a fine wine, it comes with maturity. But it was cruel of me to make you look a fool in front of the others and I am sincerely sorry. I treated you like a hardened professional instead of a sweet and enthusiastic amateur.'

'I've heard you tend to be a bit hard on people.'

Justin couldn't believe he'd just said that. But instead of being affronted, Bella laughed. 'You shouldn't believe all you hear through the media. Still, I hope you enjoy the rest of the course. Your singing is bound to improve if you practise daily and have a good teacher.'

'If you taught me, I'm sure I'd improve.'

Again Justin was amazed by his boldness, but he asked himself what he had to lose. Surely the worst had already happened. He couldn't imagine anything more traumatic than being made to took a fool in front of everyone by the woman he most idolised.

'Are you asking me for lessons?'

Bella was smiling at him but he wanted to sink through the floor. 'No, of course not! I wouldn't presume . . .'

'You couldn't afford, you mean! I am a realist, Justin. But it would be a way for me to make amends, wouldn't it? We would just have to think of a way for you to repay me.'

He could see that she was reflecting on something but it was too much to hope that she was actually going to become his singing teacher. Perhaps she was about to recommend someone else. Someone back in London, perhaps. A word from her would give him valuable kudos in the eyes of any teacher. Hope soared within him.

Chapter Two

Marina knew she would attract some male attention at the reception. She'd made a special effort with her appearance and the cloud of Schiaparelli perfume that followed her about was heady and seductive. She felt good in herself too, with that extra dash of vitality that she knew would make her stand out in a crowd. But she hadn't counted on hooking such a big fish as Signor Postoni himself.

When she first arrived Marina had wondered about approaching Justin but thought better of it. She prided herself on being a pretty good judge of men, and that one needed time and effort spent on him. He was probably the sort who needed to feel emotionally involved with a girl before he bedded her, and afterwards there might be complications. Tonight she was in the mood for a good, no-nonsense fuck and she hoped she was sending out the right signals.

So when Luigi Postoni came up to her with his suave Latin smile and asked her if she'd been to Rome before, Marina felt a buzz of sexual excitement.

'No, this is my first time,' she said, with a flirty grin. 'I'm hoping to find out just what it is you Romans do, so I can do it too.'

'Ah, "when in Rome", eh? I like that!' His laugh came from deep in his throat, making her tingle all over. God, he was good-looking! Like some Latin film star, a *divo*, who knocked the socks off any of the Englishmen present. His dark, bushy hair was worn long and inviting, making her fingers itch to penetrate its silken mass. His head was large and leonine, his features well-defined. Thick brows arched expressively over brown eyes, in whose depths reflected all the subtleties of his moods. His nose was long and narrow, his lips full and red, with the ripeness of soft fruit. Marina wanted to taste him, all of him, in one long orgy of sensuality.

'Well, one thing we Romans like to do is sing,' he smiled. 'So we have that in common, do we not?' His eyes dropped to her pert breasts. 'You have beautiful . . . posture, my dear. That augurs well for the voice. I look forward to hearing you sing. Do you have a favourite aria?'

'Not really. I love singing so much that I enjoy anything. Before I came here I was working on 'Depuis le jour' from *Louise*.'

'Ah, delightful! Louise's hymn to love. If you like that opera you must also like *La Bohème* since it has a similar Bohemian setting.'

'Yes, I love it.'

'Have you given any thought to what you might perform at the festival? I know this is only the first day of the course, but I shall be urging everyone to begin work on their presentation tomorrow. *Bohème* might be a good choice for you.'

'Do you think so?'

'Oh yes. I can see you as Mimi. You certainly look the part, with your lovely slim figure and big eyes. Not that I'm suggesting there's anything unhealthy about you, of course.'

'I should hope not!'

Marina felt the bubbling wine go to her head, but she scarcely needed its effect since she was feeling pretty high already. She and the director seemed to be getting on brilliantly, and who knew where that might end? An affair would be wonderful. She sensed that he was an experienced lover and a man who knew better than to confuse sex with love. But what if her association with him proved to be a boost to her career? A man like Luigi knew everyone who was anyone in the world of opera. His name could open quite a few doors for her. He might even invite her to study here, at the most famous voice academy in Italy.

'Excuse me, I must have a word with someone,' he murmured. The disappointment on her face must have been obvious because he added, in a low voice that thrilled its way deep into the core of her, 'I'll see you again later, I promise.'

He gave her a wink then melted into the crowd. Marina felt at a loss and went to get her glass refilled. She noticed, much to her surprise, that Justin was with Bella. She thought he'd have avoided that woman like the plague this evening. Drifting across to where two of the more attractive male students were standing, Marina made an effort at bright conversation.

'Hi! Enjoying the free booze?' she began, thinking that was about their level.

The one she fancied more gave her a wide grin. 'Don't kid yourself – we've paid for every drop of this stuff, and I mean to have my full share.'

'You're just a piss-head, Laurence,' his friend remarked, dryly.

'Well, if you think I'm only here for the *Nastro Azurro* you're quite wrong. I like this fizzy stuff too!'

'Better mind you're not too hung over tomorrow,' Marina warned. '*Maestro* told me they're going to start putting us through our paces with a vengeance.'

Laurence laughed. 'I sing better when I'm pissed. All men do, didn't you know?'

'Now that's a matter of opinion. I'm sure all men *think* they do . . .'

After passing about twenty minutes in similar inconsequential chat, Marina began to get bored. Talking about alcohol always bored her – she would much rather talk about opera. But somehow it seemed bad form this evening. Everyone seemed to want to pretend they were here on holiday, not to improve their knowledge of the art of opera or their vocal technique. She glanced around the room and caught Luigi's eye. He smiled at her, causing an immediate acceleration in her pulse. 'God, I fancy him something rotten!' she told herself.

An Italian radio crew arrived, and Marina was one of several students who gave the eager reporter some sound-bites. Luigi had a longer interview, but although she strained hard Marina couldn't quite hear what he said. It was enough just to watch him from across the room, enjoying the workings of his mobile mouth and expressive eyes.

Then, around midnight, she was aware of him edging through the crowd towards her. It wasn't obvious, he was exchanging a few words with people on the way, but she knew beyond any doubt that she was his destination and the thought sent a fizzing excitement through her veins. She felt the hard cones of her nipples pressing against her uplift bra and knew that they were visible beneath the gauzy cotton of her dress.

Luigi's eyes lighted on them as he came towards her, a faint smile on his handsome face. He raised his glass to her. 'More wine, Marina?'

'I think I've probably had enough. I feel quite tipsy.'

He spoke low, close to her ear, in that sexy murmur that had sent desire spiralling through her before. 'In that case, you'll need an escort back to your hotel.' He glanced at his elegant Philippe Patek watch. 'The party should be breaking up in a few minutes. Meet me in the foyer at midnight.'

'Do you promise not to turn into a pumpkin?'

'Shouldn't that be a frog? I thought that was the fate of handsome princes, and I'm studying the part of Prince Igor at the moment.'

Marina thought he would look fantastic as the Russian prince, decked out in some exotic costume. She looked him in the eye, her lips curving into the smile of a temptress. 'Oh, that only happens when you kiss them.'

His grin widened then he began mingling with the crowd again, playing the part of the gracious host, putting on an act. Marina found it amusing to watch him, knowing he knew she was watching him, seeing him almost camp it up for her. She noticed that Bella had already left and that Justin was looking remarkably self-satisfied, arousing her curiosity. But before she could go over to speak to him Luigi was calling for silence.

'I just want to thank you all for coming tonight, and giving our course a good start. Tomorrow, of course, the hard work begins but I hope it will also be a great pleasure for you all. It has certainly been a pleasure for me to have my dream of a summer school here in this beautiful academy fulfilled. I would like to thank all my staff who made it possible. And now, please return to your hotels for a good night's sleep, everyone – you are going to need it!'

Marina smiled and clapped along with the rest, but she hoped that his last remark had not been aimed at her. Sleep was the last thing on her mind right now and, from the way he'd been looking at her all evening, she guessed that he felt likewise.

Laurence came up and started making jokey conversation. He seemed very drunk, and Marina was afraid he might make a pass at her, the way he was ogling her cleavage. But just as his behaviour was becoming embarrassing, Luigi came to her rescue.

'Marina, would you mind coming along to my office for a moment? I'd like a word.'

'Word, my arse!' she heard Laurence exclaim as she followed the director to the door. 'He just wants to shag you, girl. You watch out for him!'

She gave a wry smile. Little did he know! Still, it bothered her slightly that their mutual attraction was so obvious.

Luigi went into his well-appointed office and switched on a table lamp. 'Actually, I thought you might want to get away from that young man,' he grinned. 'This was the best excuse I could think of. But, since we're here, would you like to listen to a recording of Giulia Veldoni singing Louise's aria?'

'Oh, yes please!' Marina's enthusiasm was genuine. She was an admirer of the Sicilian singer. 'I didn't know she'd recorded it.'

'Very few people know about it. It's on a new album of arias and chansons, due to be released for Christmas. She let me have an advance copy.'

Once again Marina was reminded that here was a man who mingled intimately with all the stars of the opera world, especially those on the Italian circuit. As she settled into the deep, leather sofa the pure tones of Giulia's voice rang out and she instantly relaxed.

'Glorious voice,' Luigi murmured, coming to sit beside her. Although the sofa was huge, Marina felt the virile heat emanating from his body, enfolding her like a shawl. There was an electric energy building between them that was almost tangible. She leaned back and closed her eyes, letting her sandals loosen and fall from her feet. This was bliss!

They listened in silence to the rest of the album, and all the while Marina was aware of the growing sexual tension between them. Although her eyes were closed, she sneaked a few glances beneath her lashes at Luigi's handsome face and felt herself becoming more aroused. Her breasts were tingling, the exposed cleavage swelling in her tight bra, and her stiff nipples ached for some stimulation. Between her thighs she could feel the soft folds of her labia moisten and slacken as her clitoris grew to throbbing prominence.

The music stopped, followed by a few tense seconds of total silence. Marina's lashes fluttered open and she saw that Luigi was smiling at her. Slowly her lips curved in response.

'Magnificent!' she breathed, stretching her arms and legs in a catlike gesture. 'I wish I could sing like that.'

'Maybe you will, one day.'

Luigi's eyes were dark and lustrous, dropping to the tight cleft between her breasts. She took a deep breath and saw his look smoulder. Casually she put out a hand and let it fall onto his broad shoulder. 'Well, I suppose I should get going.'

'Not yet.'

He turned in his seat, placed a finger beneath her chin and stared deep into her eyes. 'You are a bewitching creature you know, Marina. I spotted you right from the start. I thought, there is a beautiful woman who also has great presence. If her voice is as good as she looks, she will be a sensation some day.'

'Really?'

Marina didn't believe his flattery for one moment, but it served to intensify her desire for him. Her heart was thudding loudly, and she ran her tongue over her tumid lips then swallowed hard as his finger traced a gentle, tickling path from her chin down her throat and onto her chest. The tormenting anticipation had turned her body rigid, stopped her breathing.

'Yes, really,' he murmured, his lips slowly approaching hers. 'You have a voice within you, Marina, that has yet to be found. Your name suggests a goddess of the sea, and like the ocean you have hidden depths . . .'

His lips brushed hers with teasing lightness, setting them a-quiver. Slowly he gathered her into his arms, his hands pressing into her lean flesh, the pressure of his lips increased, pushing hers apart. His tongue slipped in to find hers and she gave a great sigh of release as the kiss became searching, passionate, and his right hand began to caress her bare arm.

'Oh!' she moaned, her skin becoming sensitised to his touch. His tongue felt like wet silk against hers.

Luigi's rich voice thrilled her with its sultry inflexion. 'Gorgeous woman! So beautiful, so passionate . . .'

She liked being called a passionate woman by a man who was not afraid of having such feelings. So many of her English boyfriends had been stolid, inhibited types. Although his compliments were over the top she was revelling in them, just as she was relishing his unashamedly sensual approach to love-making. It was a long time since she'd looked forward to a sexual encounter as much as this, and she was determined to make the most of it.

Now his lips were moving away from hers to feast on the soft flesh of her neck, making her shudder with longing. His fingers pulled at the straps of her dress until they hung down her arms, loosening the tension on the bodice. All Marina's senses were on full alert, and she could smell the spicy-citrus scent of his shampoo as he bent his head to her bosom. She touched his soft hair, her fingers slipping easily into the silken mass, and heard him moan her name. A wet sliver of tongue probed between her engorged breasts and at the same time his fingers pulled at her neckline, delved right into the lacy cups of her bra and found the tense nipples.

Marina was in blissful heaven. Her nipples were ultra sensitive and she loved having them pinched and licked. While his mouth continued to graze on the plump slopes of her breasts his fingertips tweaked at the swollen buds, scratched them lightly, rolled them around until they were pulsing out strong signals to the rest of her body that this man meant business. Her panties felt wet and clinging, and she began to crave stimulation down below.

21

Luigi's right hand dropped to her thigh. Lifting up the hem of her short dress he found the bare flesh beneath and began to stroke with a tantalising touch. His lips found a jutting nipple and fastened on it hungrily while his other hand was caressing her breast. Marina moaned, plunging her hands into the thick, dark mane. Her breath was ragged now, caught up in the heady flow of her emotions as she surrendered to the currents of excitement that were winging their way around her body.

Then she felt him slipping away from her, down past the quivering slopes of her breasts, his hot breath searing through the flimsy dress. With a groan she opened her thighs to him and his lips fastened on the delicate inner skin, notching up her desire to fever pitch. His hands crept beneath the brief panties and found her damp bush. She began to push them down and he helped her get them out of the way, laying bare her sex. Gentle fingers parted her labia, opened up her entire vulva to his gaze, while she continued to moan with soft insistence.

'Oh yes,' she heard him say, his voice raw with lust. 'Luscious, quite luscious!'

His gourmet mouth began to suck on her, treating her pussy as an exquisite delicacy. Marina found herself moving towards new heights of ecstasy as her melting flesh yielded new subtleties of sensation. Luigi's experience as a lover was evident as he played his tongue around her melting lips, avoiding the overheated clitoris – not from ignorance, she was sure of that, but only to make her want him more and more. He blew softly on her swollen tissues, caressed the convoluted flesh gently with his fingertips, found the gaping entrance to her cunt and dabbled in the fresh stream of moisture that his ministrations had provoked. Marina sighed with relief, wiggling her pelvis as his finger found her eager clitoris and began to stroke it.

Suddenly he lifted his head and, for a few seconds, Marina felt abandoned until she realised what he was going to do. His mouth returned to smother hers, his left hand played with her hungry clitoris and his right forefinger slipped inside her pussy, where she gripped him tightly. At

22

last her aching need was being satisfied.

While he slid in and out of her, Luigi pressed hard on her clitoris with his thumb and she felt her arousal spiralling out of her control. With complete abandon, Marina gave in to the accelerating waves of pleasure. Her hips circled around, thrusting her pelvic mound against his hand to increase the friction on her clitoris and soon the overwhelming tide of orgasm was upon her, making her gasp and moan as the spasms of sensual energy pulsed through her, again and again. She forgot everything – where she was, who she was with – as bodily delight enveloped her consciousness completely.

'Oh God!' she breathed at last, coming back to reality through a haze of diminishing bliss. 'That was amazing! It felt so . . . wonderful!'

Luigi returned to licking her, tasting the exotic juices as they streamed out of her, but soon it became unbearable for her over-sensitised flesh and she pushed his head away.

'Enough!'

'That word isn't in my vocabulary,' he grinned up at her. 'But if you insist.' She gathered him to her bosom, stroking the smattering of grey hair at his temple. For a while she lay in a doze, but soon the thought of reciprocating his foreplay occurred to her and she whispered in his ear, 'Now it's your turn . . .'

The thought of performing fellatio on him was suddenly very tempting. She was curious to see what kind of cock he had, and the idea of making him come with her mouth was alluring. Her hand drifted to his fly but he seized it before she could undo his zipper, saying firmly, 'No, *cara*. Not now.'

'Why not?'

'Because it is late and we should both be in bed.'

Marina grinned wickedly. 'What a good idea!'

He wagged a reproving finger at her. 'I don't know, you English girls! You have – how do you say? A "single-track mind".'

'One-track mind, Luigi dear.'

Too late, she saw him freeze at the familiarity. He got up off the couch and told her to get dressed. Marina felt as if he'd thrown a bucket of icy water over her. He turned and threw her a short-lived smile, but his eyes were cold.

'Tomorrow we both have work to do,' he reminded her.

She shrugged, pulling on her panties. 'Pity.'

'This isn't a holiday. You are here to work. I shall order a taxi to take you to your hotel.'

Marina dressed quickly, with fumbling fingers. After the heated abandon of their love-making she felt as embarrassed as a teenager on her first date. Had she said or done something wrong? In vain she trawled through her memory for snippets of their conversation but could find nothing untoward.

Even so, the idea that she'd somehow offended him grew as he phoned for a cab then ushered her quickly out of his office and into the dimly-lit corridor. They walked in silence to the deserted foyer, where he lit a cigarette without offering her one. She was surprised to see him smoking and he must have noticed because he remarked, casually, 'There's no evidence that the occasional cigarette harms the throat. Even the great Pavarotti is partial to a cigar now and then.'

Marina could think of nothing more to say, and he just stood in silence gazing through the glass door into the night. Mercifully the taxi arrived before the silence became too embarrassing. He got into the car with her, telling the driver to continue to his villa after dropping the young lady at her hotel. For five minutes she had to endure more of his silence, then the hotel came into sight and Luigi leaned across to open the cab door for her.

'Well, er . . . I suppose I'll see you tomorrow then,' she mumbled as she scrambled out.

'*Buona sera, Signorina*,' he said with crisp formality, his eyes staring sightlessly through the windscreen. Marina felt her heart sink like lead.

In the privacy of her hotel room she soon gave vent to her feelings by pumping her fists into the pillow. 'Bastard!' she exclaimed beneath her breath. She felt used and humiliated, angry with herself for being so naive as to imagine there was anything more in it for her than a quick thrill. He'd been on an ego-trip, that was all. Once it was over he couldn't wait to get rid of her, and now she had to face him for the rest of the course. What a stupid cow she'd been!

Marina undressed quickly in the small bathroom. Her body was still in a state of arousal, the scent of her love-juices assailing her nostrils when she removed her panties, but she was too tired to do more than wash herself in the bidet. She sprayed the jet of warm water on her clitoris and felt the old urges returning despite her fatigue. Seizing the soap she gave her crevices a thorough cleaning and, in the process, felt her libido rising. Luigi had only awakened her appetite, not sated it.

'Now, what do I do?' she asked herself. 'I ignore it and go to sleep, or get out my vibrator?' She decided it would do her more good to prove that she didn't need any pompous prick like Luigi Postoni to get her off, that she could satisfy herself. Besides, she thought with a smile, he hadn't made any attempt to fuck her. Did that mean he couldn't get it up? Or perhaps his dick was so small that he hadn't wanted her to see it. As she flicked the switch on her 'deluxe probe-'n-stim' Marina gave a low chuckle.

Soon the familiar feelings were reviving in her, but as the humming rubber dildo took her steadily towards orgasm Marina found herself thinking of Justin, her fellow student. He, too, had suffered humiliation by a leading light of the academy, and she felt a strong sympathy for him. The idea that they should console themselves with each others' bodies was an exciting one, and as the final phase of her climax juddered its way through her nervous system the image that dominated her mind was of the pair of them fucking like there was no tomorrow.

It won't happen, Marina told herself sleepily as she tossed the silenced dildo into the bedside drawer and pulled the sheet up over her shoulders. Justin's already made it clear I'm not in the running. He's not interested in anyone but *La Bellissima,* and she's certainly not interested in him. If I made a play for him I'd probably find myself locked into a classic eternal triangle.

* * *

The following morning Marina made her way to the rehearsal room, hoping she wouldn't bump into the director en route. When she arrived the first person she saw was Justin, who gave her a cheery grin, making her feel uncomfortable as she recalled her fantasy of the night before.

'Hi, Marina! Enjoy the party last night?'

She made a non-committal noise and sat down in the chair beside him. 'Whew, I don't know about you but singing is the last thing I feel like doing right now. It's so darned hot!'

'You'll soon get acclimatised.' His grey eyes were surveying her thoughtfully. 'Are you coming on the sightseeing trip this afternoon?'

'Oh Lord, I'd forgotten all about it!'

'Well if you want to go you'd better sign up now. The list was looking quite full.'

Marina went out into the foyer and added her name, but by the time she returned Justin was chatting to another girl. She was surprised at the unmistakable feeling of jealousy that assailed her. She saw Laurence and made a beeline for him, talking animatedly about nothing at all until Signora Bellini, the voice coach, arrived, rapping on the lectern with her baton for silence.

Renata Bellini was a small, thin woman with scraped-back black hair that looked as if it was drenched in oil, darting, birdlike eyes and a trim figure. Despite her small stature, her presence was commanding, and it was obvious that she would brook no slacking or nonsense of any kind. Marina felt instantly in awe of her and guessed the others did too.

The morning passed rapidly, with various voice exercises and, before they broke up for lunch, the students were paired off so that they could work on their presentations for the festival. The Signora said she was looking for 'voices that will complement each other' and Marina was surprised to find that her 'complementary voice' turned out to be Justin's.

'Your voice has a relatively low *tessitura*, Marina,' the coach explained, 'while Justin's tone is very mellow. I think you will perform well together. Now you should give some thought to your choice of duet. Let me know when you have some suggestions, and I will guide you.'

Marina was pleased. She had found Justin's light tenor to be very pleasing, although he lacked vocal power. She also rather enjoyed seeing the scowl on the face of the girl he'd been chatting with earlier, and who had been teamed with another girl because there weren't enough men to go round.

'Shall we talk about what we're going to perform over lunch?' Justin asked. 'I heard there's a decent place just down the road.'

Minutes later they were sitting in a nearby *trattoria* discussing their options. For Marina, however, there was no alternative. She already knew what she wanted to do. Ever since Luigi had mentioned it she had longed to sing as Mimi in *La Bohème*, and that meant the duet at the end of the first act, 'O Soave Fanciulla'.

Even so, she let Justin ramble on a bit, not wanting to seem too pushy. 'Of course we could try some Puccini,' he suggested, after going through practically everyone else.

Marina mentioned *Bohème*. He didn't take much persuasion. 'I've already done a bit of work on Rodolfo. My singing teacher ran me through some of the score back in London. That would be great!'

Marina first felt relieved, then excited. The prospect of singing a duet which expressed the feeling of 'love at first sight' was very enticing, but she couldn't resist teasing Justin a little.

'Of course, you'll have to pretend to feel passionate towards me. Bella didn't seem to think you'd be very good at that, did she?'

'No problem!' he grinned, but he wouldn't be drawn further. Marina was left wondering how they would make out together. She would love to prove the prima donna wrong, to show that Justin was eminently capable of putting on a toe-curling performance as Rodolfo when he had a sexy leading lady to inspire him – her!

There was someone *she* had to prove something to as well: Luigi. Marina knew she could hope for no special favours from him now, and it would all have to be achieved on her own merit. But if she and Justin could pull it off their mutual triumph would be sweet.

The meal over, the pair of them sauntered back through the overheated streets towards their respective hotels. The shops were closed and most Romans were indoors for the afternoon *siesta*. Heat suffused the city, pouring out of the ancient stones, and Marina was feeling restless. She wanted to see the city, but the sightseeing tour didn't begin till four.

Marina might have suggested they spend more time together, discussing the opera, but once they'd left the restaurant Justin seemed to go into a daze and she concluded he must be tired. His normally alert grey eyes had a faraway look in them as if he were dreaming of someone else, and she found being with him almost embarrassing. It occurred to her that he might be spoken for, and she felt a surprising pang of disappointment.

'See you later then,' she said, with a casual wave, before going through the glass doors of her hotel. For a few seconds she watched him wander off down the crowded street in his jeans. Nice butt, she thought, but quashed any further speculation. Her feeling that Justin was a complicated type returned, making her wary of fantasising about him too much, and she still didn't know quite what to make of him. Perhaps he would open up to her more once they were working together.

On the sightseeing tour, Marina sought the company of Laurence and his friend who kept the back of the coach in stitches with their alternative commentary on the monuments of Rome. She returned to the academy in a good mood, but as she got out of the coach Luigi appeared on his way out of the building.

'Ah, the tour bus,' he said, seeing the party descend onto the pavement. He continued, addressing no-one in particular, 'I hope you all enjoyed seeing our beautiful city.'

Marina caught his eye and was startled by the sudden coldness in his gaze. Any initial recognition was instantly quashed and he was regarding her as if she were a complete stranger. She felt a hot wave of anger flood through her. The bastard was snubbing her! The memory of how he had performed cunnilingus on her just the night before fuelled her indignation, and she gave him a contemptuous look before he turned his back on her. Oh God, she thought, I've made an enemy of him already. Some chance I've got of winning any prizes at the festival!

Chapter Three

Justin could hardly wait for the weekend. The unimaginable had happened: Bella had agreed to give him private lessons in exchange for his services. The singer spent most of her leisure time at her second home near the Pope's summer residence at Lake Albano. She would arrange for a car to be sent to Justin's hotel on Saturday morning to take him to the *Villa Gandolfini*. The question was, exactly what kind of 'services' did she have in mind?

The summer school course did not run at weekends so on Friday afternoon everyone was making their own arrangements, pairing up and swapping tips about where the best discos, bars and restaurants were to be found. When anyone asked what Justin's plans were he would give a secret smile and say he was 'spoken for'.

With Marina, however, he was more explicit. They had arranged a first rehearsal of their duet with Renata Bellini for three o'clock on Friday. It went reasonably well, although the coach told them they had 'much work to do, individually and together'. Afterwards, over lemon tea in a nearby bar, Marina casually announced that she was going with a couple of others to a disco the following evening and invited him to join them.

'Sorry, I'm otherwise engaged,' he replied with a grin. The temptation to say a bit more was overwhelming, and he gave in to it. 'Actually, I'm going to a certain eminent person's villa for the weekend.'

'Not Luigi's?'

Justin was surprised by the sudden vehemence of her question. He shook his head. 'No, not Luigi's. Why?'

'Oh, nothing.' Her blue eyes darted questioningly over

31

his face. 'Who then?' Light dawned. 'Not *Bella's*, surely?'

He laughed at her astonishment. 'I'm not saying another word.'

'Bella? My God, Justin, you don't mean . . .'

He enjoyed seeing her imagination run away with her and gave a self-satisfied chuckle, but he refused to say any more. Let her speculate. If believing he was on intimate terms with Bella made him more attractive to Marina, it could only feed back into their performance and lift it to greater heights.

Justin could act as suave and confident as he liked in front of his singing partner, but when the time to depart for Albano came he was filled with trepidation. A liveried chauffeur arrived in a sleek black limo and Justin was suddenly conscious of the inadequacy of his wardrobe. What if she had famous and sophisticated guests to stay, and he had to dine with them? His Italian wasn't up to much either. What had at first sounded like a wonderful opportunity now seemed more like an ordeal.

The chauffeur stowed Justin's shabby overnight bag in the boot with careful disdain then opened the back door for him. As they made their way through the chaotic traffic the man made light conversation in broken English, but once they were on the *autostrada* all attempts at conversation ceased and Justin sank back, relieved, into the embracing leather upholstery. He watched the countryside stream by until they climbed into the mountains and the road became more winding and hazardous.

Eventually they drew up at some elegant wrought-iron gates which slowly opened to admit them. A short drive led to a building of faded glory with ochre walls and green shutters with two heraldic beasts guarding the approach. When Justin left the vehicle a light, but very welcome, breeze caressed his forehead. He followed the chauffeur as he carried his bag towards the pillared entrance but before they got to the door a couple of hounds bounded out, lolloping around Justin in a manner that was anything but threatening.

'No good guard dogs,' the chauffeur grinned. 'No good at all!'

Suddenly Bella herself was there to greet them, her

impressive figure framed by the doorway. She wore a lemon yellow dress with a white, fringed shawl about her shoulders and loosely knotted over her chest. The pale, but vibrant, colours emphasised the splendour of her olive tan, shining dark eyes and black hair.

'*Ciao, Justin!*' she smiled, genuinely welcoming. 'You are just in time for lunch. Come and meet Olga. I've told her all about you.'

She led the way into the imposing entrance hall before Justin could ask who this 'Olga' was. He followed her into a large, light-filled lounge where a woman in a black dress was standing. His first impression was one of brittle strength and subtle power.

'Justin, meet Olga, my secretary.'

There was no embrace, no handshake even, just a curt nod. He felt chilled by the woman, but oddly fascinated too. She surveyed him with hooded grey eyes, her mouth a stern line. The grey-streaked hair was tied back into a tight bun and the black dress concealed a figure that was buxom but slim-hipped.

'Shall we dine soon?' Olga said. Her accent was not Italian, more Eastern-European, and her tone was clipped. 'We can talk during the meal. It is cook's afternoon off, and she is anxious to leave.'

Bella agreed, and Justin had the uneasy feeling that she was somehow under the other woman's thumb. Here was a relationship he would not have suspected, a hidden power behind the throne of the reigning Queen of Opera. It sent shivers of anticipation through him as he stepped through a communicating door into the dining room.

The table was huge but one end of it was laid for three, with fresh flowers in a crystal bowl. Beyond the two large windows Justin could glimpse a lakeside vista, with the volcanic mountains in the distance. He felt ill-at-ease in his jeans and T-shirt, but no-one had said anything about him going to his room first.

Almost as an afterthought, Olga directed him to the cloakroom across the hall. When he returned the two women were already seated and a third, rather portly female, was serving pasta. Salad and bread had appeared on the table, together with a huge bowl of fruit.

'Sit here, Justin,' Bella commanded.

He took his place between her and Olga, nervously eyeing the cutlery. The thought that the three of them would be alone in that house that afternoon was somehow disconcerting. There seemed to be a hidden agenda which the women knew about but he didn't.

As soon as the cook was dismissed and they began eating, Justin said, 'It's very good of you to invite me here, Signora. It's a beautiful house.'

Bella threw her companion a complicit smile. 'And you are a very special house guest – isn't he Olga?'

'Guest? Have you not told him about the arrangement, Bella? I thought . . .'

'Not yet.'

Bella spoke sharply, but her manner softened as she turned towards him. 'This dish is *pasta puttanesca*. Do you know what that means, Justin?'

He shook his head. 'My Italian's not up to much, I'm afraid.'

'It means "food for whores".'

She accompanied her words with a flourish of her white silk scarf. The flimsy garment drifted away from her bodice to reveal her bosom. Justin only just prevented himself from gasping aloud as the design of the dress came into view. The two halves of the bodice were only just held together by some flimsy cross-lacing that clearly showed the rounded swell of her breasts and the deep cleavage between. There was a teasing indecency about it that punctuated her words and made him blush, averting his gaze.

Both women were obviously amused by his discomfiture. While Justin tucked into the *fettucini* dressed with a pungent sauce of olives, anchovies and capers, they exchanged a few words in rapid, fluent Italian which he found totally incomprehensible.

Suddenly Bella said, 'Olga thinks I should tell you exactly what you must do in exchange for voice lessons.'

'You are very privileged, you know,' Olga put in. She was

almost scowling at him and Justin had the distinct impression that she resented his presence. 'Singers all over the world would pay a great price for just one hour of the *Signora's* precious time.'

'Oh yes, I know!'

'Well, Justin, the price *you* must pay is this,' Bella continued, breaking off a chunk of bread and dipping it in the rich sauce on her plate. 'If you agree, you will have a lesson on Saturday and Sunday afternoons until the end of the summer school. But after each lesson you will place yourself completely at the disposal of Olga and myself. Whatever we ask you to do you will perform impeccably, without complaint.'

'And if we feel the need to chastise you, you will accept your punishment like a man,' Olga added. She was smiling, but in a way that made Justin's flesh creep.

'Well, I'm not sure,' he heard himself saying. 'I mean, it's a bit vague, isn't it?' Olga rapped her fork on her plate, making him jump out of his skin. 'Ungrateful boy!' She spoke to Bella in Italian again. Both women were frowning and Justin felt most uneasy. There was a peculiar vibe between the pair of them and he felt caught in the middle, like a mouse being tossed between a pair of cats in play.

When Bella turned to him again, however, her smile was sweet. 'If you would prefer it you may leave immediately, Justin. Enrico is on hand to drive you back to Rome. You will have had a pleasant journey and a free lunch. Tonight you can join your friends at some sleazy discothèque and forget all about my offer. It's entirely up to you.'

'But if you refuse,' Olga said, 'you will spend the rest of your days wondering why you turned down the opportunity of a lifetime. You will wonder how your singing career might have progressed if only you had been coached by the wonderful Bella Conti. You will wonder what exciting new experiences you might have missed by refusing to become our slave. And, most of all, you will wonder how far *La Bellissima* might have gone in rewarding you for services rendered.'

The women laughed, a tinkling cadenza of female

conspiracy that held Justin enthralled. He couldn't help staring at the seductive plumpness of Bella's breasts in their lemon corset, simultaneously unlacing them in his imagination and blushing at his own daring. This, he reminded himself, was the woman who had vast audiences hanging on her every note, entrancing them with her exquisite voice and wonderful stage presence. Yet here she was right beside him in the flesh, making him an offer he would be an utter fool to refuse.

If only the two of them had been involved he wouldn't have hesitated, but the unknown factor in the equation was Olga. She sat at the table like a black crow, repellent yet also strangely magnetic. Although Bella had described her as a secretary she was obviously a good deal more than that. There was a peculiar tension between this daunting woman and her mistress that defied analysis. Justin found the idea of putting himself at her mercy terrifying, but he was curious too. Just what made a woman like that tick?

'Well, Justin?' Bella said.

He gulped and nodded. 'Okay. Maybe we could regard this as a trial weekend? On both sides, I mean.'

To his dismay, Olga shook her head vehemently. 'Oh no, it must be all or nothing. Either you agree to come here every weekend, without fail, until the end of the course, or you leave now.'

Justin glanced at Bella, who nodded. Her dark eyes were gleaming at him with an excitement that seemed almost sexual. When she looked at him like that it was impossible to resist. 'All right.'

'Good!' Olga rose from the table with the air of a bargain sealed. 'In that case I shall leave you alone. I have some thinking to do. Enjoy your lesson, Justin!'

The dishes were left for the maid, Lena, to clear. She seemed a timid little thing, excusing herself and scurrying about as if she wanted to be invisible. Bella beckoned Justin back through the communicating door into the lounge, where Lena brought them coffee. She opened the windows and it was pleasantly cool in there, with a light breeze wafting in from the mountains. An imposing portrait of Bella as

'Queen of the Night' in a midnight blue gown studded with moons and stars dominated the room from above the fireplace.

'Now, Justin, we can talk about your aspirations,' Bella began, the porcelain coffee cup poised on its way to her lips. She had flung the shawl over her bosom again but through the fringe Justin could still glimpse her cleavage. His cock swelled inside his tight jeans, making him squirm uncomfortably on his chair. 'You have ambitions to be an opera singer, yes?'

Their talk lasted quite a while and proved surprisingly wide-ranging. Bella showed that she had good knowledge of the English opera scene. She knew which companies preferred to sing in English rather than Italian or French, and was able to discuss the pro's and con's. She knew about the controversy over awarding lottery money to Covent Garden, and vehemently defended it. The new stage at Glyndebourne was discussed in detail, along with the rising public enthusiasm for the art which the 'Three Tenors' had inspired. It was remarkable, she said, that while England and Italy had always shared a love of football now they were starting to share a love of opera too.

When talk turned to personalities, Bella could name-drop with authority. Justin was impressed by her knowledge not only of established singers and directors, but of up-and-coming ones too. He thought of himself being added to her list of 'promising young tenors' and a heady wave of euphoria swept over him. But there was much work to be done first.

'Every morning, as soon as possible after waking, you must test your voice,' Bella told him. 'Only then will you know which exercises to perform. You must know your voice intimately, recognise when it needs loosening up – I find lemon juice in a glass of warm water invaluable – and take throat remedies as soon as you detect the slightest soreness. You must check your English weather daily, and know when to muffle your throat and when to give it air. Here it is not so much of a problem, but cold and damp are terrible for the throat. You must learn to . . . cosset your vocal cords, for if you become successful they will be your most valuable asset.'

They finished their coffee and moved across the hall into the practice room, whose walls were covered with shelves containing scores, posters from the world's most famous opera houses, all showing Bella at the head of the bill, and many framed photographs. A music stand, holding an open score, stood beside a grand piano. Bella took her place on the piano stool and played a few opening chords.

The afternoon passed swiftly, but Justin was aware that he was getting far more than a mere hour of tuition. Through the large window he watched the sunlight fade until it was almost dusk, and all the time Bella was pushing him mercilessly. They worked on posture, breathing, scales. She was not pleased with the way he had been previously taught and he had to alter everything to her satisfaction. By the end of the session he was thoroughly exhausted.

'Now you may go to your room, shower and rest,' Bella smiled at last, rising from the stool. She came up and kissed him softly on the cheek, sending tingles of anticipation down his spine. 'At eight, Olga will help you get dressed.'

The thought was unpleasant. Justin said, 'Well, I . . . er . . . don't have anything smart.'

Bella laughed. 'Don't worry, Olga has her own ideas. She will provide you with something . . . appropriate. Now hurry along. I wish to practise by myself.'

Soon the villa was ringing with the mellifluous sound of Bella's singing, and Justin's elated mood returned. As he showered his head was full of the complimentary phrases she had thrown at him that afternoon: 'Nice phrasing . . . good diction . . . excellent tone . . .' She liked his voice, she really did, and as the lesson progressed he had felt it developing under her expert tuition.

He hadn't yet told Bella about the piece he and Marina had chosen for their festival presentation. For some reason he wanted to keep that a secret, and she hadn't asked. They were working on the 'the basics' but Justin had a feeling that if things continued to go as well as they had that afternoon there might be more on offer than just four weekends of lessons. He didn't want to let his hopes range too high, however, and the outrageous idea that he might be invited to study at the academy on a more permanent basis was kept firmly at bay.

After the cooling shower, Justin lay down in the attractive guest room at the back of the villa. The bed was covered with crisp, white linen smelling faintly of lavender, and the view of the distant mountains at dusk was peaceful. Soon the delicate scent of the bed linen soothed him into slumber.

He was awoken by a sharp rap on the door and as he sat up, bleary eyed, Olga entered briskly, some garments hanging over her arm. She wore a black rubber dress with a mandarin collar and a flap that fastened over her right breast with red buttons, like the greatcoat of a Russian general, and high-heeled black patent boots. A short-handled whip was thrust into the belt at her waist.

At first Justin stared at her in amazement, but then he became aware that he had nothing on. He tried to pull the bedcover over his nakedness, but she gave a snort of derision and her blood-red lips made a thin curve in her pale face.

'No false modesty in front of me, young man! Now get up and try this on for size. Hurry up, we haven't got long. You'll be serving dinner in half an hour.'

'*Me*?'

'Of course. Remember our little bargain? You do whatever you're told, and look smart about it. Stand up, now, and get into this.'

Justin gaped at the leather harness, chains and assorted straps that she held out for him. There was a dildo-shaped tube of rubber attached to a pair of black leather mini-briefs with just a thong to slip between the buttocks behind. Straps and chains were designed to link the garment to other parts of the anatomy, and studded neck collar, bracelets and anklets completed the outfit.

'What's this?' he gasped.

'Your slave uniform, of course. You will perform all duties wearing it. Now stop wasting time and step into the pants.'

She held them out for him and, overcoming his distaste, Justin put them on. The feel of the cool leather against his bare flesh was alien, but when he tried to get into the rubber cock-harness it felt even weirder. Some talc had been dusted into it but he found it difficult even so.

'It will be easier when you get an erection,' Olga informed him, matter-of-factly. 'Just pull on the buckle for now, to tighten it around your scrotum.'

He fumbled, but the thing wouldn't stay on properly. She slapped his wrist impatiently. 'Let me do it.'

Olga pulled the strap so tight his eyes watered. 'Ouch!' he complained.

To his horror, she slapped him again – on the cheek this time, where it stung. 'You'll get far worse than that if you don't behave yourself. It has to be tight, you'll just have to get used to it. Now I'll fasten the rest. Just stand as still as a statue. If you even breathe I'll be very displeased and you'll soon discover it's not a good idea to cross me in any way.'

Already Justin felt a deep dread of the woman seep into his very soul. He longed to see Bella again. She had been sweet to him that afternoon, and if he had to go through this torture for one of her smiles it would all be worthwhile. Yet the thought of being handed over to this sadistic female for punishment was horrific. He had a feeling it wouldn't take much to upset her, either.

He stood stock still while the buckles were made uncomfortably tight. The criss-crossed chains ate into the flesh of his chest and the leather collar was too tight over his Adam's apple, but he didn't complain. Perhaps he would get used to the discomfort after a while. The anklets were joined with a chain that hobbled him and he wondered how he was going to get as far as the door, let alone any farther.

'Here, bite on this!' Olga commanded.

Justin had thought his accoutrement was complete, but now she was giving him a rubber gag. It was too late to protest. The solid wedge of rubber went between his teeth and the straps were fastened tightly behind his head, effectively silencing him. Olga walked around his immobile form, studying her handiwork, and gave a final nod of approval.

'Good! Now listen very carefully. You will move around on your hands and knees unless given permission to stand upright. You will not attempt to do anything unless specifically requested to do so. Think of yourself as a robot, an automaton, whose entire existence is dedicated to serving your two mistresses. I can see you already worship the ground Bella walks on, so it shouldn't be too difficult for you.'

She went over to open the door then stood beside it, beckoning him over. 'Down, slave! Let me see you on all fours as befits your lowly status.'

Clumsily, Justin got down on his knees. It was difficult to maintain his balance, but he managed to get to the door by moving his knees within the limits imposed by the harness and shackles. At the door, Olga clipped a dog-lead onto the eye at the back of his collar.

Now, forward!' she said, yanking his head with the chain.

As he began to crawl along the carpet runner towards the stairs, the sound of familiar music came from the dining-room below. Justin strained to hear and soon recognised the piece from Verdi's opera *Nabucco*: 'Va, Pensiero', the chorus of Hebrew slaves. He couldn't help smiling at the appropriateness of the music, but Olga saw his grin and gave him a sharp tap on his bare behind with the whip. The pain stung him acutely, but he bit hard on the rubber in his mouth and avoided making any sound which, he was sure, would only have elicited a second cruel lashing.

'Down to the kitchen!' she commanded him. 'Go!'

It was hard negotiating the stairs, but somehow Justin managed it. In the kitchen his knees were hurt by the stone flags, but Olga made him stay very still while she tied a tray onto his back and began to load it. When it became clear that he was expected to act as a 'dumb waiter', moving between kitchen and dining room, his spirits sank. Now it would be even harder to avoid making a mistake. As soon as he began moving, the hot dishes that Olga had placed on the tray beneath silver domes started clashing around and he was terrified that the whole lot would go sliding onto the floor.

'This way!' Olga barked. She held the door open while he moved very slowly out of the kitchen. Fortunately the dining-room was on the same floor. His knees slid over the carpet, following his hands, but already the skin on his knee-caps was raw. If they wanted him to play these silly games they might at least have provided him with knee-pads!

But it was soon obvious that neither Olga nor Bella regarded this as a silly game. He half expected the singer to burst into laughter when he entered, half naked, with the tray on his back. Instead she pointed to the floor beside her saying, 'Here, slave!'

The dining-room was softly lit and Justin guessed that there were candles on the table. He made his way carefully over the carpet and came to a halt beside her chair. His eyes feasted on shiny black leather boots with impossibly spiked heels and beringed hands capped with vermilion talons, resting on thighs covered in black fishnet stockings. If he strained his neck Justin could get a glimpse of skin-tight panties in fabulous sky blue latex. Much as he longed to see what her top half looked like he couldn't lift his head entirely without de-stabilising the tray. Olga lifted the lids off the dishes and Bella helped herself. She dropped a little sauce onto his nose in the process and he longed to lick it off, but he contented himself with breathing in her heavy perfume, so laden with exotic aromatics that it was almost incense.

Olga took her place at table too, and Justin had to carry the tray round to her. It wobbled precariously because Bella hadn't put the dishes back with the weight evenly distributed, and Justin concentrated with all his strength to prevent an accident. He felt ridiculously exposed, with his naked buttocks up in the air and his cock hardening inside the rubber dildo, but neither woman seemed to find it in the least untoward. The suspicion that they'd put other young men through similar ordeals struck him with unpleasant certainty.

He waited like a patient hound while the women ate their meal. His knees felt as if they would give way any moment, and his thigh muscles were stiff and aching, but he daren't give in. Taking his frustration out on his rubber gag, Justin bit down hard and did his best to endure the unintelligible stream of chatter that passed from one woman to the other as they completely ignored him.

At last Olga rose from her chair. 'Time for dessert, I think,' she said, in English so he could understand.

Justin's heart sank. The way back to the kitchen loomed long and arduous. However, this time he was to be spared. Taking the chain that dangled from the back of his neck, Olga led him over to the large sideboard. She removed the tray and began to lay out an assortment of fruit and pastries over his naked back, arranging them between the straps and chains. Then she told him to remain between their chairs so they could help themselves to whatever took their fancy.

The fruit and gateaux soon warmed up on his skin and began to ooze juices and cream. The women thought nothing of scooping up a fingerful of goo from his back, or even licking it up. They chatted and laughed, often with a lascivious note as if they were exchanging hot gossip, and Justin felt his libido rising, slowly but surely, making him forget his aching limbs. Being there in the rôle of an inanimate piece of furniture was oddly exciting, like eavesdropping. He only wished his Italian was more fluent.

Then, just when his mind as well as his body were becoming numb, he suddenly realised that Bella was talking in English.

'I think the slave has done well, don't you, *cara*? Perhaps he deserves some reward. What do you think?'

'A small one, perhaps. It is as well to encourage good behaviour as well as discourage bad, I always say.'

'In that case, how about a little . . . titbit?'

Cool hands swept away the last of the delicacies from his back and wiped his damp skin with a napkin. Olga tugged on the chain attached to his collar and he was able to lift his aching neck. It creaked and pained him horribly at first, but what he saw as he lifted his eyes soon made him forget his physical ills.

Bella's waist was nipped in by a blue corset in the same sky blue latex as her panties, but her bosom was completely exposed, with just a strap between them leading up to a tight collar. The large breasts spilled out voluptuously with their nipples fully protruding, and the incipient erection that

Justin had been harbouring all evening instantly reached its full potential. He watched incredulously as Bella leaned forward in her chair and lifted the plump swell of her right breast towards him.

The greenish hue of her eyes sparkled with secret, electric light and the pair of miniature silver daggers dangling from her ears caught the glow from the two candelabras on the table. Justin stared at the pale mound of flesh with its tempting, rosy bud and felt his heart thudding wildly. Removing the gag, she placed her bud between his lips and he gave a long moan of longing.

'Not too greedy!' Bella warned, as his mouth closed over the tender morsel and he began to lick and suck at it.

'He is full of carnal lust,' Olga said with disdain. 'What else do you expect from a male slave? Female ones are much more sensitive to our needs as well as their own.'

'We had a female last time, to please you,' Bella reminded her. 'Now it's my turn.' Justin scarcely heeded their words, although the conversation struck him as bizarre. He was far more wrapped up in the blissful taste and texture of the nipple. If only he could stroke and knead the breast as well, he would be in heaven. But there was no way he would risk taking any liberties.

Then, in his eagerness, Justin's teeth grazed the wet nub and Bella gave a sharp cry.

'He bit me! Little devil! He bit my nipple, *cara*!'

'Did he indeed?'

The menacing tone of Olga's voice made him turn his head in alarm. She was taking the whip out of her belt. Justin cringed, alarmed by the severe scowl on her face. Her eyes were black malevolent points in a white mask, her lips a red gash.

'Do you wish to administer the lashes?' she asked Bella, over Justin's head. 'Six, I think.'

'Let's share it. You give him three, then I'll do the rest.'

'Very well.'

Justin braced himself, aware that his tender buttocks were fully exposed in the minimal suit. He heard the singing of the whip before it landed, and then the stinging impact made him wince and gasp. While his right cheek was still smarting, Olga brought the whip down again on the left one so that the burning pain was equalised. The third stroke was the worst, falling where he was still raw and defenceless. He moaned aloud as the two women changed positions and the whip was handed to Bella.

'You see, it is not just your voice that must be trained,' he heard her murmur. 'Your body, too, must learn subservience to the will – not yours, but mine. And there is only one language that the body understands.'

'One language, but two dialects,' Olga added. '*Dolore e piacere* – pain and pleasure.'

She was standing right in front of him as Bella wielded the whip. Justin could see his own face in the shiny dark boots, could witness his grimace of pain as the leather snake stung his sore flesh once again. He bit hard on the wedge of rubber now back between his teeth and somehow managed to endure to the end of his punishment without crying out.

'Good!' Olga said, going to take the whip back from Bella. 'He took that well. Let him lie face down on the couch in the other room and I'll fetch some ointment. We don't want any nasty weals developing.'

Still on all fours, Justin was led out of the dining-room and across the hall. Bella threw a silky shawl over a sofa that was upholstered in dusky pink satin and he lay on it, relishing the cool touch of the material against his fevered skin. His bum was smarting horribly now, hot and throbbing, but the prospect of having gentle hands rub cream into it was very pleasant indeed. Maybe it would be worth all the torment, he thought.

With a sigh he relaxed and closed his eyes, releasing his grip on the rubber gag which fell from his mouth. It was luxurious to be able to rest and stretch his limbs after their cramped position of the last hour or so. Sweet relief flooded through him, preparing him for the sensual delights to follow. He heard the door open and a whispered exchange took place, then the door was quietly closed again.

A soft, greased palm caressed the aching cheeks of his behind and soon he began to feel much better. Whatever

45

medicament she was using seemed to be anaesthetising him, and instead of flinching Justin relished the delicate touch as the ointment was rubbed over his buttocks and into his crack. A feeling of utter voluptuousness went through him, and his cock began to fill out the rubber dildo as his erection became more substantial.

'There, that's better isn't it?' Bella's voice crooned in his ear as her fingers slipped between his thighs and beneath the thong to caress his balls.

He gave a wild moan of response. She chuckled and smoothed the cream all over his rear, her fingertips lightly probing his anus. Justin could barely stand it. He began to thrust against the silk throw, longing to feel its coolness caressing the naked flesh of his shaft, but he could not find the relief he craved.

Eventually the teasing caresses stopped and he heard Bella leave the room. Feverishly he turned over and tore away the rubber dildo, grasping the hot flesh of his prick with both hands, and proceeded to manipulate himself to orgasm. It took less than a minute. Hot milk spurted from him onto the silk beneath and his whole body felt voided, blissfully released from the tormenting tension that had been building in him practically all day. Utterly spent, he turned onto his side and sank into an instant slumber.

When he awoke it was pitch dark and the house was silent. Feeling disorientated, and full of an oddly exciting sense of shame, Justin slid from the sofa and made his way gingerly to the door. His mind struggled to recall the way back to his room. He was terrified of opening the wrong door and intruding on some scene of lesbian debauchery, for by now he was convinced of the nature of the relationship between the two women. His brain was too tired to speculate on the implications of this so he just plodded on. When he reached the top of the stairs, his feet made their way to the guest room almost of their own accord. After stripping off his strange accoutrements, he sank wearily onto the bed and was soon soundly asleep once more.

Chapter Four

With her hopes of becoming closer acquainted with Justin dashed, Marina decided to make the most of whatever opportunities offered themselves at the disco on Saturday night. She'd been intrigued by her singing partner's hints of a 'special relationship' with Bella, but now she was convinced that the pangs of jealousy she'd felt were not sexual but related to her ambition to be 'discovered' while on this course. It was starting to look as if she'd been upstaged by Justin already.

Even so, as she prepared for her night out on the town, Marina felt bubbles of excitement rising within her. She selected a satiny blue mini-skirt with a skimpy silver top which made the most of her blue eyes, long legs and honey-tanned skin. The top would not accommodate a bra, so the rounded contours of her breasts with their small, firm nipples were clearly evident, and beneath the swirly skirt she wore a pair of high-cut tanga briefs in matching silver. After spraying a spice-laden perfume into her cleavage and flicking a brush through her shoulder-length fair hair, Marina felt ready to dance the night away.

The gang who were going out together were meeting in the foyer of her hotel, so Marina had only to go downstairs in the lift. She wasn't sure exactly who would be there, but when she saw Laurie and Tim amongst the crowd she gave a sigh of relief. The pair of them were good fun. She saw their eyes light up as she walked towards them, and gave Laurie a wink.

'You look sensational!' he said.

'Good enough to eat!' Tim added. He often said daft things like that, which vaguely irritated her, but she knew he was a good sort. She wasn't quite so sure about Laurie, although he was the one who attracted her more.

'Shall we go?' someone said, and Marina realised they'd all been waiting for her.

'Where are we heading?' she asked, to cover her embarrassment.

The plan was to head for the *Cocomero* disco, near the Coliseum. If that didn't seem quite the thing there were some others nearby that they could try, not to mention several bars.

'There's supposed to be one of those topless places round there too,' Tim said, his eyes gleaming. 'You know, lap dancing and stuff.'

'Trust you to know about that,' Laurie grinned. 'Where do you get such information from?'

'Barmen. They always know everything that's going on. You should talk to Toni at the hotel. He said he can get you anything, from girls to cocaine.'

'Yeah – at a price!'

'*Naturalmente!*'

The laughing group left the hotel and began to walk along the noisy street, hailing passing cabs. Eventually they got two taxis together and were whisked off to the bright lights. The *Cocomero* was approached through a narrow entrance, but when they descended the stairs they found themselves in a huge cellar bar with flashing lights and gyrating bodies. Marina soon found herself confronted by a grotesque cocktail in a livid green colour.

'It's called a *pappagallo ubriacho* – that's "pissed parrot" in English!' Tim grinned.

'What's in it?'

'Not sure. Some kind of melon liqueur, lime cordial. Sounds like an alcopop to me.' Marina sipped the concoction through a straw. It did have a fruity taste but it was also very alcoholic and went straight to her head. She let Laurie drag her up onto the dance floor, hoping some activity would clear her head, but all he wanted to do was hold her close and smooch. For a while she gave in, finding his deep, sensual kisses very arousing. Their tongues mingled, hot and sweet, and since their crotches were hard up against each other she could feel the outline of his erection clearly through their clothes, making her want him even more.

Then Tim came up and tapped his friend on the shoulder. Laurie pulled away, leaving Marina feeling dazed and unsteady on her feet.

'Look, mate, I've decided to go on to this topless bar. If all you want to do is maul each other . . .'

'No way! Let's all go. All right with you, Marina?'

She nodded. Their steamy embraces had been getting her so worked up that she'd started to feel frustrated there in the disco, with no possibility of going the whole way. Another five minutes of that and she'd have been dragging him into the loo for a screw, which would have been most undignified. After her experience with Luigi, which still rankled, Marina wanted everything to be right next time.

Besides, she was curious to see what went on in such places. As the three of them walked towards the *Bar Fantasia* her excitement grew. There was a lot of loud music coming through the door, and a couple of heavy-looking bouncers who regarded them with unsmiling stares.

'You know what to expect?' one of them asked, in an Italian-American accent. 'Naked girls acting sexy. The lady won't be offended?'

'Oh no!' Marina giggled. 'Some of my best friends are strippers!'

It wasn't true, some demon had made her say it. But she was pleased by the look of alarm that crossed the faces of Tim and Laurie. The bouncers regarded her impassively and stood aside to let them in. At once they were accosted by a tall woman in a black leather dress who demanded quite a large sum of money off them.

'For this you get two drinks tickets,' she told them.

The men hesitated, but when Marina offered to pay her share they agreed to give it a go.

'It had better be worth it,' Laurie said as they moved down the dark corridor towards swing doors.

The scene that met Marina's eyes vaguely resembled the film 'Showgirls' which she had seen. Two leggy beauties

49

wrapped themselves around silvery poles on a small stage while equally scantily-clad girls moved amongst the customers as topless waitresses.

'Gor Blimey!' Tim murmured, betraying his cockney origins. 'What do you have to do to get one of those to squirm in your lap?'

'Pay them,' Laurie said.

They sat at a free table and, within a few seconds, one of the girls approached. She had luxuriant red hair, hazel eyes fringed with long lashes, pouting orange lips and large, pert breasts that were studded with tiny gold and silver stars but otherwise naked. Her bottom half was clad in gold hot pants. Her mouth curved into an automatic smile as she greeted them.

'*Buona sera, Signore, Signorina*. What would you like to drink?'

'How much is a lap dance?' asked Tim.

The hostess frowned slightly and Marina feared she was insulted by this direct approach. She said hurriedly, 'I'd like a champagne cocktail, please.'

'And me,' Laurie grinned.

'Make that three,' Tim said. 'And what about the other?'

The figure named for the lap dance made Tim gasp. 'Well that's out then. Shame.'

'Wait a minute, we could probably afford it if we clubbed together,' Laurie said.

'One lap only!' the girl said.

'No, that's not what I meant. Couldn't you do it for one of us while the rest watch?' The girl looked dubious, but she was obviously tempted. After all, she'd be gaining a customer who would otherwise not be able to afford her services. At last she nodded. 'Okay, but we go next door. I'll bring your drinks first.'

The three of them put their money on the table. 'We'll toss for it!' Laurie grinned.

He won the toss, but then Tim said, 'Hey wait a minute, what about Marina? Her money's as good as ours. I reckon we should include her in.'

Marina had assumed she would not be in the running for

the lap dance, although she was willing to pay her share. It would be interesting to watch, anyway. But Tim insisted and, when the coin was tossed a second time, she won.

'She'll never agree to it,' Marina said, laughing. The idea of having some nude woman gyrating on her lap was weird, but exciting too. Although she'd never had an out and out lesbian experience Marina had always been secretly fascinated by the idea, and sometimes fantasised about it. The red-haired girl intrigued her, with her deadpan manner and sexy body.

'We'll see,' Tim said, archly. 'Look, here she comes.'

The girl put the tray of glasses down and took their tokens. 'Two for each drink,' she told them. 'Cocktails come expensive.'

The men grumbled a bit but handed them over. They were ogling the woman's breasts, their eyes practically on stalks. 'Where do we go for the lap dance?' Tim asked.

'Through that door,' she said, pointing to the other side of the room. 'Have your drinks first then wait for me in one of the private cubicles at ten-thirty.'

They watched her swaying butt as it wove between the tables. On the small stage two new girls had arrived, each wearing nothing more than a spangled G-string. One was black and one was Chinese, and they made an attractive sight as their slim legs wound around the slowly revolving silver columns. Sometimes they threw back their torsos, in the style of trapeze artistes, so that their breasts were outlined against the wall of light behind.

'Blimey, this is some place!' Tim exclaimed. 'If I hadn't had that chat with Toni I'd never have found out about it.'

'Pity it's so bloody expensive,' Laurie sighed. 'Going back to the hotel and having a wank is going to be a bit of an anti-climax after all this.'

'Oh, ha ha! Anti-climax, geddit?'

Marina was scarcely listening to their banter. The raunchy atmosphere of the place was beginning to get to her too, but the prospect of being involved in a lap dance was daunting. She was half hoping the girl would refuse to do it with a woman. In that case, it would be Laurie's turn. Yet she knew she would be disappointed if that happened.

The cocktails were powerful, reducing Marina's brain to cotton wool in a few minutes. She was amazed when she heard Tim say he'd like a beer.

'Are you sure that's a good idea – mixing drinks?'

'I can 'andle it,' he grinned, clicking his fingers at the hostess. She nodded, but took her time coming over. She raised her brows a fraction when he asked for a large beer, but made no comment.

'I'd like a mineral water please,' Marina said. Laurie had a coke.

When Tim got up to go to the gents, Laurie said, 'Look, Marina, once we've had the dance I think we should go. If we hang around here much longer we'll have to carry Tim back to the hotel.'

'That's what I'm afraid of.'

'Right, soon as he comes back we'll find this cubicle. Are you sure you want to go through with this? I mean, I don't mind standing in for you!'

Marina smiled at him. The spark of attraction between them was making her feel very randy. She moved her face close to his and murmured, 'But will you stand up for me?' He gave a throaty laugh. 'Well now, that depends . . .'

Before she knew it they were kissing again, their tongues duelling with suddenly released passion. She realised that she wanted him, badly, but that they would both have to wait.

Meanwhile, it was fun to fantasise. She imagined that active mouth on her breasts, her pussy, making her come with darting movements of that agile tongue, and a shudder of deep-rooted desire went through her.

'Hey, you two!'

Tim's outraged voice split them apart. He was glaring down at them, flies still undone.

'Zip yourself up!' Laurie snarled at him, annoyed at the interruption. 'Let's take our drinks through to the other room.'

The hostess saw them go, Laurie made sure of that by giving her a wave. Through the door was a long hall with curtained cubicles down both sides. Many were closed, with the sound of music coming from inside, and Marina guessed that dances were going on. She glimpsed the occasional flash of flesh where the curtains gaped a little. It was quite arousing.

They found an empty cubicle and piled in. There was room for little more than a chair, a shag-pile rug and a small cupboard on which a cassette player and box of tissues stood.

'We're not going to see much in here,' Tim grumbled.

They sat on the rug to finish their drinks, and by the time Tim had quaffed his beer he looked ready to keel over at any minute. Laurie threw Marina a look of despair. It clearly said, 'How the heck are we going to get him back to the hotel?'

Suddenly the curtains were swished aside and their hostess stood there, smiling. 'Here you are! Now which one of you is to be the lucky one?'

'She is!' Tim guffawed, pointing at Marina.

'You are joking, yes?'

'No, he's not joking,' Laurie explained. 'She won the toss. You don't mind doing it with a woman, do you? I mean, a lap's a lap, surely?'

Light seemed to dawn within the woman's tawny eyes. 'Oh, I see. You like to watch your girlfriend with another girl.' Laurie didn't deny it. The hostess put both hands on Marina's shoulders, smiling wickedly. Marina felt a thrill of sexual anticipation pass through her. Her shoulders were burning where the soft hands were touching her skin. 'Okay, darling. If it turns you on. Sit on the chair please, and remember – you can look all you like, but don't touch.'

Marina's legs were trembling and she was more than ready to sit down. Feeling like an awkward schoolgirl she sat with her hands in her lap avoiding the dancer's eye as she gyrated before her. The taut breasts bobbed with tantalising allure and she was stroking her own thighs suggestively as she moved her hips in a swaying arc. Aware of the two men watching in the wings Marina felt acutely embarrassed, yet she was mesmerised by the sight of the other woman's body, so lithe and active, and unashamedly sexual.

'Enjoying this are you, darling?' she heard her murmur, below the tinny music.

Marina swallowed. Her throat felt dry and taut and she could hear a wild pulse thundering in her ears. Nearer and nearer came the semi-nude body, with fingers plucking delicately at the nipples to bring them into prominence. Then, to her horror, those same fingers began to unzip the hot pants, disappearing down the front to toy with whatever was down there. The blatant exhibitionism of the dancer knew no bounds, and when Marina dared to snatch a glimpse of her face it was contorted with lust, open-mouthed, her eyes dark slits of concentrated passion.

Slowly the satin pants slid to the floor to reveal the merest whisper of a G-string. It was obvious that her mound was completely shaven and the scrap of lace that covered her pussy was damp and clinging. Marina caught her eye and a look of collusion passed between them. They were scarcely aware of the two male voyeurs but inhabited a feminine world of their own, a subtle, shared universe of pleasure that only women can understand.

Their relationship was taking on the nature of a celebration of female sexuality. Marina felt utterly exhilarated and when, finally, the dancer came to rest across her thighs she breathed a long sigh of satisfaction at their physical contact. The woman was radiating heat and as she writhed and moaned in front of her Marina felt her own libido increasing to boiling point. She couldn't keep her eyes off the pale globes of her breasts with the provocative nipples. The urge to touch or lick them was almost unbearable. She even had the feeling that if they had been completely alone, anything would have been permitted.

Furthermore, Marina had the distinct impression that the woman was enjoying doing this for another woman instead of a man. Was she a secret lesbian, hating the men she performed for, doing it only for the money? Marina knew this was true of some prostitutes. The idea was intriguing. She could feel herself overheating at the very idea, her heart skipping beats, the torrid pulse between her legs accelerating inside as the dancer glided up and down, round and around, on her tense thighs. Glancing down, she saw that the woman's nipples were firm and huge, taunting her with their nearness. She wet her lips with her tongue, imagining how it would feel to lick and suck at those provocative buds. The faint, but recognisable, odour of another woman's musk reached her nostrils.

'Oh God! I can't stand much more of this!' she heard Tim moan, his voice thick and slurred. There was a thud and he landed sideways on the mat. Laurie shook him but his friend had gone down like a lead balloon and there was no response. He threw Marina a despairing look, but she grinned and winked at him. His gaze returned to the lithe buttocks of the dancer as she thrust her pelvis back and forth.

Now Marina could clearly smell the heady mix of sweat, scent and pheromones that the woman was giving out. It swamped her senses, driving her to the edge of desire so that she thought she would soon climax. She was both attracted and repelled by the idea. If they had been alone she might have been less inhibited, but with Laurie's eyes on her she didn't dare react too obviously. It was a strain, though, keeping her distance. She was filled with a perverse urge to plant her own lips on those plump orange ones, to fondle those glistening, star-studded breasts, to divest herself of her own clothes and indulge in some intimate bump and grind with this woman who was dominating her so completely, teasing her so mercilessly, so near and yet so far.

The woman fixed Marina with her amber eyes, as if she knew exactly what she was feeling, what she was wanting. Her mouth was curved into a sardonic smile but, just as Marina felt she could stand it no longer, the pressure was taken off her thighs and the woman stood up, backed off, her body glistening with perspiration. She pulled on her hot pants and whisked herself through the curtain with a fluttering wave of her hand before either Marina or Laurie realised that the show had ended.

'Whew! Hot stuff.' Laurie exclaimed, but Marina was still in shock. She sat there with her mini-skirt hitched up to her crotch, damp and creased, her thighs still tingling with the after-effects of their brush with alien, yet familiar, flesh. The raucous music drifted to a close then the cassette player switched itself off with a loud click. Suddenly the whole experience seemed sordid and distasteful. Marina was filled with a horrible disappointment.

'What are we going to do with him?' she asked, to deflect Laurie's attention from herself. Tim lay slumped on the mat. He had begun to snore.

'Will you help me get him back to the hotel? He and I are sharing a room.'

Marina's brow raised itself quizzically, but he gave a derisive laugh.

'Oh no, nothing like that. We're sharing for economy reasons, that's all.'

'I'm relieved to hear it.'

'Why? Do you fancy me?'

Laurie had caught her by surprise. Marina decided it was best to come clean. 'You know I do,' she said, throatily.

'Well, I'm relieved to hear that, too!' They both laughed. He bent towards his friend, lifting his right arm around his neck. 'Let's go, shall we? You take his other arm and we'll try to drag him to his feet.'

A cab came along in a few seconds and soon they were speeding back towards the hotel with Tim sprawled between them on the back seat. During the journey, Laurie's arm crept along the top of the seat and played with Marina's hair, making her spine tingle. She felt as if she were filled with warm jelly, from top to toe and found herself wondering what the chances were of her ending up in bed with Laurie that night. Pretty good, she decided, as long as they could dispose of the corpse-like Tim.

The prospect cheered her. She felt like a good, no-nonsense screw after that weird lap dance business. Perhaps because she wanted to convince herself that she still fancied men, not women. Yet there was a haunting regret lurking somewhere within her, a feeling of unfinished business that both titillated and dismayed her.

As soon as they arrived at the hotel a porter was summoned to help get Tim into the lift. The man showed his distaste for the operation, but made sure they arrived at the third floor. He hung around until Laurie gave him a tip and then sidled out, evidently wondering whether the young *signorina* intended to spend the night in the room of the two young *signore*.

'Nosy bastard!' Laurie grinned, as he finally shut the door on the man. 'We'd better get Tim into bed. You take his feet and I'll hold his armpits and we'll swing him. One, two, three . . .'

They managed to get him onto one of the twin beds and stripped him to his underpants, then pulled the sheet up over him. Almost as soon as it was done, Laurie took her into his arms. In the moonlight that drifted in from the window, his eyes were large and luminous. He kissed her gently on the lips and a surge of fiery longing went through her.

'You know,' he whispered, 'all the time I was watching that lap dance I was wishing you were doing it to me. I don't suppose you could give it a go, could you? I mean, you know what to do now, don't you?'

It wasn't what Marina had expected. She'd imagined they would fall upon each other hungrily once Tim was put to bed, devouring each other's flesh with their lips and tongues and hands. Instead he seemed to want to prolong the agony.

'Please, Marina,' he cajoled. 'I've been aching for it all evening.'

'Okay.'

She made Laurie sit on a chair with his legs together while she began to pirouette in front of him. Although her head still felt woozy Marina was more relaxed now and ready to raise her own sexual temperature along with his. Beneath the skimpy top her nipples were already hard, pushing out the silver fabric, and as she moved her hips the blue skirt brushed against her naked thighs with silken caresses. She put her hands beneath her top and lifted it a few inches until the bare undersides of her breasts were just visible. Laurie groaned, the outline of his erection clearly visible beneath his light summer trousers.

Marina moved slowly towards him, lifting the top until it

lodged just above the nipples. Then she undid her skirt and slowly stepped out of it so that she wore only the silver tanga, slung low on her hips. Laurie's eyes stared at the naked curves of her body with hungry intent and Marina was sure she could see his penis twitch. Between her labia she could feel a tell-tale moistness and knew that she was becoming deeply aroused as well.

It was time to make contact. Marina sidled up to his legs and gradually lowered her bottom onto his horizontal thighs. She could almost feel the sexual energy oozing out of him as she began her routine of pelvic thrusts and self-massage of her breasts. He was perspiring terribly, giving out little groans and exclamations of 'Oh, my God!' as her body was presented to him, almost nude and full of obvious libido.

It was turning her on a treat, too. Marina put one hand down the front of her pants and felt her swollen clitoris with the tip of her forefinger. She slid it down into the wet chasm below, smiling at Laurie all the while.

'You're torturing me!' he complained.

'At least you don't have to pay for it.'

'I'm paying, all right!'

She took pity on him then and, flinging off her top, put one of her nipples between his lips and let him suck. His mouth fastened there greedily, provoking exquisite tingles of pleasure in her as the hotline from nipple to clitoris was activated. Her grinding over his thighs became harder, more focused, as she felt the familiar throbbing in her cleft and the aching emptiness within. It would soon be time to do something about both.

'I have to touch you!' Laurie pleaded, tearing his mouth away from her breast with obvious reluctance. 'Let me touch you down there, please!'

'Okay.'

His fingers were rough on her, making her wince. 'No, not like that! More gently.'

He stroked her mons, his fingertip just reaching the hooded top of her clitoris, giving her light stimulation. Marina knew she couldn't put up with that for long, but it was better than having him maul her mercilessly. She knew from experience that drunken men make clumsy lovers, yet she wanted a screw so badly.

So, it seemed, did he. He broke off and felt in his pocket, pulling out a condom. 'Here, put this on me, won't you?'

She nodded, removed her pants then deftly undid his zipper, pulling out his short, thick organ. Once she had dressed it in rubber Marina raised her mound above it and let the glans engage with her entrance. Then, when she was sure there was enough lubrication for an easy ride, she slowly slid down onto him.

Laurie moaned so loudly when his cock finally entered her up to the hilt that she was afraid he might wake Tim, but he seemed dead to the world. After giving his meaty tool a few squeezes of encouragement, Marina began to move up and down with agile grace, enjoying the intimate contact at last. 'This is so good!' she whispered, lusty feelings surging through her.

Laurie's hands and lips were busy with her breasts and buttocks, devouring her as if he hadn't had a woman in years. Perhaps he hadn't. She was afraid he might come too soon, but his erection proved surprisingly robust and as she felt the first earthy signals of her approaching orgasm she knew that she, at least, would be thoroughly satisfied that evening. Exulting in her own sensuality she threw her head back as the moment of climax arrived, let the wild flurries of passion inflame her entire body through and through until she collapsed onto him in total exhaustion.

The juices ran from her pussy and over both their thighs, but Laurie was still hard. 'Amazing!' she murmured.

'I can't come like this now,' he muttered, much to her dismay. 'Will you suck me off?'

They disengaged and she stood up, legs trembling. 'Give me a chance, I'm knackered.'

'Okay.'

They lay down on the single bed but Marina really was tired. It was almost two in the morning, and she felt as if she'd been on the go all night. Laurie took pity on her.

'Okay, you don't have to do a thing. Just lie there and

push your gorgeous tits together so I can come between them.'

She was amazed Laurie had the energy. He knelt astride her and placed his hot cock into her cleavage while his fingers pulled her flaccid nipples back into hard cones. She reached round behind his thighs and found she was able to fondle his balls while he wanked. Over-stimulated as he was, Laurie took less than a minute to come into the condom and afterwards they lay in each others' arms. There was no question of Marina being able to return to her own hotel bed. All she could do was lie there, cradled in Laurie's firm embrace, until sleep overtook them both.

In the morning they were awoken by Tim's cries of envious amazement.

'You lucky bastard!' he exclaimed, shaking Laurie awake.

Marina gave him a rueful grin, rubbing her eyes. 'We had to bring you home, you were so drunk,' she explained. 'And afterwards I was just too tired to go back to my hotel.'

'Oh yeah, I bet you were!'

She felt sorry for him. It couldn't be easy playing gooseberry, even in retrospect! But she wasn't prepared to do anything about it. When she got up from the bed, ignoring Tim's goggle eyes, she made straight for the bathroom. A shower would wake her up, she decided.

By the time she came out, draped in a towel, she found the two men eating croissants and drinking coffee. Laurie waved at her, inviting her to join them at the low coffee table.

'I ordered breakfast in our room. It's a bit expensive, but what the hell! I don't think any of us are up to traipsing downstairs, are we?'

'Certainly not!' Marina grinned, quaffing a small glass of orange juice. 'Whew, that's better. I'm starving.'

'Well you must have used up a lot of energy last night, one way or another.'

'It's not fair!' Tim grumbled. 'I want to know exactly what I missed.'

'Marina practised her lap-dancing technique on me. I can recommend it, any time!'

She said nothing, hoping they would change the subject, and they soon did. The conversation turned to speculation about what the others in their party might have done last night.

'I reckon Andy was set to get off with Jill,' Tim grinned. 'They've had the hots for each other since the first day of the course. Anyone could see that.'

'Patricia fancies Luigi,' Laurie said. 'But I rather thought he was interested in you, Marina.'

'No comment.'

Laurie continued, recklessly, 'It would be quite a good career move, I imagine, sleeping with a guy like that. What do you reckon?'

She shrugged. 'Maybe. I wouldn't know.' Some devil made her add, 'How about the lovely Bella, then? Don't either of you fancy your chances with her?'

Tim giggled. 'Don't you know about her, Marina? I thought it was common knowledge.'

'What do you mean?'

'She's a lezzie! Lives with this weird dyke who poses as her secretary. I think you might be more her type than me or Laurie.'

It was Marina's turn to giggle, much to the men's bewilderment. But she couldn't help thinking about Justin's obsession with the woman. Had he discovered the prima donna's predilections yet? Her glee was almost spiteful as she recalled how adoringly he had spoken of her. Well if he did harbour a sexual passion for her, he would soon be disillusioned, that was for sure.

And when that happened, Marina thought, giving a catlike smile of satisfaction, maybe there would be room for someone else in his life, after all.

Chapter Five

Waking in a strange bed, it took Justin a few seconds to remember where he was. When he ran through the events of the previous evening he was overcome with excruciating embarrassment. How on earth could he have agreed to take part in such bizarre goings-on? Tempted as he was to imagine that he'd dreamt it all, the weals from his beating and the heap of leather, rubber and metal on the floor were proof positive that his memory wasn't deceiving him.

He rose slowly and opened up the shutters, letting the pure morning light flood into the room, then went back to bed. The sight of that grotesque rubber dildo contraption revolted him, yet he could still recall how excited he had felt when his cock had filled it. The straps and chains that had imprisoned his flesh looked ridiculous now, but the effect of being so tightly constricted had been strangely arousing.

Most of all he remembered how the two women had looked, how they had behaved, and his prick gave a sudden leap of enthusiasm. There had been something wickedly voyeuristic about being with the pair of them, even in such an inferior capacity. The idea that Bella was having a lesbian relationship with that awful Olga woman was incredible, but perhaps it was all some kind of act, a conspiracy to put him in their power.

At any rate, he would go through a lot to feel her gentle hands caressing his bum again. That had been fantastic! And his climax afterwards had been extremely satisfying. Was he one of those peculiar types who like to be dominated? The idea had never occurred to him before, but if it was true then he'd come to the right place. After a few weekends at the *Villa Gandolfini* he would know whether being bossed around by a couple of dominating women really was his cup of tea. Of course, the fact that it was the Divine Bella who was doing the bossing made it all the more exciting.

He was tempted to remain in bed for a while, fantasising, but curiosity made him get up. After a shower he dressed in jeans and T-shirt then went downstairs. It was ten o'clock, the sun was streaming through every window and the villa was as quiet as the grave. Justin sauntered out onto the terrace to admire the view, but he hadn't been there long before a voice behind him called, '*Buon giorno, Justino!*'

It was Bella. She came towards him clad in a magnificent floral silk housecoat, her hair hidden beneath a matching turban. Gold sandals were on her feet and her face was devoid of make-up. She was holding a tray with a cafetière and two mugs.

'I thought you might like to have coffee with me,' she smiled.

Justin was nonplussed. She was behaving as if nothing unusual had happened last night. Well, he would play it cool too. They sat down at the wrought-iron table and Bella poured them both a cup of rich, dark coffee.

'Would you like orange juice, croissants?' she asked him.

'No thanks, this is fine.'

Bella sat back in her chair and sipped thoughtfully from her cup. Then she said, 'What did you think of your lesson yesterday?' Justin wondered which 'lesson' she was referring to. She saw his hesitation and smiled. 'I meant your voice lesson, of course.'

'It was wonderful, marvellous. To be taught by someone like you . . .' He tailed off, afraid of sounding too gushing.

She leaned over and touched his arm. 'I can't work miracles, you know. All the hard work must come from you. The inspiration you must find inside yourself. You have promise. If you dedicate yourself completely you may succeed in becoming a great singer. But you must be able to forget yourself, to bury yourself in the part, the work. That is why we played our little game afterwards. Dedication, passion, discipline . . . do you understand?'

'I . . . think so.'

'Good.' She patted his hand. 'This morning you are free to walk around the village, visit the lake, as you will. I have to practise. Lunch is at noon, then we shall work.'

Bella rose, giving a brief glimpse of naked thigh before sweeping her long gown around her. She smiled at him, her eyes intense in her lightly tanned face, then she wandered back into the house. Almost immediately the maid appeared to clear away the coffee tray.

'You want anything more, *signore*?'

Justin looked closely at her, wondering if she was also mixed up in the charades that took place in that household, but her peasant face was completely neutral, innocent.

'No, thank you. I think I'll take a walk now.'

Olga didn't appear for the rest of the day. When Justin returned after a pleasant stroll by the lake he found only two places laid for lunch. Bella brought in a CD player and they listened to her recording of 'One Fine Day' all through the meal, which she played over and over. She seemed intent, her mind still on work, and Justin felt like an intruder. He was glad when the light meal was finished and he could escape to his room for half an hour.

Their second lesson got off to a shaky start, when Bella tetchily accused him of forgetting everything she had told him about posture and breathing. However, he soon rectified it and they made some progress. Having her as his teacher again was mildly arousing, since Justin was reminded of the way she'd behaved towards him the night before. When that subtle note of command, almost menacing, came into her voice it sent shivers of anticipation through him. She had only to fix him with a look of faint displeasure and he would feel his bowels curdle deliciously with a tantalising mixture of fear and lust.

As the afternoon progressed the tension within him grew until Justin was longing for some relief. He was singing to the best of his ability, all his pent-up energy pouring out through his voice, and when Bella at last clapped her hands together and cried, '*Bravo!*' he knew he was making headway. Filled with exhilaration, he listened impatiently to her summing up while his imagination leapt forward to that evening, wondering what new delights she had in store for him. Surely he was due for some reward after working so hard!

At last she turned to him with an enigmatic smile. 'So, you will take a rest now and we shall meet again at dinner. Olga will come to help you dress, as before. I hope you will find your second night with us as stimulating as your first.'

She swept from the room, leaving him to tinker with the piano keys before drifting upstairs. The intensive voice work had drained him, and he lay down to rest. He was imagining Bella in her most famous rôle as Queen of the Night, resplendent in a midnight blue gown scattered with moons and stars like the portrait in the lounge. How divine she truly was! He still couldn't believe he was privileged to be so intimate with her, to receive her help and guidance. The way she'd caressed him had been even more incredible. If he had to abase himself before her in abject gratitude, take her scorn and punishment without flinching, then it was only fitting. He would do that, and a lot more, to be with her like this.

By the time Olga entered his room, without knocking, Justin had already showered. He confronted her draped in a towel and she held out his clothes for the evening: a parody of a waiter's costume, with a bow tie fixed to a white collar, tight fitting black leather briefs with a window in the back to show off his buttocks, stiff white cuffs and lightweight black laced boots, the sort boxers wore.

'Come along!' she told him, sternly. 'The mistress wants you impeccably dressed for tonight. She is expecting guests.'

Justin was horrified. It just hadn't occurred to him that their kinky little scene might expand to include others, but of course it made sense. A woman as famous as Bella would be used to entertaining. The question was, just who might these 'guests' be? For one awful moment he wondered if Luigi Postoni might be amongst them. If word got around the summer school that he allowed himself to be humiliated in this way he would head straight home, the shame would be too great.

Olga sensed his apprehension and gave a tight smile. 'Don't worry, no-one you know will be there. I think you might even enjoy the company, provided you are a good boy and don't make any silly mistakes.'

There was an extra spice to Justin's excitement as he followed Olga downstairs that evening. This time he was allowed to walk upright, but she had bound his wrists with a white silk scarf over the cuffs, so his arm movement was restricted. She took him to the pantry, where a tray was placed on his upturned palms and glasses of sweet and dry vermouth were arranged, along with dishes of black and green olives.

'You will take that up to the sitting room,' she informed him.

Justin counted only four glasses. That was a relief. A couple of guests would not be as intimidating as a big dinner party. Even so, he was full of trepidation as he walked along the corridor with Olga casually strolling behind, his elbows tucked in and his forearms stiffly horizontal. His forehead and bare chest were already perspiring a little and his stomach felt queasy with apprehension.

His entrance was greeted by a cry of delight from Bella, who turned in her chair to survey him. She beckoned him over with a smile.

'Ah, the new butler has arrived. Doesn't he look splendid, Annaliese?'

While he waited for the trio to come forward and take their drinks, Justin gave them all a discreet inspection. Bella herself was dressed in a pair of loose, turquoise velour trousers and matching top – rather informal, Justin thought, for a dinner party. But she had gone to town on her jewellery. Diamonds and sapphires gleamed at her ears and throat, while her fingers were heavy with glittering stones.

The girl she had called Annaliese was very pretty indeed. Her short, curly hair was very blonde and her eyes were a sparkling, greeny-blue. The floral silk shift she was wearing had a bodice that emphasised her small, but shapely, breasts. When their eyes met she smiled at him, showing small, perfectly white, well-formed teeth. Justin grinned back, instantly smitten.

So it was a while before he took notice of the other guest, a lanky, rather lugubrious-looking man with stringy black hair and a melancholy expression. He looked as if he was going to be a bit of a skeleton at the feast and Justin wondered why Bella had invited him. Could that man and the lovely Annaliese possibly be a couple? He did hope not.

'Yes, he is certainly very splendid,' the girl said, as she took a dry vermouth off the tray with a delicate touch, sending his libido into overdrive. She had a slight accent, one which Justin guessed was either Scandinavian or Dutch. Their eyes met and he saw the pent-up amusement lingering there, ready to erupt into laughter at any moment.

Justin gave a bow and was about to retreat when Bella called, 'Over here! Come and be admired.'

Obediently he went to her. When he was standing by her chair she turned him round and displayed his naked behind to her guests.

'Lovely rotund buttocks, don't you think, my dears? He loves to be spanked, you know. Maybe one of you will have that privilege later on.' She gave him a playful slap on the behind. 'Now run along, back to the kitchen with Olga. You'll be needed at table soon.'

'You think you're quite something in that outfit, don't you?' Olga snarled in his ear, as soon as they'd left the room. She gave him a pinch on his right buttock which was quite painful. He winced, but didn't drop the tray. She went on, spitefully, 'Well, let me tell you who's the boss around here – it's me, see? Just you remember that.'

Not for the first time, Justin was aware of a certain tension between his two mistresses, as if they had made an uneasy truce with each other. He was intensely curious about their relationship but doubted whether he would ever find out the whole truth. Meanwhile, the thought that he was obliged to play 'piggy-in-the-middle' was rather disconcerting.

He followed Olga into the kitchen, where the cook was busy with the first course. She was making a minestrone soup, which was soon poured into a large tureen.

'You will take this to the dinner table, then go back to the drawing room and announce that dinner is served,' Olga told him. 'During the meal, your duty will be to serve the wine.' Justin held his bound wrists up before him. 'How can I?'

To his dismay, Olga slapped his cheek hard, making the spot sting badly. Cook, busy with her saucepans, pretended not to notice, 'Impertinent man! Of course I shall make it possible for you to perform your duties. Don't you trust me?'

'I'm sorry.'

'So you should be. Come here.'

She loosened the scarf until it was no more than a token restraint. Then she placed a tray containing the hot tureen into his hands. 'Now go. And don't give me any more cause for complaint this evening, or you will deeply regret it.'

Justin made his way to the dining-room taking care not to spill a single drop from the tureen. He placed it on the table then went to knock at the drawing-room door. Bella's voice summoned him in.

'Dinner is served, *Signora*,' he announced, bowing slightly. Annaliese jumped up. 'Oh good, I'm starving!'

Her infectious enthusiasm made him smile at her and she returned it openly. But when Justin saw the frown that passed over Bella's face he grew alarmed. As they all filed out of the room she took him aside, muttering crossly in his ear, 'A butler should avoid over-familiarity at all times, especially with guests. Is that quite clear?'

'Yes, mistress,' he said, suitably humbled.

To his relief the maid served the soup, but he had to go round with the decanter. Terribly afraid of spilling red wine on the pristine white tablecloth, Justin concentrated really hard as he poured. When he had filled the glasses of Bella and Olga, he moved towards Annaliese with some trepidation, afraid that his attraction to her would make his hand wobble.

'Just a little wine, please,' she said, in her deliciously accented voice. He leaned forward and then, much to his amazement, felt her hand on his bare buttock. For a moment he wavered and it looked as if he was going to spill the wine, but he recovered himself and proceeded to pour, doing his best to keep a straight face and a steady hand while she caressed him intimately. As he straightened up he felt her finger slip into the crack between his cheeks for a brief moment and his anus involuntarily tightened, keeping it there. She giggled and he backed away, letting her finger go.

'Now Ettore's glass,' he heard Bella say. 'We must lubricate dear Ettore's vocal cords, mustn't we? So he can entertain us later on.'

There was something decidedly spooky about the man. He spoke little, and when he did it was almost in a whisper. He gave off a strange odour too, like old-fashioned cologne. Justin filled his glass then retreated to the side table, just behind Bella's chair, from where he could be a silent witness to the proceedings.

At first the conversation was about people he didn't know and it soon became clear that the guests were both, or had been, pupils of Bella's. Her protégés, in fact. He remembered reading that she took a keen interest in young singers and helped to foster their talents. But what was the exact nature of her interest in these two? There were sexual currents whirling back and forth across the table that he couldn't quite analyse.

Olga, too, was behaving in a peculiarly coquettish way. She was in a rather sombre black dress but she kept fingering the string of pearls around her neck and playing with the matching earrings, drawing attention to herself in subtle ways. Once or twice he caught her eye and she gave him a reproving look, as if he wasn't supposed to be taking any interest in the goings-on. But what else was he to do, standing there like a lemon?

Soon his services were called on again, as they finished the soup course and he had to take the empty tureen back to the kitchen. Olga followed, hard on his heels.

'Try to conduct yourself with a little more decorum,' she said, icily. 'What goes on between your mistresses and their guests should be of no concern to you.'

He bowed his head in acquiescence while she continued, 'You will serve the Barolo with the main course. There is a sweet wine for dessert. When you are not busy you will stand with your eyes lowered away from the table and as still as possible. Is that clear?'

'Yes, mistress.'

'Later, we may invite you to join in our party games, if you are very good.'

The prospect thrilled him enormously, but he was careful not to show it. He knew if he went about his business like a regular butler, doing exactly as he was told, he might escape the punishments and reap the rewards. But a perverse voice inside him argued that wouldn't be nearly so satisfying. Remembering how he'd felt last night, first being chastised and then cosseted, he realised that it was all part of the same game and you couldn't have one half without the other.

The meal proceeded without incident until they all left the dining-room and Justin brought the coffee into the drawing-room. He spilt a drop on the silver tray as he was pouring it into one of the dainty cups and Olga pounced on him at once.

'What is that mess on the tray?' she snapped.

Justin was nonplussed and reacted automatically. 'It's only a little spillage. . .'

She took the tray from him and set it down on a small table. 'Insolent creature! See how he answers back? What shall we do with him, Bella?'

'Let us draw lots for the pleasure of punishing him.'

'Oh yes!' Annaliese clapped her hands together in glee. 'That shall be the first of our party games. We can play "Smack the Butler on the Bum"!'

'I think it would be better if he were blindfolded,' Bella suggested.

The silk scarf that had been used to bind his wrists was now tied over his eyes. Justin was made to kneel over a chair with his buttocks exposed while the lots were drawn and he heard Annaliese give a giggle of triumph. 'Oh good! I was hoping it would be me!'

'We'll give our other guest the choice of instrument,' Bella said, coolly. 'What is it to be, Ettore: whip, rod, slipper, or bare hand?'

There was a pause, during which Justin did his best to calculate which would be the most and which the least painful. At last Ettore's whispering voice came, 'Bare hand. For a slight misdemeanour.'

'Very well,' Bella said. 'Annaliese, give him three on each buttock. First the left, then the right.'

Justin braced himself. The girl's slaps were light at first, but became bolder, more punishing, as the count continued. Soon his posterior felt warm and tingling all over, and he could feel his prick hardening in response. In his imagination he could see the flush on Annaliese's face, her cheeks becoming as pink as his own nether ones, and her small breasts bobbing with each stroke. He could hear her gasping clearly, her breathing accelerating to match her effort. She sounded just as if she were in the throes of orgasm.

'There!' he heard her gasp, with much satisfaction. 'Six of the best!'

'Well done!' Bella said. 'You managed that spanking like a true devotee of the art. Didn't she, Olga? Now, I think it is time for you to sing, Ettore.'

'For my supper, yes?' he said, dryly.

'If you like. But you know how we all adore to hear you. And perhaps you would permit our servant to remain in the room and enjoy your exquisite voice too? I doubt he has ever heard such a rarity.'

'Nor ever will again,' Annaliese added.

Justin's blindfold was removed and he was permitted to sit on a small footstool while Annaliese went over to lift the lid of the grand piano and Ettore took up his position nearby. A few baroque-sounding chords were played, and the whole room sank into hushed expectancy. Ettore took a deep breath, opened his rather cherubic lips, and began to sing.

Justin had expected to hear a fine tenor voice, perhaps even a baritone. So he was totally unprepared for the sound which came forth from Ettore's mouth. It was pure and sweet, and as the song progressed it became obvious that his range was far above the normal for a tenor. Unable to help himself, he muttered under his breath in astonishment, 'A *castrato*?'

Only Bella, who was sitting nearest to him, overheard. She frowned and shook her finger at him. Justin was completely mystified. He had never heard a man sing in such a high vocal range before. Yet, as far as he knew, the last man to sacrifice his manhood for his voice had been the cele-brated Moreschi, who had died in the Twenties.

Once Justin had got used to the sound, he found Ettore's voice very beautiful, with an ethereal, almost angelic, purity of tone. He was certainly a rarity. While he listened his brain buzzed with questions. Did the man perform in public, or only at private parties like this? If he wasn't a eunuch, how was such an incredibly high voice produced: was he born with the gift, or was it some specially acquired skill? Did the fact that his speaking voice was almost a whisper have anything to do with it? Had Bella been tutoring him as she would a soprano?

The man ended his pretty song, accepted the applause gracefully then went to sit between Bella and Olga while Annaliese also obliged, accompanying herself on the piano. She sang well, but unremarkably, and after Ettore's per-formance it was something of an anti-climax. Justin half expected Bella to rise to sing but she remained seated and the piano lid was closed, putting an end to his hopes.

'Now what shall we do?' asked Olga, with the air of a master of ceremonies. 'How about a game of "Butter-fingers"?'

'Don't you mean "Butterballs"?' Annaliese said, with a sly wink at Ettore, who responded with, 'Buggerballs?' Everyone seemed to share the joke except Justin, who smiled out of politeness but felt bewildered.

'Go to the pantry and fetch a dish of butter,' Olga said, looking at Justin with her dark, direct gaze. He felt a faint dread stirring within, but left the room without demur and was back a few minutes later, bearing a silver butter dish. He set it down on a low table and awaited further instructions.

'For those who have not played this game before, here are the rules,' Bella began. 'Each of us will take three slips of paper. On one we write the name of a part of the body. On the other we write the name of someone else in the room.' She held up two silk bags, one black and one scarlet. 'All the name slips are put in the red bag for the draw, and the body parts go into the black one. First we draw the name of the person who is doing the buttering. Then we draw the name of the person to be buttered. Finally we draw the part of the body. Is that clear?'

It sounded a weird game. The way everyone was looking at each other and giggling gave Justin the impression that something was being kept from him. Was this just an elaborate hoax, intended to humiliate him? Yet the thought of being 'buttered' was quite sensual. Shades of 'Last Tango'. His bowels contracted at the thought.

Justin wrote 'Annaliese' on both his slips. He didn't much care whether he got to do her, be done by her, or watched her with someone else. He then wrote 'pussy' on the third and the slips went into the bags with the others. There was a moment of dramatic suspense while Bella shook the bags around. Then she held them open for Olga to make the draw.

'Olga!' she read out, with a sly grin. 'I shall be buttering someone up, then. And who is to be my lucky victim?' She made a show of delving around in the red bag then pulled out another slip. 'Justin. Well, well. What a surprise!'

She crumpled up the two slips and tossed them into the grate. There was a suspense in the room that seemed conspiratorial. Justin had the distinct feeling that they were all laughing at him, secretly, all dying to break out into hysterical giggling. But Olga read out the final slip with a completely straight face. 'Arse!'

'Lucky you!' Ettore said, lugubriously. It was the first time he had directed a remark to Justin but now there seemed a weird kind of complicity between them. He couldn't help wondering if Ettore had been through the same kind of treatment that he was getting. Perhaps it was some kind of initiation, to test the mettle of Bella's pupils.

Further speculation was curtailed as he was spread-eagled over a footstool with his bottom in the air. It occurred to him that someone – Olga? Bella? – must have a fetish about men's behinds. They certainly seemed to relish having his on display.

'Ettore, sing that rude song about the arse-lickers!' Annaliese begged.

'Oh yes!' Bella giggled. 'Perfect!'

Justin heard them move to the piano and soon Ettore was

singing in a mincing falsetto that had the company in fits of laughter. Then he felt the firm hand of Olga applying the grease to his buttocks. At first he thought the experience was going to be similar to when Bella had caressed him, but soon she was delving deep into his crack and he knew she was going to penetrate him.

He groaned as her relentless finger slid further into him, its way eased by the sticky lubrication, filling him with a sensual warmth that was nevertheless tinged with shame. He didn't want anyone to know that he was relishing it, and hoped the rest of the party were intent on Ettore's singing. The ridiculous-sounding song went on and on, and all the time Olga was digging in and screwing her finger around in his anus until he was in a state of high excitement.

His cock was fully erect, pressed hard against the up-holstery of the stool, and he was afraid that if she continued to stimulate him in that way he would soon come. He didn't want to, not in front of the others. Acutely embarrassed, he did his best to squeeze his muscles tight and not give in to the irresistible arousal that was forcing him towards a con-clusion.

'There, my little buttered bun,' he heard Olga croon, below the music.

Justin wriggled helplessly on the stool as the final spasmodic surrender came. His cock pumped furiously, all the tension spilling out of him, and he had to snort through his nose to avoid making a more obvious noise. His one prayer was that the others wouldn't notice.

Perhaps they didn't, but Olga certainly did. 'Dirty little beast!' she whispered in his ear, as Ettore's mocking voice reached a crescendo. 'I knew you couldn't resist it. If you've made a mess everywhere you'll get a good spanking, I'm warning you.'

He jumped up as if he had been scalded and stared down at the pink velour of the footstool which, mercifully, was unstained. But he could feel the wetness tricking down his thighs beneath the saucy *lederhosen* and knew it would only be a matter of time before his emission became obvious. If only they would dismiss him he could go to the toilet and clean himself up, but there seemed little chance of that.

Ettore's song ended, with amused applause, and then Bella asked what they should play next. Olga murmured something in Italian then gave Justin a shrewd look and said something else. Bella nodded. She turned to Justin and said, 'Your services are no longer required for this evening. You are dismissed.'

She spoke coldly, and he had the sudden feeling that he meant nothing at all to her, or to anyone else in that room, that he was being regarded as little more than part of the furniture. Miserably he walked towards the door. His buttocks stuck together with the butter and moved as he walked, making a slight squelching sound that he found acutely embarrassing. Olga followed and caught up with him once he was outside the room.

'Tomorrow you will need to get up at five, in order to return to the Academy in time. Lena will bring coffee to your room, then Enrico will drive you to your hotel. We shall see you again next weekend.'

Justin wondered whether he should thank her but her demeanour discouraged such niceties. She turned back towards the drawing-room door and then, as an afterthought, said with a strange smile, 'Bella and I are satisfied with your progress, but you still have a long way to go.' With that she entered the room again and he had a tantalising glimpse of Annaliese sitting on Ettore's knee before the door was firmly shut once more.

Chapter Six

Justin was acting weird. Marina had tried to get a smile out of him when they re-assembled on Monday morning but all she got was a scowl. Then, at coffee time, she asked if he'd had a good weekend and he practically bit her head off. Maybe there was something in that rumour about Bella after all, and he'd found out the hard way!

Far from putting her off, however, his surliness only intrigued Marina more. She sensed he was an iceberg type, nine-tenths of him below the surface, and she never could resist a mystery man. So when they gathered outside the academy for the afternoon trip to Caracalla she sidled up and engaged him in conversation. When Laurie butted in, saying he hoped the coach would be full so she could sit in his lap, she froze him off.

'Sorry I spoke!' he moaned, batting his eyes in fury at her.

Marina was sorry too, but she knew it was no use encouraging Laurie. Whatever attraction she'd felt towards him had been provoked by alcohol on Saturday night and, in the clear light of Monday afternoon, he was looking decidedly unsavoury. As far as she was concerned, he was yesterday's news. But when she turned around Justin was talking to someone else and she thought she'd lost her chance with him.

So she was pleasantly surprised Justin came to sit beside her in the coach. 'Hi!' he grinned, more like his usual self. 'Fancy rehearsing in a real amphitheatre then?'

'Will we get the chance?' she asked, excitedly. The *Terme di Caracalla* were ancient Roman baths, used during the summer months as a fantastic setting for opera.

Bella, who had just joined the coach, overheard. 'Not

today,' she smiled. 'They are rehearsing for the current production of *Aida*. It's only through my influence that you are allowed to attend, so you had better behave yourselves!'

Marina saw the strangely arch look that the *diva* gave to Justin before she passed on down the aisle. It made him blush. Even more intrigued, Marina whispered, 'Did you really spend the weekend at her villa?'

He nodded, tight-lipped, in a manner that suggested he wouldn't be drawn further. Marina vowed to bring it up again at a more opportune moment. Meanwhile she was looking forward to a nice drive through Rome and an interesting afternoon watching the professionals rehearse. Maybe she and Justin could pick up a few tips for their own performance.

The remnants of the old baths were an impressive sight, the ruined walls flushed with gold in the late-afternoon sunshine. The rehearsal had already been resumed, and the Irish tenor Michael O'Donaghue was singing Radames' aria, 'Celeste Aida', when they arrived. Quietly they took their seats at the back of the auditorium, high up amongst the banked rows.

'Oh, it must be wonderful to sing here!' Marina whispered to Justin as the rich tones echoed all round the amphitheatre.

'Maybe one day,' he smiled back.

Marina relaxed, glad he was being friendly again. Sitting there with their knees touching she felt a certain excitement. Knowing that he was appreciating the music as much as she was helped. Once again she began to warm to him, glad that fate had thrust them together, made them singing partners. They hadn't had time to rehearse since Friday but she was half hoping for a run-through that evening, when they got back to the academy.

Her motives weren't entirely pure, either. Although Marina told herself that she wanted to get him alone so she could find out more about his weekend exploits, in reality she knew that she fancied her chances of seducing him. The nearness of him was making her dizzy, and she could feel all her pulses throbbing with excitement at the combination of heat, magnificent singing and the physical proximity of a man she found enticing.

The conductor stopped the singer and explained some points to him that were unfortunately spoken too quietly for the onlookers to hear. Then O'Donaghue resumed the aria at a slower pace.

'That's better,' Justin said. 'I thought he was rushing it a bit.'

'Really?' Marina's eyes met his, quizzically. 'You're familiar with the part, then?'

He nodded, diffidently. 'Will you sing the same aria for me sometime?' she asked. 'It's one of my favourites.'

'Maybe.'

They were speaking almost in whispers and Marina found his low, slightly husky voice very arousing. She pressed her thighs together beneath the thin cotton of her summer skirt and squeezed so that her vulva squelched a little. Her clitoris was making itself evident, and she wondered if Justin had noticed. Didn't they say that a man could smell female musk keenly whenever it was exuded, becoming subliminally aroused?

She decided to stick to him like a limpet all afternoon, pressing home her advantage. If what Laurie had said about Bella was true, Justin would be a very frustrated young man right now and ready to relieve himself with almost any willing female. She glanced down the rows to where Bella was sitting, her statuesque form very upright on the bench. Was she really a dyke? Remembering her experience with the lap-dancer, Marina found herself becoming surprisingly hot and wet at the thought. Yet the idea of becoming involved in a lesbian scenario with an international opera star struck her as so ludicrous that she had to stifle a giggle.

'What's the matter?' Justin asked, reprovingly.

'Oh. Nothing. Just a thought.'

He was frowning at her so she did her best to recover. It wouldn't do to put him off her, not now that she was determined to have him as soon as the opportunity presented itself. The heat was making her perspire, and she could feel a small rivulet travelling down between her breasts, tickling her sensitive skin. She wiped the material of her dress against her cleavage but she wasn't wearing a bra and the dampness made her nipples stand very obviously. Justin glanced at them and looked away again quickly, as if he were embarrassed. Marina smiled. A man who wasn't at least thinking of bedding her would not have been quite so disconcerted, she was sure of that.

Feeling as if she were on a taut wire, Marina was scarcely aware of what was going on far below, on the wooden stage. She was suddenly jerked into attention when Bella stood up amidst sporadic applause, and began to descend the steps.

'What's going on?' she asked Justin.

His expression was radiant, adoring, and Marina felt a stab of jealousy. 'Michael has invited Bella to sing with him. Isn't that marvellous? They'll be doing it specially for us!'

As Bella reached the stage, the *répétiteur* played an introduction on the piano which Marina instantly recognised. 'Oh no!' she groaned.

Justin stared at her, perplexed. 'What's the matter? Don't you want them to show us how it can be done? I think it's a marvellous coincidence that they're going to do our duet.'

'Yes. Yes, of course. You're right.'

She settled back to listen, but still felt uneasy. Already she felt horribly inferior, afraid that she would never shape up as a singer. Now, in Justin's eyes, she would come a very poor second to Bella when they came to rehearse the same piece. The fact that he was already besotted by the world-famous soprano made Marina's dreams of seduction seem foolish.

Once the exquisite singing began, however, Marina felt she could forgive that woman anything. Bella's voice contained a unique blend of passion, playfulness and charm that could win over the most recalcitrant crowd. For a group of her greatest fans, who had been lured onto the summer school by the mere mention of her name in the brochure, it was an experience to die for. Scarcely had the last note died away than the students were on their feet, whooping and cheering her with all the wild enthusiasm of a *claque*.

'Fantastic!' Justin exclaimed as he turned to her, his eyes like flaming beacons. 'Isn't she just sensational?'

'Of course,' Marina murmured. She watched Michael

bowing low before the *diva*, kissing her hand with as much reverence as if she were the Pope.

'I hope you feel inspired, rather than put off,' Justin went on. 'I thought we might have a run-through later on, when we get back. If you've nothing else on, of course.'

Marina threw him a broad grin. This was exactly what she'd been hoping for. 'That would be great! Shall we see if we can use one of the practice rooms at the academy?'

He nodded, his eyes swivelling back to where Bella was acknowledging the applause with mock-staginess. Marina felt the urge to win his sole attention grow acute. If she could only distract him for five minutes from his obsession with that woman she knew she would stand a chance. But it was a tall order. How could she hope to compete with a phenomenon like her?

On the way back to the centre of Rome everyone was buzzing around Bella. Even Luigi was being sycophantic, saying what an honour she had paid them that afternoon. He marvelled that she had not sung the part for three years, had never sung with that young tenor before and yet had delivered a consummate performance. That, he said, was the mark of a true *diva*, a real professional and a generous spirit. It made Marina want to puke.

Things began to look up when they disembarked outside the academy. Justin actually took her by the hand and led her up to Luigi, where he asked for permission to practise.

'Inspired by greatness?' he said, with a hint of a sneer in his voice. His eyes lowered to where the tips of Marina's nipples were still nudging through her dress, and a look of disdain came into them. She felt a warmth rise in her cheeks, not of lust but of indignation and shame. How could she have been so naive as to make a play for that self-obsessed bastard?

Still, he allowed them to use one of the practice rooms on the second floor. They picked up two scores from the library and one of the pre-recorded accompaniments that the academy students used. Then they entered their allotted room and Marina found herself totally alone with Justin for the first time. Her sudden awareness of the emptiness and silence was overwhelming, making her half-suppressed desire for him rise swiftly to the surface of her consciousness like a bubbling spring.

'Okay, let's run through it from the top,' he said.

She could tell, from the slight huskiness in his voice, that he was affected in the same way by their being alone together. Nervously she held onto the score-sheet, and when the time came for her to sing she sounded so wavery that she collapsed into giggles.

'I think we should do some exercises first, don't you?' she suggested.

First Justin played the scale for her to sing to, then she did the same for him. Arpeggios followed until both their voices had limbered up and they were singing freely. Marina felt her spirit fill with the special joy she felt whenever she was using her voice to good effect. She trilled and warbled her way up and down the scale, then took off at a tangent and began to incorporate all kinds of silly tunes.

Justin joined her and they began to play with sound like a couple of kids, improvising together, having fun. All pretence at serious rehearsal vanished as they got to know each others' voices in a crazily impromptu fashion, the notes spilling out of them in promiscuous abandon. In the process, Marina felt herself warming to him immensely, and guessed it was mutual. He was glowing at her, vital and aroused, looking extraordinarily handsome.

It was impossible to say which approached the other first. As the accompanying music swelled to a climax an irresistible urge thrust them into each others' arms where they kissed hungrily, tongues raping each others' mouth. Justin was holding her to him in a kind of desperation, his hands roving down to the taut curves of her behind. She was thrust hard against him, feeling the satisfying evidence of his lust against the flat of her stomach. God, how she wanted him!

'Marina!' he gasped, trying to pull the shoulders of her dress down.

She struggled out of his embrace. 'Not *here*! Someone might come in!'

'Where, then – my hotel, or yours?'

Something in her was disappointed at this blunt approach. She had wanted the pleasure of a lingering seduction, of winning him by stages. Now it looked as if she would have the whole of him on a plate, in one ravenous session. Yet she feared that if she played hard to get he would slip from her grasp forever, and she did want him. Oh yes, she was quite sure of that!

'Your place,' she grinned, picking up her discarded bag. 'It's nearer.' Minutes later they were racing along the pavement, raising eyebrows as they went, until the glass and gilt foyer of the hotel came into view. Marina took Justin by the hand and slowed him down, wary of attracting attention from the hotel staff.

'Look, they won't like it if they think we're using the hotel like a pick-up joint. I'll go in first and head straight for the Ladies. You wait a few minutes then get the key, and I'll come up later. What's your room number?'

'Thirty-two. Third floor.'

'Okay.'

Feeling nervous, Marina entered the artificially cool foyer and tried her best to look as if she belonged there. Her chief worry was that she would bump into someone else from the summer school. She quickly spotted the sign for the cloakrooms and headed confidently in that direction, looking straight ahead. No-one challenged her, and as soon as she was behind the closed door she breathed a sigh of relief. She went into a cubicle and pulled down her pants. The gusset was already soaked with her juices.

After she'd peed Marina touched the swollen tip of her clitoris with her finger and the warm relief that flooded through her felt so good that she continued to stimulate herself, impatient to assuage some of the hungry need in her. She had seldom wanted a man so much, and her lust had taken her by surprise. It took scarcely a minute of rapid friction to bring her to a climax and then the throbbing flooded through her abruptly, sharp and sweet, making her groan out her satisfaction, leaving her spent and gasping. She hoped no-one else had come into the Ladies meanwhile.

Just to make sure, she lingered a bit longer and then

flushed the loo. It seemed pointless to replace her sodden underwear so she rolled the damp rag into a ball and put it into her bag, then came out of the cubicle and washed her hands. Seeing no-one else around she took a glob of liquid soap and wiped her pussy with it, then douched herself with water. Much as she would have loved to open her legs and let the warm air dryer do its work there was no way she could contort herself into that position, so she had to be content with drying herself on a paper towel.

Her legs felt weak as she went out into the foyer again, but she resumed her confident attitude and made for the lift. She got in and pressed the button for the third floor, but it stopped at the first and two men got in. They looked at her rather strangely, and she wanted to giggle. Did they know she was wearing no knickers? Could they smell the residue of her love-juice, even? The thought excited her unbearably and she began to fantasise about letting the pair of them take her right there. But the idea of the lift making endless journeys up and down while the men screwed her made her want to laugh out loud, and she stuffed her fist into her mouth to prevent it.

Justin was waiting for her in his room, visibly on edge. His dark hair was dishevelled where he'd run his fingers through it, waiting for her. She did hope he wasn't having second thoughts. Maybe some alcohol would be a good idea. But before she could suggest it he launched himself at her, pressing her into a forceful embrace.

'Hey, wait a minute!' she laughed. 'Talk about a rib-crusher!'

'Sorry!' he mumbled. Then his face dropped. 'Maybe this isn't such a good idea . . .'

Marina's heart made an abrupt dive. 'What's the matter? You were hot for it just a few minutes ago. What's a girl to think if . . .'

'I'm just a bit screwed up, that's all.' He gave a self-mocking laugh and went to sit on the edge of the bed, looking dejected.

Marina sat beside him, taking his hand in hers. 'What is it? Tell Aunty Marina.'

He gave her a rueful smile. 'I suppose it's Bella.'

'*Bella*?' Despite herself, Marina was intrigued. 'You did spend the weekend with her after all, didn't you? Did she give you a good time?'

She sounded more bitterly sarcastic than she'd intended. Ashamed, and wanting to salvage the situation, she added softly, 'I'm sorry, Justin. I know how you feel about her. But I'm afraid that if you become too emotionally involved you'll get hurt. She's an international star, for God's sake. She wouldn't . . .'

Justin snapped, 'I know what she is, and I know what I am! I'm a bloody fool!'

Marina put her arm around his shoulders. 'You're infatuated, that's all. It happens to the best of us at some time or other. If you can't get her out of your mind I suppose there's nothing more to be said. I'm disappointed, because I really fancy you. But I like you too, Justin. I want you to know that.'

He turned his soft grey gaze towards her. His eyes looked sad and distant, a far cry from the laughing eyes that had turned her on a treat in the practice room. Perhaps they should have thrown caution to the winds and got down to it there and then, before they'd both had time to reflect on what they were doing.

Marina held him close and whispered, 'Never mind, Justin. If you want to talk about Bella, about your feelings for her, I'll listen as a friend. I won't judge you or anything, I promise.'

His face turned towards her with a look of desperation. 'I had a really strange weekend, Marina. I can't . . . go into detail. But every time I think about it, it freaks me out.'

'So you did go to her villa?'

'Yes. It was amazing. She offered me singing lessons if I'd . . . well, I can't talk about that.'

Marina felt herself growing excited again. 'You mean, in exchange for sex? Is that what this is about, Justin?'

He shook his head. 'Not exactly. Anyway, there are others involved . . .'

'Others? Who, another woman?'

'What?'

She almost laughed at his startled expression. 'Oh I just heard some rumours. That's all.'

'Well they're not true!' he said, vehemently. 'You shouldn't listen to gossip, Marina. Bella is a goddess, on stage and off. When you get to know her a bit she's wonderful, more wonderful than I'd have imagined.'

'Are you in love with her, Justin?'

He turned away, his cheeks colouring. 'I don't know. I've never felt anything like this before. I mean, I was already a big fan of hers, as you know. But to be invited to her villa, to have her giving me private lessons. I can't tell you how that makes me feel.'

Marina thought of how she'd felt, at first, with Luigi. He wasn't of Bella's calibre, of course, but he was still famous in the rarefied world of opera. And she'd had sex with him, of sorts. She gave a small smile. 'I think I can understand, a little.'

'Can you?' He kissed her cheek. 'Do you know what it's like to worship the ground someone walks on?'

Impelled by some mischievous, yet powerful, spirit Marina got to her feet. 'Show me!'

'What?' His face looked up at her quizzically, making her want to smile, but she remained stern and aloof. 'Show me how you would worship me if I were Bella. Pretend I'm her.'

Justin stared at her incredulously. 'I can't.'

'Yes you can. Close your eyes and picture her. Imagine what you would do if you were with her, just the two of you, alone.'

'But I don't know. It would be up to her, I mean . . .'

Suddenly Marina realised that he needed her to take the responsibility, wanted her to tell him what to do. She gave a faint smile and lifted her skirt up to her waist. Justin's eyes widened in a mixture of alarm and arousal as he saw her neatly trimmed pubic hair with the outline of her vulva beneath.

'Close your eyes!' she commanded him. 'Then kneel down, and open your mouth.'

She saw him kneeling like a supplicant on the carpet

before her and a heady wave of delight rushed through her. Slowly she approached him until her mound was on a level with his face. Could he smell the traces of musk below the soap? She began to regret her attempt to clean herself in the loo.

Justin looked faintly ridiculous kneeling there with his mouth open, as if he were about to receive the blessed sacrament. Perhaps he was, in a way. She spoke softly to him, her words hanging in the air like tempting fruit. 'Justin, I want you to use your tongue on me, to give me pleasure. Do you understand?'

He nodded, evidently too confused to speak. She came closer, parted her swollen labia with her fingers and thrust her steamy pussy towards his moist lips. When they finally made contact he gave a shuddering sigh and was soon thrusting his tongue into her with complete abandon. Marina stroked the dark thatch of his hair, encouraging him with gentle firmness, pressing him close.

After his earlier diffidence, she was surprised by Justin's eagerness to perform cunnilingus on her. He was good at it, too. His tongue flicked back and forth over her still-erect clitoris with rapid, light friction that was guaranteed to bring her to a swift climax. She felt the dizzying spiral begin and rocked back on her heels, almost tumbling over as the final spasms of orgasm took hold, rocketing her into instant bliss. Her moans seemed to excite him because, as the echoes of ecstasy died away in her, she could hear him groaning too.

Collapsing onto the carpet she took him into her arms, cradling his head against her chest. 'Did you like that?' she murmured. He gave an incoherent moan. Feeling unbearably hot she untied the straps of her dress at the shoulders and let the bodice fall until her breasts were bare. Justin gave another loud moan and tilted his head towards her, his eyes pleading. She smiled and lifted the heavy globe towards him.

The dark pink nipple was semi-tumid, full of soft ripeness. Marina pinched it into a stiff peak and placed it between his lips, enjoying the rapid return of her desire as his lips and tongue went to work on it, licking and sucking until fierce shivers of sensation were zipping down her spine, rousing her again. She slid down until she was flat on the floor with her dress scrunched around her waist exposing her above and below.

'Lick me again down there,' she told him. 'But keep pinching my nipples and stroking my breasts. Make me come again, even better than last time.'

It was what he wanted, to be told what to do. Suits me fine, Marina thought, smiling to herself, as his dark head descended once more. The touch of his tongue on her overheated vulva was exquisite, cool as balm and yet inflaming her at the same time. She lay back with a contented sigh and waited for the delicious cycle to resume.

Justin was indefatigable. He feasted on her like a glutton, bringing her to the edge time and again but then slackening so that she was left hanging there in tantalising torment. Marina wanted to beg him to finish her off but she knew that the longer she held out the more intense her orgasm would be, so she let him subtly take control of her libido. Meanwhile his fingers tweaked and plucked at her aching nipples, compounding her unsatisfied longing.

Then, when she thought he was set to go on all night and she would die of frustration, he plunged one finger inside her while continuing to lick her clitoris and the unstoppable rise towards oblivion began. Marina squirmed with unfettered delight, her vagina convulsing over and over as his slim finger rubbed against the cushioned walls. She was on fire from head to toe, revelling in the prolonged climax that had her bucking and moaning through what seemed like several long minutes. Heedless of where she was or who she was with, scarcely conscious of her own identity, she rode the slowly diminishing waves of her orgasm until the tremors finally ceased and she was left utterly spent, a throbbing mass of molten flesh.

Flopping back onto the carpet, Marina relaxed completely and was soon dozing. When she came to and sat up Justin was lying on the bed with his hands behind his head and his eyes closed. She crept over to join him and, for a while, they just lay there embracing. Outside she could hear the sounds of Rome's frenetic traffic but inside the room they seemed to be in a bubble of calm, with a little sunlight creeping through the slats in the blind and onto the floor.

Marina gazed at the ornate plaster work on the ceiling and a profound sense of joy filled her, a feeling that it was so very good to be alive. She wanted to communicate that thought to Justin, but she was afraid of breaking the spell. So she lay there for minutes more, listening to the soft rhythm of his breathing, synchronised with her own.

It was Justin who broke the spell first. Without saying anything he rose from the bed and went into the bathroom to take a leak. While he was absent Marina felt unaccountably sad. She'd just experienced the best orgasm she'd ever had, but with a man she scarcely knew. And how weird it had been to play the dominatrix like that, to make him do it to her. Now that it was over she felt a pang of regret, wishing he'd overpowered her instead, but it was no use wishing for the moon. Probably this was the only sexual encounter they would have. She'd been hot for him and he'd been full of frustrated lust after seeing his beloved Bella. It was the classic eternal triangle, and if she thought otherwise then she was in for a fall.

Briskly Marina rose and put on her crumpled dress. It looked terrible, but it was all she had. Her instinct was to get away from Justin's hotel and back to her own, as soon as possible. She picked up her bag and crept to the door. The sound of the shower came from the bathroom, drowning any noise she might make. She closed the door behind her and slipped along the corridor to the lift, praying it would be empty.

Her prayer was answered and she got down to the foyer without being seen by anyone. Instead of getting out of the lift, however, she noticed there was a button for the basement and pressed that. It was probably for employees only but there might be an inconspicuous door she could slip out of. The thought of walking through the main door in that state was embarrassing, to say the least.

Luckily there was a back door with a fire bar across it that opened at once when she pushed it. Outside she was faced with several huge dustbins in a yard, but through an archway opposite she could see the street. She flitted out, pulling her shoulder bag across the front of her dress to hide as much as she could of its wrinkled state, then found herself in a side street that she didn't recognise. She walked down to a cross-roads and then realised she was not so far from her own hotel. Feeling the strength returning to her legs as she got into a striding rhythm, Marina hurried along the narrow, almost-deserted street with her mind in a turmoil.

Chapter Seven

When Justin came out of the shower he couldn't believe Marina had gone. All the elation he'd felt dissipated at once, leaving him flat and disappointed. He thought he'd given her a really good time. Surely she hadn't been faking those two long orgasms? There was no way he could come to terms with her abrupt departure.

Lying down on the bed he tried to dismiss the horrible thoughts that were whirling around in his head and think of Bella instead. Next weekend he would be going to her villa again, for another lesson followed by some 'payment'. He didn't know which he'd enjoyed more. Seeing his idol again that afternoon had been a bonus, but now the high he'd been on was abruptly over. Resentment welled up in him. Why did that Marina have to piss on his parade?

The thought that he was stuck with her as his singing partner rankled. He didn't relish facing her again after this. Maybe they could swap with another couple, pretend their voices didn't blend well or something. From the way she'd reacted to his efforts to satisfy her sexually it seemed likely that she'd jump at the chance to have nothing more to do with him.

But when he turned up at the academy next morning she greeted him with a sunny smile, much to his amazement. They had no chance to talk at first since they were attending a lecture on stagecraft, but as soon as coffee break came round she made a beeline for his table.

'Hullo, Justin. I'm sorry I rushed out on you yesterday,' she began. 'I just remembered I'd promised to see Laurie about something.'

Justin didn't know whether to believe her or not. If she

was lying then there was some other, darker, reason why she'd wanted to get away from him. If she was telling the truth, then he had every reason to feel jealous. It was not reassuring, either way.

'That's okay,' he said, adding on impulse. 'I was expecting a call from Bella, anyway.'

'Really?' Her tone was cool.

'Yes. She said I could go to her villa again next weekend and would ring to confirm it.'

Marina's blue eyes turned as grey as an overcast sky. 'I see.'

'Actually, after seeing her and Michael give such a wonderful performance of the "Soave Fanciulla" duet, I thought of asking her if she'd coach us.'

Marina's gaze warmed. 'Do you really think she would?'

'She might if I asked her.'

'You sound very smug. Just what is going on between you and her, Justin?'

'Aha, wouldn't you like to know!'

He enjoyed teasing her, seeing those expressive eyes widen with fascination and a burning desire to know the truth. She would probably be astonished if she knew exactly what went on at the *Villa Gandolfini*!

Bella didn't appear at the academy for several days. Officially she was taking a break, learning a part that had been specially written for her in a new opera by a Swiss composer that people were comparing with Michael Tippett. Justin and Marina had several more chances to rehearse their duet, but although they both sang competently it was somehow uninspired. Perhaps Marina was right, Justin mused, and they needed some input from a woman of passion like Bella, because whatever passion there might have been between them seemed to have fizzled out, for some unknown reason.

Marina was friendly towards him, but that was all and he'd begun to look elsewhere for romance. Many of the other students had paired up by now, though. Besides, his every waking thought was directed towards the magnificent Bella and no other woman could hope to compete with her. Justin decided he would feel guilty about forcing another girl to play second fiddle. No doubt that was why Marina was keeping her distance. She knew just how much the opera star meant to him.

The *diva* herself appeared on Friday afternoon and when Justin bumped into her in the corridor she smiled sweetly and asked to see him in her office on the second floor in half an hour. When, after an interval of extravagant fantasising, he finally stood in her small, elegant room he felt thoroughly bedazzled by her. She was wearing a pink shift dress that skimmed her generous bosom and fell, tent-like, to her knees. Not the most flattering of garments for a woman of her stature, yet she carried it off with aplomb. Round her neck and wrists flashed silver chains of various widths: a subtle reminder of the way she liked him to be? The knowing smile she gave him certainly hinted as much.

'Justin, I simply want to confirm with you that you will be ready tomorrow morning when Enrico calls. About ten o'clock, I think he said. He'll be running Olga into town first.'

'That's fine. Thank you.'

She gave him a look that was almost maternal. 'And how have you been getting on this week?'

'Okay.'

'Just okay? What about your piece for the festival, how's that coming along?'

'Not too well, actually.'

'Then we'll have to see what we can do about it. I don't believe you've told me what it is yet.'

He mumbled the name, and she gave a tinkling laugh. 'Really! Then you had an object lesson on Monday afternoon, didn't you dear? But who is to sing with you?'

'Marina Stewart.'

'Ah, is that the girl with the pretty blonde hair and smiling blue eyes?'

He nodded, smiling himself at the romantic portrait Bella was painting of her.

'She has a sweet voice, she'll make a lovely Mimi. How many rehearsals have you had so far?'

'About half a dozen.'

'Then perhaps I should step in before your mistakes become too ingrained. When is your next rehearsal?'

'Monday afternoon.'

Bella frowned. 'Only two more weeks, how time flies! Perhaps a better idea would be for her to come to the villa with you. Then I can see you both in the afternoon. Enrico will take her back for the Saturday night disco, or whatever she wants to do. But you, of course, will stay for the whole weekend, yes?'

Justin was full of mixed feelings. The idea of having Bella coach them as a couple was fine, but he wasn't sure that he wanted Marina to go to the villa. What if she found out how he was treated by Olga? It seemed terribly risky. She might even be invited to stay to dinner, and that could be disastrous.

When he approached Marina he was relieved to hear that she had already agreed to go on an excursion round the Roman ruins next day. She seemed disappointed to miss the lesson with Bella, though, and eventually it was arranged that she should come out to the villa on Sunday afternoon instead. Justin relaxed, and began to look forward to his own excursion into the unknown.

Saturday morning found him ready for another magical mystery tour around his own psyche. He'd had the most weird erotic dreams all night and when he awoke the sheets were stained with his nocturnal emissions. That hadn't happened to him since he was at school and, in a way, that wasn't surprising. What he felt for Bella was not unlike a teenage crush, with all its crazy swings from elation to despair and wild longings for unknown pleasures.

The drive to Albano was becoming familiar. Justin sat back in his plushly upholstered seat enjoying the curious glances he got from other people as the liveried chauffeur whisked him through the Roman suburbs. It was good to feel important for a while. Once he entered the secret world of the *Villa Gandolfini* he would become the lowliest of the low, a sycophantic servant to his divine mistress. Both states were oddly attractive to him.

Bella was waiting for him in the drawing-room when he arrived. She was dressed casually, in jeans and a T-shirt, and wore no make-up but to Justin's eyes she looked as gorgeous as ever. Her brown eyes sparkled at him seductively while Lena offered him some sparkling wine.

'We have a guest for lunch,' she told him. 'Someone you've met before, and who will stand in for Marina at your lesson this afternoon.'

'Stand in?'

'Yes. Lena, tell our lady guest that Justin is here.'

'*Si, Signora.*'

'I want you to try out the part of Rodolfo with someone else playing Mimi. I think it will give you a new perspective. Then, when we rehearse with Marina tomorrow, you will have something fresh to bring to the rôle. I think you are in danger of going stale, yes?'

He nodded, well aware that his sessions with Marina that week had lost their impetus. He wondered if Bella could have guessed why.

When Annaliese entered, Justin gave a smile of recognition. Of course! He knew that she was another of Bella's pupils. The thought of performing his duet with her instantly filled him with excitement. She was looking radiant, the turquoise top she wore accentuating the vivid blue-green of her eyes. There was a butterfly hair slide clipped into her short, curly hair and her smile was generous, welcoming.

'Hullo again, Justin,' she said, placing her small hand in his for a few seconds. 'I'm looking forward to performing with you.'

The innuendo was not lost on him, and his excitement mounted. Automatically his eyes dropped to skim her breasts, small and pert beneath the loose top. She was perfectly petite, a doll-like, pretty girl of the kind that he had never dared to approach for fear of rejection. Now it felt as if she were being handed to him on a plate.

Lunch was the usual salad and pasta with Olga conspicuous by her absence. Justin was relieved. He soon loosened up in the company of Annaliese, who was like a breath of fresh air in that rather stuffy mansion. For a while she chatted animatedly to Bella about her fellow pupils, conversation which Justin should have found boring since he knew none of them. But she spoke with such theatrical gestures and in such charming broken English that he was completely fascinated and scarcely took his eyes off her for a moment.

They moved into the practice room after lunch and Bella made them go through some exercises. Annaliese sang with a light sweetness that delighted Justin and brought out the best in his own voice. It was not just her singing that encouraged him, either. All through the lesson she was giving him flirty little looks and seductive smiles, making it very easy for him to imagine that he had fallen suddenly and rapturously in love with her, like Rodolfo with Mimi.

He wished she could be his partner for the summer school festival, but she was a regular student at the academy and so wasn't eligible. He vowed to make the most of their time together all the same. Exulting in the flowing strength of his singing, by the end of the afternoon he felt he had surpassed himself and Bella confirmed it.

'Your promise is beginning to be fulfilled,' she said. 'There is real passion in your voice. Annaliese obviously inspires you.'

'She certainly does!' he replied, with feeling.

A peculiarly smug look came into Bella's eyes. 'I knew you two would hit it off. Perhaps you would like to show Justin around the garden before dinner, Annaliese.'

Justin was startled. It felt as if she were trying to pair them off. But then, who was he to complain? Willingly he allowed her to lead him out onto the terrace where the early evening sun was bathing everything in a golden glow.

'Isn't this beautiful?' she exclaimed, raising her arms above her head and stretching on tiptoe, as if making obeisance to the sun. 'Shall we go for a swim?'

'Is there a pool?'

She laughed. 'Yes, but I meant in the lake! Bella has her own private beach, didn't you know? We can swim there quite unseen if we stay close to the shore.'

'I don't have any swim trunks.'

She laughed again. 'Who cares about those? Come on, I'll race you down the path.'

She set off, darting across the lawn, daring him to follow. He felt his erection grow at the sight of her lithe, petite body running before him and when he took up the chase it felt as if he were following his cock. The path led down to a lakeside area that had been planted with trees to make it completely secluded. There were grassy areas and rocks, artfully placed, with seats and a small gazebo.

'This is great!' he exclaimed, slowing to a halt. 'Bella certainly knows how to live well, doesn't she?'

But Annaliese was already stripping. Off came the turquoise top to reveal bare, tanned breasts with nipples pert and tawny. They were delightfully firm and rounded, even though small in size, and Justin was itching to take hold of them at once. His eyes widened as she stepped out of her skirt and panties, revealing a totally shaven pubis. She smiled at his surprise. 'Have you never seen a naked girl before?'

'Not quite *that* naked!'

'I have to shave every day, just like a man. But it's worth it to feel my pussy so sleek and soft. I'm aware of it all the time, when I sit and when I move. And above all, when I make love, of course.'

'Don't!' he groaned.

She laughed and ran towards the sparkling water over which evening shadows of the trees were starting to fall. Without ceremony she threw herself into the lake, landing with a big splash, then turned round to face him. 'Come on, don't be slow! I want you in here with me, playing mermaid and merman!'

Eagerly he stripped, leaving his clothes in a pile on one of the seats, then moved towards the water's edge. More cautious than Annaliese, he waded in slowly, feeling the lukewarm water flapping about his ankles. She rose from the waves and came towards him in giant leaps, splashing furiously.

'Don't be such a scaredy-baby! Make the plunge, like me!'

She took hold of his hand and pulled him so that he toppled straight into the water. He felt her lithe naked body slide on top of him, cold and wet as a fish. She giggled as he spluttered in the water. Then they swam out together, side by side, in a calmer mood. There was a strange solemnity about the lake at twilight, pale stars shimmering and the sky turning a dull red-gold beyond the blue.

'Isn't this beautiful?' she breathed. 'I feel so romantic. Kiss me, Justin.'

He obliged at once, feeling her clammy breasts squashed against his chest as they both trod water to keep afloat. His hands crept down between her thighs, felt the wet folds of her smooth vulva and the slithery silk of her thighs. She looked up at him with huge, lucid eyes and he knew they would soon be making love on dry land, like beached creatures of the lake.

'Shall we go back ashore?' he asked, huskily.

She nodded, swimming back with easy grace while he followed the darkened yellow of her head. She got out, covered in goose pimples, and rubbed herself with her cotton top. Then she pointed to the gazebo. 'I think there's towels and stuff in there! Let's find out.'

The place was well equipped. There was a small shower-room with towels and toiletries, a kitchen area and conservatory-style wicker chairs. Justin also noticed what looked like a sofa bed, covered in padded upholstery.

Annaliese smiled at the door of the shower room. 'I think we'd better wash off the lake water. It seems clean, but you never know. Will you join me?'

Soon they were standing together beneath the shower, hot water cascading over their shivering bodies. Justin was shy with her at first but she made him take some of the orange-scented gloop and soap her breasts, his hands gliding smoothly over the firm curves and small, stiff nipples. She closed her eyes and sighed, lathering her curls, so he grew more bold and let one hand slide down over her flat stomach to her cowrie-like mound. It felt so slick that his finger slipped further into her before he knew it.

Annaliese parted her legs with a more satisfied sigh, her hand reaching for his tumid prick. 'Mm, nice one!' she murmured, fondling it gently. Violent tremors passed through Justin's body, turning him weak at the knees. He put one hand against the shower wall for support.

'It's a bit cramped in here, isn't it?' she said. 'Come on, let's wrap ourselves in these towels and go next door.'

The huge, fluffy towels were miraculously heated by electric rails on the wall. Cocooned in soft warmth Justin felt a vibrant sensuality fill his body. He went over to where she had pulled out the sofa bed and plumped up the pillows. She patted one of them invitingly.

'Come here, and let me massage you. I found this lovely scented oil in the shower cabinet.'

Willingly he stretched himself out on the padded couch and put himself at her disposal. He was used to being passive around the *Villa Gandolfini* but this time it felt completely different. He had the feeling that he would be called on to play an active rôle quite soon. Very active indeed! For the moment, however, he was content to relax under her sure fingers, allowing the subtly scented oil to work its magic on both his skin and nostrils.

She worked from his temples down, soothing any stress lines from his face and then reaching over to his chest with her breasts dangling tantalisingly over his face. Her touch was so sure that he wondered if she'd been professionally trained. Her fingertips found the deeper muscles and gave them a good working over, sending him into a more profound state of relaxation. Her busy hands circled around on his stomach but by-passed his loins, ignoring his very obvious erection. Despite the passivity of the rest of his body his mind was active, imagining how it would feel to have Annaliese's svelte body beneath his, bumping and grinding her way towards fulfilment, and his cock was responding accordingly.

'Turn over!'

Her voice startled him but he obeyed sluggishly, re-arranging his tackle as he did so. She began at his feet this time, pushing into the soles with her thumbs and awakening new flurries of desire in him. Justin could feel his erection straining into the padded upholstery and it reminded him of the time when Bella had caressed his backside on that other couch. The memory was potent. He could feel premature juices leaking out of him and gave a groan of frustrated lust. The sense of anticipation was almost unbearable.

Annaliese's sly, knowing hands were kneading the mounds of his buttocks, pressing hard into them and then describing light circles around the circumference. He heard her pour more oil into her palm and tensed his muscles, not knowing where she was going next.

'Relax!' she cooed. 'I'm not going to hurt you.'

Carefully she pushed his thighs apart and began to run an oiled finger up and down his cleft, opening him up. The sensitive hairs around his anus quivered with delight as she probed a little, found the hard rose within and teased it with her soft finger. Justin didn't know whether he wanted her to penetrate him or not. To have her fingertip perform such a delicate dance around the rim was an exquisite pleasure in itself.

With her other hand she began to oil his balls, doubling his satisfaction. The whole of his rear end was alive with feeling now and attracting the full attention of his mind. He revelled in the sense of total abandon to her ministrations, happy to let her go wherever she wished. Then, when she sat astride him and began to rub her wet pussy all over his buttocks, he voiced his joy in a loud groan, making her chuckle naughtily.

'You like this, eh?' she murmured, leaning forward to nibble at his ear. 'Well, so do I!'

She spread her female body all over his back so that he could feel the hot tips of her nipples against his shoulder blades and the steaming heat of her pussy against his arse crack. Inside, his body had reached melting point. The urge to make contact with her insides was insistent now, and he didn't know how much more teasing he could bear.

At last, after she'd pushed his self-control to the limit, there came the words that released him. 'Turn over!'

He did so and at once she swung round to let the pale fruit of her vulva hang over his mouth while she took the tip of his glans between her lips. Giving a huge sigh he tongued the length of her exposed pussy and found the hard bead of her clitoris bursting from its sheath like a bud in spring. When his tongue made contact with it she exhaled with a sharp, hissing sound and he knew that she was as far gone in arousal as he was.

Annaliese's parts tasted first of the orange-flavoured shower gel but once he had licked that off her own luscious juices filled his mouth and he sucked them down hungrily. His fingers found the hard, ripe breasts and he squeezed them in rhythm, making her gasp with heightened feeling. Soon, though, he was on autodrive as his awareness shifted to what she was doing to him. Her hot little tongue was moving up his shaft with agile grace, licking all around his glans and then moving down again. Every so often she would give his bollocks a catlick, then resume servicing his prick. Sometimes she would take the whole of him into her mouth for a few ecstatic seconds before returning to her fellatio routine.

It was all Justin could do to retain control. He wanted to stop himself from coming too soon, wanted to prolong the action for as long as possible, but once he felt her throbbing pussy escalate towards orgasm he knew he had lost the fight. There was a powerful stirring in his balls and a prodigious quantity of love-juice pumped its way up into his straining penis and out through his glans, filling her warm mouth with the gushing fountain. She seemed to relish it, for as the accompanying ecstasy took hold of his consciousness he was dimly aware of her swallowing it down, sucking him dry.

Soon everything was blotted out as he succumbed to the final shuddering bliss of his climax. He came to and found her snug against him, her golden head on his chest.

'Mm, that was so good!' she murmured. 'And if you're good, very good, we might just do it all over again in a minute.'

'Yes, that was very nice. But I can think of one or two other things that might be even nicer to do.'

'You mean . . . the f-word?'

'I thought you'd just done that!'

She giggled. 'So you noticed, then?'

'Eventually. Most of the time I was too busy myself.'

'I know the feeling . . .'

They were suddenly shaken out of their conversation by the shrill ring of a telephone, close at hand. Justin sat up with a jerk and eventually saw the receiver, half hidden behind a pot plant.

'What the hell . . . ?'

But Annaliese sprang up, deftly pulled the damp towel around her, and skipped over to the phone. She answered in monosyllables, then replaced the receiver. 'Olga. Telling us dinner is almost served and would we please return to the villa.'

'How did she know we were here?' Justin asked, alarmed.

She shrugged. 'I suppose she just hoped we'd be within earshot of the phone. Anyway, the system worked, didn't it? Come on, we'd better get a move on!'

Justin felt deflated and vaguely annoyed as he struggled back into his clothes. He'd been looking forward to a prolonged session with his new-found lover, and resented the interruption. Still, with luck there might be another chance later on.

When they reached the dining-room Bella was already seated at the table, looking splendid in a black dress and pearls. Olga was standing behind her chair, looking disapproving. She said nothing, however, but rang the bell for Lena who soon appeared with a silver soup tureen.

Conversation during the meal was strangely stilted, apart from when Bella and Annaliese gossiped again. Justin wondered how he would be required to 'pay' for his lesson this time, but nothing had yet been said about what Bella or Olga wanted of him. The suspense made him anxious and, in the aftermath of his love-making with Annaliese, vaguely guilty. Had either of the women guessed what had been going on in the gazebo? He was disturbed by the way Bella kept looking from one of her guests to the other with a faintly mocking smile. Could she possibly have set up his seduction that afternoon? It seemed more than likely. But why?

It was a relief when the meal ended and they adjourned to the drawing-room for coffee. There Annaliese played Chopin for them, which Justin found very soothing. He closed his eyes and imagined the feel of her hands upon his naked body, but the imperious presence of Bella soon led his fantasies away from the younger girl and towards the older woman, his irresistible *femme fatale*. He began to imagine that it had been Bella in the gazebo with him, letting him anoint her intimate parts with the scented oil, allowing him to caress her splendid bosom. When he caught her eye he flushed, giving himself away, and then coloured all the more.

'That was delightful, Annaliese,' Bella said. 'You play with your hands almost as well as you perform with your mouth. Don't you think so, Justin?'

'Er . . . yes. Yes, very much so.'

He felt like a babbling idiot. How these women could run rings around him! Yet even in the midst of his shame and confusion he felt a deeply erotic thrill. What if both of them should set upon him at once, making use of his body for their own pleasure with shameless lust. The thought sent quivers of burning arrows through him and his prick stirred impatiently.

Justin's attention was drawn back abruptly to what Bella was saying to her guest. 'Enrico will take you back to Rome shortly, then.'

'What?' Justin said, startled. 'You're not going back tonight are you, Annaliese?'

She gave him a sardonic smile. 'Of course. I was only invited for the day. Besides, I have a rehearsal at the academy first thing tomorrow. I'm singing in the chorus for a summer gala performance.'

'Oh.' His disappointment was almost tangible.

Annaliese came over and offered him her hand. 'I'm sure we'll meet again, Justin. Good-bye for now. And good luck with *your* performance, at the festival.'

He mumbled thanks, good-byes, his mind in a turmoil as he felt the sexual withdrawal symptoms take hold: aching balls and a hollow emptiness in his stomach. Bella rang for Lena who took Annaliese away with her.

'Such a lovely girl,' Bella commented, picking up the cafetière. 'And one of my most promising pupils. More coffee, Justin?'

'No thanks. It'll only keep me awake.'

He spoke abruptly and saw Bella lift her right eyebrow a fraction. She poured herself a small coffee then sat back in her chair with the cup suspended daintily in mid-air. Her searching gaze was embarrassing him and he looked away. The silence became elongated, then Justin suddenly remembered what he had meant to ask her.

'This afternoon's lesson,' he began awkwardly. 'Did it count as a normal lesson? I mean, being the two of us . . .'

Bella's laugh cut through him. 'If you mean do you owe me any "payment" the answer is no. You have already paid, in full.'

He looked up with a frown. 'What do you mean?'

'Never mind. The slate is clean, I think you say in England. Someone told me it means the same as "quits". Such a subtle language, English. If only it sounded like Italian it would be the most perfect language in the world!'

The door opened and Olga entered. Justin felt the hairs on his nape prickle. Whenever those two women were together he felt uneasy. But this time, it seemed, they wanted no sport with him.

'Olga and I need to be alone together,' Bella said. 'If you'll excuse us, Justin. My villa is at your disposal, of course. You will find television in the lounge opposite, videos, CDs. But mind you are fresh for your lesson with Marina tomorrow afternoon. You haven't forgotten that she is coming, have you?'

He started, guiltily. No thought of Marina had entered his mind since early that afternoon, when he couldn't help comparing her to Annaliese. He gave a wry smile and rose from his chair, taking his leave of the two women.

The videos on offer were mainly of opera performances, with a few feature films that he had already seen. The television seemed to be all Italian game shows and dubbed foreign films. Justin felt a great weariness overtake him. He was missing Annaliese, regretting that they'd not had a chance to explore each others' bodies further, and not even the thought of seeing Marina next day could compensate. Feeling profoundly dissatisfied, with himself as much as anything else, Justin finally went out into the hall.

There was flickering light under the door opposite, and the sound of whispering. Justin was intrigued. Were they really a couple of dykes, those two? He was tempted to put his ear to the keyhole but that seemed very ungrateful behaviour from a guest. Besides, he was afraid Lena might suddenly appear. So he crept upstairs to the guest bedroom to drown his sorrows in the night-cap of brandy that was provided as a courtesy for all guests at the *Villa Gandolfini*.

Chapter Eight

Marina stared at the back of Enrico's glossy dark hair as he whisked her smoothly through the suburbs of Rome. She was wondering what Bella's chauffeur would be like in bed. His physique suggested that he could easily double as her bodyguard, and his hands on the wheel seemed firm, yet sensitive. She drifted into a pleasant fantasy where they made a detour into the Roman countryside for a spot of impromptu dalliance.

Something had happened to her since she arrived in Italy. She wasn't normally this randy, but the presence of so many handsome Latin men had certainly got her going. Not that they were her type, not really. She preferred the more understated English looks of a man like . . . well, Justin, for example. Marina gave an involuntary sigh at the thought of him. If only he hadn't been so obsessed with that Conti woman she really could have gone for him, but she wasn't going to waste time mooning over a lost cause.

Even so, he was great at you-know-what! A self-satisfied smile crept over her face. When she looked up she caught Enrico staring at her in the driving mirror and hastily re-arranged her features. 'Is it much further?' she asked, innocently.

'Another hour, perhaps.'

'What's the villa like?'

'Beeg. Very nice. You will like it there.'

He was right. The minute she saw the *Palazzo*-style building, standing in its own landscaped gardens beside the lake, Marina knew that she was entering a more elegant and luxurious world. The car swept up to the front door, where a severe-looking woman was waiting to greet her.

Was this the infamous Olga? she wondered.

Her guess proved right. 'Bella asked me to show you to your room, *Signorina*,' the woman said in clipped, Eastern-European tones. She was looking at Marina in a manner that made her feel uncomfortable, as if she were being assessed in some way. Remembering the rumours that this woman was a lesbian, Marina felt an unexpected twinge of sexual excitement.

Not that she fancied Olga in the slightest. She seemed most unattractive, with her hair smarmed back and her clothes making her look like the proverbial sack tied in the middle. Yet she was curious to know what was going on behind those bright, black button eyes. Did she have special ways of making love to women, ways that would produce their own novel delights? Did she and Bella share some kind of weird sexual relationship? Marina was disturbed by the prurient nature of her thoughts. What business was it of hers what Olga and Bella might get up to in the privacy of their own home?

Olga led the way up an impressive staircase and Enrico followed with the overnight bag she had brought with her. She was taken to a small but attractively furnished room at the far end of the upstairs corridor.

'If there is anything you need, just ring this bell and Lena will attend to you,' Olga told her. 'You are expected down-stairs in half an hour for coffee, before your lesson.'

'Thank you,' Marina said, and again those penetrating eyes sent prickles down her spine for a few seconds, before the woman turned to leave.

The house seemed quiet. It was almost noon, but possibly the others were only just rising. Marina wondered how Justin had got on the day before. He'd seemed strangely reticent about what went on during his last weekend there. There was something about the atmosphere of the *Villa Gandolfini* that hinted at secret assignations and perverse pleasures. Secluded in its grandeur, it reeked of the decadence of Venice and Rome in the declining years of the Renaissance.

Bella and Justin were waiting for her in the lounge when she went down. She was intrigued to see that her hostess was dressed casually, in a loose printed silk top with pink velour trousers and gold sandals, her face devoid of make-up. Justin looked very fetching in an open-necked denim shirt that showed off his growing tan.

They both seemed pleased to see her. Yet there was an air of slight embarrassment about Justin, as if his new intimacy with the opera star was something he didn't want to share with anyone else.

'Nice place you have here,' Marina said, wryly, examining the gilded splendour of the ceiling.

'Yes, I love this house!' Bella declared with a naive enthusiasm that made Marina warm to her. 'It was in a dreadful state when I bought it. I engaged the finest workmen to restore it to its former glory.'

The small talk, coffee and sandwiches were soon over. Bella was evidently a woman who believed in getting down to business. She made her two pupils sing the same scale repeatedly until their notes were as a clear as a bird's. Then she put them through their paces one by one.

Marina had never worked so hard in her life. No matter how satisfied she felt herself with the way she was singing Bella always demanded more of her, coaxing her voice to attain heights she would never have believed possible. She was an equally hard task-mistress with Justin. Then, when it came to the pair of them singing together, their duet began to fall into place beautifully.

At the end of three hours Marina sank, exhausted, onto the couch. Bella rang for tea, a wry smile on her lips. 'Now you know what a real singer has to go through,' she told them. 'It is hard, my dears. Far harder than you imagined, yes?'

'Do we stand a chance?' Justin asked her, bluntly. 'In the festival, I mean.' But Bella just put her finger to her lips, smiling mysteriously.

Justin invited Marina to walk with him in the garden but Bella intervened. 'You go by yourself, Justin. I want to talk to Marina. Girl talk, you know?'

He looked surprised but did as he was told. Marina thought it decidedly odd too, and wished that she could have spent some time with him. Maybe he would have opened up to her about his relationship with Bella. But Bella evidently had other plans. As soon as he'd gone she poured them both a glass of *grappa* from the decanter on a small table.

'Isn't it a bit early for this?' Marina said, eyeing her glass doubtfully.

'Not at all. When your throat has been working hard you need to relax it and this will do the trick I think. Cheers!'

'Cheers, then! It's so kind of you to invite me here. . .'

Bella's brown eyes were sparkling dangerously at her. 'Nonsense! I had a motive. I always have a motive. And right now you are going to tell me about Justin.'

'What about him?'

'Is he good in bed, for example?'

Marina was not often shocked but the question floored her, coming out of the blue like that. She spluttered into her brandy then said, 'I've no idea!'

'You don't have to pretend to me. I know you went back to his hotel room on Monday.'

'How did you know?' Marina gasped.

She giggled. 'My spies are everywhere! So, is he a good fuck?'

'We didn't do that. Honestly.'

Marina felt decidedly uncomfortable. She wanted to tell this woman to mind her own business, but she couldn't forget who she was. And there lurked, in the back of her mind, an idea that if she was open with her she might get some juicy titbits in return.

Bella was obviously amused. She crossed her legs as she sat in the big armchair and swung her gold sandal from the end of her foot, coquettishly. 'But you did *something*, yes?' Marina nodded, embarrassed. 'Now, let me guess. You performed on him . . . no? He performed on you! Ah! Good with his tongue, is he?'

By now Marina was squirming. She was unused to such frank talk even with intimate girlfriends. From a woman as famous and admired as Bella it seemed incongruous, to say the least. So she merely nodded.

'You are a sexy girl, Marina. You should use it far more

when you perform. That is the secret of every *prima donna*'s success, sexual passion.'

Marina recovered her wits enough to say, archly, 'Is that on or off stage?'

She laughed. 'Both, I guess!' Her eyes grew reflective. 'I was in love with the great Mario Vespiani when I was starting out in my singing career. We had a *grande passion* that lasted almost two years. During that time he made me a star.'

Marina found the courage to say, 'If that happened to me I think I'd be always wondering whether I'd have made it on my own.'

'Of course not. In this business, everyone needs a helping hand. There are many good singers, a few great singers, but it is very competitive. You need the protection of a mentor, someone who can tell you which parts to try for, which productions to audition for. Someone who knows your strengths and weaknesses. I had Mario, and now I have Olga.'

'Olga? But I thought she . . .'

'Is my secretary, yes. And of course I have a manager and agent, but Olga is the one who knows me best, the one I listen to when everyone else is telling me different things.'

Marina was feeling decidedly uneasy. 'I . . . I'm not sure why you're telling me all this.'

'Because I think you have a future, my dear. You need someone to guide you, and I may be that someone. But only if you are prepared to work like the devil. Justin has the potential to be good, but you . . .'

She could hardly believe her ears. Was Bella offering to be her personal coach? It seemed incredible after so short a time.

The door opened and Olga entered. She glided across the carpet in her lace-up shoes and came to sit on the arm of Bella's chair. Marina was struck by the way she seemed to dominate the star, even though Bella sat there with impressively elegant grace. Her sense of discomfiture intensified as she caught Olga's eye and was subjected to her cool, appraising gaze. The prickling sensation at the nape of her neck made her shiver involuntarily.

'I was just telling Marina how important it is to have an ally in the opera world,' Bella said, looking up into the other woman's eyes. There seemed to be an amused understanding between them.

Olga nodded. 'Oh yes, opera can be very cruel. Very cruel indeed!'

Bella said, 'Perhaps because it deals in extreme emotions.'

Marina tried to contribute usefully to the conversation despite feeling out of her depth. Her own voice sounded distant and strained to her ears, full of suppressed tension. 'Are you suggesting that opera attracts certain types of people? More emotional ones, for instance?'

Bella seemed to make a point of smoothing down the velour that covered her thigh as she said, 'More sensual, I would say. Wouldn't you, Olga?'

'Oh yes, definitely more sensual.'

'We can tell that you have that special quality of sensuality, Marina. It comes out in your eyes when you sing. And in your voice. That's how I know you have great potential.'

'Really?' She felt giddy and sick, partly with elation and partly with apprehension. The feeling that the two women were ranged against her, playing some cat-and-mouse game of their own, was now overwhelming. She longed for Justin to return and break the spell, but knew he was unlikely to enter the room without an invitation.

'I . . . er . . . think I'd like to go up to my room for a bit, if you don't mind,' she said at last.

'No, we don't mind at all. You've had a tiring morning and I expect you'd like to rest before dinner. Take a shower, and . . . oh, perhaps you'd like Olga to treat you? She is a fully qualified masseuse.' The women exchanged a smile as Bella added, 'Just one of her many talents.'

Marina felt a fluttering panic. 'No, it's all right thank you. I . . . j . . . just need to rest.'

'There is no more relaxing experience than one of Olga's wonderful massages. She uses the finest oils, obtainable from an exclusive boutique in Florence. I can promise you, Marina dear, that you will greatly benefit.'

After that it was hard to refuse. Olga insisted it would be

no trouble; Bella repeated her insistent praise and, somehow, Marina found herself talked into it. She was still wary of the woman as she went upstairs and ran the shower, reluctant to undress in case Olga suddenly walked in. Miserably she gave herself a quick wash and then put her underwear back on. There was no way she was going to appear stark naked before that lesbian. She would play it as if she expected to get a 'therapeutic' massage out of her and no more. That way she would feel safe.

The door opened as Marina was lying on her bed, vainly hoping that Olga would think she was asleep and tiptoe away again. No such luck! The woman advanced into the room and plonked her bag down on the antique marble washstand. Watching from beneath semi-closed lids, Marina saw her withdraw some phials from her bag and mix them in a small bowl. Suddenly she turned around and placed a chair next to the bed.

'Here we are,' she said in a jovial voice. 'I've mixed up a special recipe, just for you, with geranium, frankincense, melissa, neroli. Tell me, dear, do you have any trouble sleeping?'

Marina opened her eyes, knowing it was useless to feign sleep any longer. 'Sometimes.'

'Then I shall give you a special preparation to take away with you. Do you have one of those light-bulb rings?' Marina shook her head. 'Then I shall give you one also. To take back to England, for your bedroom. It will perhaps remind you of me.'

Marina wasn't at all sure she would want to be reminded of Olga, but she was determined to play this whole thing straight. She told herself that the woman was being kind, that was all. As long as she could convince herself that her motives were entirely above board she had the superstitious belief that nothing untoward would happen to her.

Olga was pouring some of the massage oil into her left palm. Marina waited uneasily to be told to remove her underwear, but the order never came. Instead, the masseuse came to perch behind her on the bed and her fingers began smoothing across her forehead in long, firm strokes, releasing the subtle aromas into her nostrils. She closed her eyes and did her best to put all disturbing thoughts aside.

To her surprise it was easy, after the first few minutes, to drift into a state of utter trust. Olga's touch was so sure, so sensitive over the delicate planes of her face, and the scent was so deliciously sedative that Marina found herself hovering all the while on the verge of sleep. Her head felt clear and light, untroubled by her former nervous fears, and she settled down to enjoy the experience without a qualm.

The confident fingers inched their way down her chest towards her cleavage, arousing her subtly, but still she heard no alarm bells ring. She was now in a delicious state of drowsiness, almost hypnotic, and her body felt warm and faintly buzzing all over. Olga was using a variety of techniques on her, now kneading gently with her knuckles, now pressing with flat palms, now prodding softly with her fingers. Her breasts, inside the constricting cups, were full and firm but her nipples were still flaccid.

Moving on, the massaging hands made circles around her navel, working on her internal organs. Marina had the impression that the latent energy in her solar plexus was being moved around, moulded like some plastic material. She felt all hot and melting, inside and out, with the faint tingling growing more pleasant by the minute. The caressing fingers followed the ridge of her pubic bone and she felt a slight stirring of her clitoris as the flesh moved upward. It was nothing overtly sexual, just a reminder that the organ of pleasure was lurking nearby and capable of being stimulated.

Olga shifted her position so that she could gain access to her legs and was soon working on her thighs. Again and again the deft fingers probed to within an inch of Marina's pussy and she was disconcerted to find herself wanting them to reach her vulva. Desire crept up on her and, although she had no intention of doing anything about it herself, she couldn't help reversing her earlier resolve. Now she was hoping that this strange woman did have a predatory interest in her. It wasn't long before she was dying for some more direct stimulation of her sexual organs.

But along with the desire came the shame. How could

she want such a thing, from such a woman? Marina's previous composure vanished as she realised that if Olga made some obvious advance she would not rebuff her. On the contrary, she was dying for it. The idea that she could be so hungrily aroused by someone she was not attracted to hit her with devastating force. Was she just a randy animal, with lusts that anyone could satisfy? She'd always pretended otherwise, always told herself that there must be a spark of chemical attraction before she could be sexually fulfilled, but perhaps it wasn't so.

The massage of her thighs seemed to last an eternity, and Marina found herself willing the woman to move up, up, closer, closer. Her body was a finely-coiled spring, waiting for a release that never came, and she felt her nipples harden in a mute and desperate appeal for more stimulation. Every time those kneading knuckles or stroking fingers moved up to within a centimetre of her pulsating clitoris Marina's hopes soared, only to be disappointed when they moved back down.

Eventually they stopped at knee level, then passed on down her shins to her feet, and Marina felt the aching need redouble inside her as the strong hands worked on her soles. Yet there was no way she could beg Olga to give her what she craved. She would die rather than suffer the humiliation of pleading with that dyke to rub her clitoris or perform cunnilingus on her. Already she felt at the woman's mercy, but she would rather keep her shameful need a guilty secret than confess and be exposed to Olga's gloating lust.

When the time came to turn over Marina was reluctant to do so, but if she had said anything her secret would have been exposed, so she obeyed without a word. The silken coverlet on the bed felt cold against her over-heated flesh and she gave a shiver. Olga's hands smoothed their way up her calves to the backs of her thighs and the expectation of sexual pleasure returned, despite herself, silently willing the masseuse to venture into the aching folds of her vulva from behind. Instead, she came up to her buttocks and began to press hard into them with her fists. Marina gasped, feeling her mound grind against the mattress beneath her, and the

115

hot waves of her arousal returned in force.

Every time the hard fists pressed into her Marina's excitement escalated until she was once more buzzing with suppressed libido. Surreptitiously she moved against the bed, providing friction for the jutting nub of her clitoris which remained, tantalisingly, on the edge of exploding into orgasm. She was waiting for Olga to move on but the woman kept pounding her behind, almost as if she knew what was happening on the other side of that prone body. The tension built up, spreading from her arse to the whole of her lower region and then up to include her aching nipples.

Inevitably, as Marina reached such a state of high excitement, her mind became fogged and spacey, overwhelmed by the heightened sensations that had taken over her flesh. She gave herself up to the experience, no longer in control but floating helplessly in the warm currents that were sweeping her on. If there was a destination she had long lost sight of it. It was enough to be floating in bliss, letting herself drift mindlessly as Olga swept up her back and across her shoulders with the same sure strokes, the soothing scent of the unguent dissolving away any latent stress.

There was no climax, no urgent spasms of relief, only a prolonged and deeply satisfying glow that lasted into timelessness. When the touching finally ended it took Marina a few seconds to realise that the massage was over and even then she remained in her highly-charged state for several minutes. During that time Olga left the room and it was only when she returned about half an hour later, bearing a herbal tisane that Marina began to return to normal.

'I hope you feel refreshed after your massage,' Olga said.

'Refreshed' wasn't exactly the word Marina would have used. She felt as if she'd taken a journey into another world and her body would never be quite the same again. But she nodded brightly and sipped the herbal tea, content to let Olga do the talking.

The other woman settled into a blue velvet armchair near the window, which had a view of the lake. At night the reflections of myriad lights from buildings and lamps along the shoreline gave the water a magical appearance. A calm settled on the room, producing an atmosphere conducive to the exchanging of secrets. Marina began to feel vaguely uneasy again. Olga had intimate knowledge of her body, she had the advantage over her.

But when the other woman spoke it was about Justin. She first asked Marina whether she liked singing with him.

'Oh yes, very much. I think we're well matched.'

'And you have . . . feelings for him?'

The question was spoken in a neutral tone, but Marina was wary. 'I'm not sure. I find him attractive, but it's probably not a good idea to think along those lines. I've got quite enough to think about on the course, without getting entangled in a holiday romance.'

Marina felt hypocritical to be saying that, knowing that if he'd shown real interest in her following their encounter at his hotel she would still be hot for him. But the feeling that he was besotted with Bella persisted and she had no wish to play second fiddle to such a powerfully charismatic woman.

Olga's next remark surprised her greatly. 'Bella is playing games with him, you know. He is what you might call her toy boy, except she plays with him like a cat, you understand?'

'No, not really.'

'Ah, she is a strange one, is Bella. She enjoys playing the *voyeur*. Yesterday she watched Justin and another girl, a very pretty *protégé* of hers. It gave her great pleasure.'

'What do you mean? Surely you're not saying what I think you're saying . . .'

'They made love of a kind, yes. And Bella loved to see them. She has special places, you know, with cameras.'

Instinctively Marina looked around the bedroom. Olga laughed. 'Oh, not in here! You're quite safe. Besides, nothing happened between us, did it?'

Those dark, staring eyes did nothing to reassure Marina. She felt momentarily sucked into a world that was alien, decadent, and it gave her the shivers. She drank the dregs of her tisane and felt the tepid liquid travel down her throat.

'I . . . I think I'd like to go back to Rome quite soon. Will Enrico be able to drive me?'

Olga was unable to hide her disappointment. 'Bella took

it for granted that you would stay for dinner.' She looked at her watch. 'It will be in half an hour. Won't you stay that long?'

'I'd rather get back, honestly.'

'You are upset by what I have told you.' It was more of a statement than a question. 'You do not like to think of Bella, the great *diva*, spying on the sex games of others. That is why you can't wait to leave the villa, yes?'

'Look, it's no business of mine what you get up to here. But involving outsiders . . .'

'Justin is a willing victim, I can guarantee that. And poor Bella, she is unable to find satisfaction without watching others. It is difficult for her to find a partner – the way you and Justin might be together, for example. For her that is impossible.'

'Why?' Marina asked sharply.

She expected Olga to mention her lesbian inclinations but instead she said, 'She is in love only with herself, you understand? No man will ever win her heart. She has given her heart and soul to her work, to the opera. She is a goddess; no man can be good enough for her. When she was young, yes, perhaps. But now she is too famous, she can trust no-one to love her and not her image. Can you understand that?'

'I . . . I think so. But why are you telling me all this?'

Olga rose from her chair and came to sit beside Marina on the bed, taking her hand. Marina's first instinct was to shrink from the contact, but she forced herself to remain still, watching as the woman's mouth curved into an odd smile.

'I want you to know something of what it is like to be one of the top three singers in the world,' she said. 'It is a lonely life, terribly lonely. If she did not have me, I don't know how Bella would survive. She lives for her work and everything else is play, including her relationships. Nothing else matters but the words and the music, the great rôles. I tell you because if Bella decides to take you under her wing, you, too, could end up in that lonely place where your only satisfaction is the roar of the *claque* after you have poured out your soul. I hope you can understand, a little.'

Marina stared at her, unable to speak. She had painted a bleak picture of the life of a *prima donna*. Surely it was not always like that.

Olga seemed to read her thoughts. 'Oh, there are other singers for whom it is not so. Lucrezia Vicenza, for example. She has a devoted husband and three children. But if she has a choice between a great part in a new production and a holiday with her family, she will often take the holiday. She is a good singer, but she is not a supreme one. That is the difference.'

Marina nodded. She had never thought that far ahead, never considered the consequences of her desire to be a famous singer. The picture Olga had painted struck a bleak chord in her, a buried fear that in pursuing her dream she would somehow be sacrificing her own happiness, and it made her uncomfortable.

'So,' Olga said briskly, rising from the bed, 'will you stay for dinner? Bella will be disappointed if you don't. Enrico will take you back to your hotel afterwards.'

It would have seemed churlish to refuse after that, so Marina agreed to stay. She was pleased to see Justin when they met in the lounge for pre-dinner drinks. His presence was a breath of fresh air in the close, secretive atmosphere of the villa.

'Did you enjoy your stroll around the grounds?' she asked him.

'Yes. The gardens are lovely. Typically Italian, quite formal, but with lovely unexpected corners with statues and herb-beds.'

'Will you stay the night, Marina?' Bella asked. 'Then you could see the gardens early in the morning, before you return with Justin.'

She was only half tempted. It would be easy to accept but she was, perhaps absurdly, afraid of what might happen in the night. If anything were to happen between her and Justin she didn't want it to be here, in this weird villa full of spy cameras and lonely, narcissistic women. What if some kind of unholy alliance occurred between Justin, Bella and Olga, turning her into their joint plaything? For the first time in her life Marina was in the grip of sexual terror.

'Thank you for the invitation,' she replied, evenly, 'but I really ought to get back. I'm not very good in the mornings unless I've had an early night and I also wanted to write some postcards back at the hotel.'

It seemed a lame excuse and she was mentally crossing her fingers against Bella trying to persuade her but, mercifully, she didn't try. They went into the dining-room where a table was beautifully laid with a swathe of fresh flowers trailing down the centre. At least, Marina thought, she could look forward to a decent meal.

The food was more than decent. Bella admitted that she had sent out to an exclusive restaurant nearby as it was the staff's night off, and the food was of cordon bleu standard. As the meal progressed and the talk grew animated and amusing, Marina felt more and more tempted to linger. But she drank only modestly so that she kept a clear head and when they moved into the next room for coffee she reminded Bella, tactfully, that she must soon leave.

Her hostess was obviously disappointed and Justin looked downcast too. For an instant Marina happily considered the possibility that he'd been hoping to seduce her that evening. Then she remembered that he was supposed to have had sex with another girl just the day before, and a pang of outraged jealousy hit her. If anything was to come of their relationship he would have to convince her that she mattered to him, that she meant more than just a passing fuck. Instinctively she knew that he was the kind of man she would want to have a serious affair with and, in her experience, there weren't enough of them around to squander.

Bella rang the bell to summon Enrico. 'Perhaps you will visit us next weekend, then?'

Marina murmured her thanks, but avoided committing herself. Even that one day at the villa had left her feeling disturbed and unsettled. She would need to reflect seriously on what had happened before she exposed herself to such strange experiences again.

Chapter Nine

Justin was sorry to see Marina go. Not that he had designs on her or anything, but while she was at the villa he'd felt safe from the machinations of the two Italian women. Besides, he enjoyed her company. Fancied her too, although after their session at the hotel he had wondered just what was going on between them. She was a mystery, but he couldn't cope with two enigmatic women in his life. Bella was more than a match for anyone.

They adjourned to the lounge and Justin wondered whether he would be involved in any more strange games, but for a while the two women just chatted amiably with him. Then Bella said how pleased she was with the progress he and Marina were making.

'You sing very well together, perhaps because there is that vital spark of attraction between you. I think it could be developed into something electric, something wonderful. Tell me, Justin, do you have sexual fantasies?'

The question shocked him. Visions of his masturbatory imaginings floated into his mind, things too personal and private to be revealed. 'Sometimes,' he hedged.

'Then use them. Imagine yourself with Marina in some of those situations while you listen to recordings of the aria. Then, when you come to sing with her, revive those thoughts. It will give your singing a secret power, make words and music come alive in a special way. Believe me, it is the key to certain success.'

'Is that what you do?' he asked, fascinated.

'I used to. I don't need to any more, because I have developed my voice to its highest extent and I know how to achieve excellence by other means. But you need to harness the power of your subconscious, Justin. Make it work for you in the realm of the imagination. Then you will transport your audience into a world beyond their wildest dreams.'

It was an interesting theory, but Justin doubted whether it would work quite so neatly. Nevertheless he promised to give it a try. His ambitions had grown since the great Bella Conti had boosted his confidence and he'd begun to believe that he really could make a great singer one day. If this was Bella's recommendation he would try it. He would try anything.

The two women retired at ten, leaving Justin to ponder alone in his room on the events of the weekend. His memory of Annaliese was almost eclipsed by what had happened since. There was a heady excitement whenever he re-lived his afternoon lesson with Marina. Bella had brought out new qualities in his voice, subtleties wrung from the depths of his psyche that he never knew were there. Maybe he should take her advice and focus on his fantasies, bringing them into line with the part of Rodolfo that he would be singing on the final night of the course. He lay down on the bed and closed his eyes.

Could he use his favourite scenario, that of being seduced on stage by a beautiful *prima donna* in front of a vast audience? It seemed appropriate, and there was just that element of danger to add spice. Yet he had always cast Bella in the rôle of his seductress before. He tried to imagine Marina as an exotic temptress, but she didn't quite fit the bill. Then he thought of her as a siren, singing like the Lorelei, luring him to his doom. She certainly had the eyes for it, and the svelte, voluptuous figure. Then there was her voice, high and sweet, just the kind that alluring maidens ought to have.

There was just one problem: in *La Bohème* it was hard to see Mimi as a sex goddess. A flirt, perhaps, but an innocent one. What scope was there to imagine her as some kind of doomed heroine, sensing that she was bad news and that whoever loved her would suffer for it. Eagerly Justin picked up the copy of the libretto that he had beside the bed and scanned it for clues. There was an English translation beneath the Italian, but he knew it more or less by heart. As

122

he scanned the pages it seemed to him that a kind of sub-text was feasible, that he could see the character of Mimi as playing the innocent in order to entrap the gullible Rodolfo. It was not a conventional interpretation, but it would serve his purpose.

Justin settled down again and imagined himself on the stage of Covent Garden with a full house. Opposite him sat Marina/Mimi in her simple dress, a ragged-fringed stole around her shoulders. He could see her breasts jutting beneath the thin material, firm and enticing. Her lips were very red, her mouth round and inviting as she began her aria, 'They call me Mimi'. She turned in the chair where she sat and her skirt parted and fell open, revealing her slim thighs. He felt his cock harden.

As her song progressed towards its emotional crescendo, Mimi began to stroke her own breast through the thin fabric, a faraway look on her face. Her passionate singing was accompanied by increasingly abandoned gestures until she had torn her bodice down to expose her well-rounded breasts, the nipples puckered into firm points which she fingered with nervous energy.

By the time Justin imagined himself joining in, turning the aria into a duet, she was flushed and aroused, her thighs moving restlessly and exposing more and more of her bare flesh. When her skirt rode up he thought he could glimpse the dark vee of her pubic hair.

'O sweet girl . . .' he sang, moving closer, his longing for her providing a strong counterpoint to the words and music. Out there, in the darkened auditorium, the suspense was almost tangible. They were willing him to consummate his love-at-first-sight there and then. When he looked at the glowing face and flushed throat of his heroine, her breasts heaving with more than just the effort of singing, it seemed as if that was her desire, too.

He knelt before her as he sang, his face close to the object of his lust. He imagined that he could scent the faint perfume of her sex beneath the perspiration induced by the effort of singing. Justin's penis was forcing itself out of his clothes so he hastily took off his underpants and it sprang to attention.

He pulled it to ease the foreskin and then began to fondle himself with a firm hand while he continued with his fantasy.

He knew what Marina's pussy tasted like so it wasn't hard to imagine licking it right there on stage with all those people watching, envying him as he ventured in beneath that tented skirt. While his tongue slipped between those hot, fleshy grooves to find the hardened tip of her clitoris she would still be singing, and he would break off to join her from time to time. His hands would take firm hold of her naked breasts while he sang, caressing the fleshy globes and pinching the erect nipples, urging her on to greater vocal heights and greater pleasure.

Then, as their duet moved rapidly towards the final crescendo, he would thrust into her without further preparation, finding her smooth and wet as he slid his cock home. His thrusting would synchronise with the music and he would strain to keep singing as his hips worked for their mutual pleasure. Then, when the music reached its tumultuous, emotional peak, they would climax together in a flurry of ecstatic notes that would bring the crowd to their feet, stamping and clapping with a tremendous ovation. He would look down at the woman's flushed, utterly satisfied face and know that he had achieved the supreme performance of his life.

With a series of convulsive shudders Justin's cock began to spurt, filling him with sensations of deep satisfaction together with a faint underlying shame. He had followed Bella's instructions but the experience left him feeling vaguely uneasy. There was something dubious, almost sacrilegious, about abusing Puccini's much-loved opera in that way. Yet the power it had induced in him was enormous. It was a primitive kind of magic but it might just work, in which case perhaps the end justified the means.

When Enrico drove him back to Rome early next morning, Justin felt very optimistic. He felt sure that he and Marina could build on the good work they had done under Bella's expert tuition, even without her further help. He was looking forward to seeing her, but when he did he was disappointed. She was deep in conversation with Laurie, and the way they were talking it looked as though she didn't want anyone else to interrupt. He felt absurdly put out, and when she greeted him with a smile at lunch-time he responded with a surly lack of grace.

'What's the matter?' she asked him, sounding genuinely mystified.

'Oh, nothing.'

'Didn't you enjoy your weekend at the villa? I thought our lesson went really well.'

She seemed bright and upbeat. Justin wished he didn't feel quite so fed up. He knew it was ridiculous to be jealous of Laurie but he couldn't help it. The good feelings he'd had first thing had faded and his hopes of building on the rapport he and Marina had established now seemed futile. 'Yes, the lesson was good,' he said, sulkily.

'Shall we have another run-through this afternoon, then?'

'Okay.' Justin brightened a little. Perhaps if they rehearsed together some of the magic there had been between them would be resurrected.

They met in the practice room at five. The presence of a *répétiteur* (Marina's idea) dampened Justin's ardour somewhat and the idea of summoning up his previously-nurtured fantasy seemed absurd. He went through the motions, but the glorious sense of re-discovering his own voice that had occurred at the villa just didn't happen.

Afterwards, when the piano-player left them alone, Marina gave a rueful smile. 'Good, but not *that* good! Why don't we forget it for now and go for a pizza or something.'

Justin was relieved that she wanted to stay with him. They ate at a small *trattoria* near the academy. Halfway through the meal the conversation turned to Bella and the *Villa Gandolfini*.

'I thought there was a weird atmosphere there,' Marina admitted. 'What do you reckon?'

Justin shrugged. 'It's never going to be your normal family home, is it? Not with Bella in residence.'

'Well that's it. And that creepy secretary of hers. Do you think they really are a couple of lesbians?'

'It's none of our business, is it?'

'I'm not so sure. After you'd gone into the garden, do you know what happened to me?'

'No?' Justin's curiosity was roused, but he was also afraid. What if Marina had found out about the way those women liked to treat their male guests?

'That Olga woman gave me a massage.'

'What? Did she . . . ? I mean . . .'

'I know what you're thinking.' Marina gave a nervous giggle. 'The strange thing is, although she didn't actually do anything – you know – lesbian, I definitely got off on it.'

'You mean . . . you climaxed?'

'Not exactly. It's hard to explain. I felt very aroused, kind of floaty and sensual. I've never felt quite like that before. But afterwards she told me a few things about Bella.'

Justin tried to hide his eagerness to learn more. He faked a casual tone. 'Did she now?'

'Yes. Did you know she gets her kicks from watching other people doing it?' An instant chill went through him. He thought of Annaliese, and the way Bella had seemed to thrust them together. He remembered how the girl had suggested they should use the summer house. Had all that been some kind of plan for Bella's secret gratification? He didn't want to believe that the Dutch girl had been conspiring with their hostess.

'Is that what Olga told you?'

'Yes. She said Bella is too narcissistic to have a normal relationship with a man. I thought you ought to know that, Justin. Just in case you had any illusions about her.'

'I think I know her rather better than you do,' he said, huffily. 'I've been there for two whole weekends and you only stayed a few hours.'

'But Olga chose to confide in me.' There was a hint of triumph in Marina's voice that annoyed him intensely. What did she know of that pair's predilections? Still, her news had disturbed him – if it were true.

'She could have been lying.'

'I doubt it. Why would she have done that? She said she wanted to protect me from ending up as some kind of ice queen, like Bella.'

'I can't accept that. Bella is full of passion. It's just that she hasn't met the right man.'

'And you reckon you might be her Mr Right, is that it?'

Justin glared at her. 'Of course not! I just value her friendship. Which is more than you seem to do.'

They were quarrelling over their *tiramisu*. Justin felt waves of fatalistic gloom sweep over him. How stupid he was to think that he and Marina could ever get it together. She was horribly jealous of his relationship with Bella, and keen to spread poison whenever she could. While he hated the way she encouraged that Laurie character, flirting with him even though he was patently the wrong type for her. For the first time he began to regret that they'd been paired up to perform together.

But then she took his hand across the white tablecloth, a regretful smile on her pretty face, and his heart melted. 'I didn't mean to upset you, Justin. I don't want to see you hurt, that's all.'

'Don't worry, I'm keeping my feet firmly on the ground as regards *La Bellissima*. My interest in her is purely professional. I thought she could help me in my career, that's all.'

'Me too.' Marina put a forkful of the gooey dessert into her mouth and licked the spoon with sensual thoroughness. 'Actually, she sort of hinted she might take me under her wing.'

The jealous feelings that had been simmering quietly inside Justin now redoubled and rushed to the surface like poisonous bile. He swallowed, then said, 'You too, eh? Maybe she's planning to coach us as a pair, like Torvill and Dean.'

Marina gave him a doubtful look, then giggled. 'Or maybe she's just having us both on a string. You never can tell with a woman like Bella, can you? Just what makes her tick, do you reckon? Apart from sending an audience into operatic ecstasy, of course.'

'Power.'

'Yeah? You think she's a power junkie?'

'I'm sure of it. And so is Olga. That's why the pair of them get on so well. They like having power over men.'

'You should know, I suppose. Exactly what do you get up to at the villa, Justin, after the lessons are finished and dinner is over? I'd love to know!'

'Oh, we just play a few games.'

'Games? What sort of games?'

He grinned. 'The usual sort. Gin rummy, whist, back-gammon . . .'

'My arse!'

'Is a very nice arse indeed!'

'Honestly, Justin, you can trust me. Tell me what happens there. I know it's something out of the ordinary. Olga said there was another guest on Saturday, too. A girl.'

'Yes. She often has other guests at the weekends. So what?'

Marina's eyes looked very blue. For some reason Justin found their intensity frightening. Just what had Olga been telling her?

But she suddenly pushed another mouthful of dessert down and then crumpled her napkin onto the table. 'It doesn't matter. Shall we get the bill now? I ought to get back.'

He looked at his watch. 'It's only half seven. What were you planning to do this evening?'

'I've . . . er . . . some postcards to write and a book to finish. I also wanted to listen to a recording Bella gave me.'

'Can't we at least have a drink or something? Later, perhaps. We could meet in your hotel bar around ten . . .'

'No, Justin,' she said, firmly. 'I want an early night. I'll see you tomorrow morning, okay?'

He was terribly disappointed. They'd seemed on the verge of regaining their former intimacy, but then she'd pulled back and he hadn't a clue why. He clicked his fingers for the waiter and they shared the bill, but she kept to her word and went off in the direction of her hotel leaving him at a loose end.

Justin ended up drinking in his own hotel bar, chatting to some English tourists and feeling sorry for himself. Although he tried not to take what Marina had said seriously – it was second-hand information, after all – the idea that Bella could possibly have set him up to have sex with Annaliese while she watched was sickening. How could he find out the truth? Annaliese was one possibility, but he had no way of knowing where she was or if he'd ever see her again. Olga was another. If she'd been prepared to talk so frankly to Marina she might do the same to him. But the mistress/slave relationship that she'd established between them made such revelations extremely unlikely.

His thoughts returned, as they usually did, to Bella. Whatever kinky desires the woman might have he was still obsessed by her. Justin thought he knew what a man must feel like when he sold his soul to the devil. Bella's heavenly voice, her divine body, had captured his own soul and he was helpless to resist her commands. She was truly the Queen of the Night, and he was her willing slave.

For the rest of the week Justin had the feeling that Marina was avoiding him. Why, he had no idea, except that he caught her looking at him oddly once or twice during lectures and classes. He deduced that she was stopping herself from becoming too involved with him. Maybe their intense and emotional singing at the villa had unnerved her. At any rate, although they had several more rehearsals they didn't approach such heights again. He didn't know whether he was disappointed or relieved.

On Saturday morning he set out for the villa in Enrico's car, feeling more apprehensive than he had on the previous occasions. Bella had been absent from the academy that week. He gathered from Enrico that she'd been away from Rome, visiting friends. Did that mean there would be other guests at the *Villa Gandolfini* that weekend? The thought that he might be called on to behave in some bizarre fashion, as before, filled him with dread.

If Marina had been right and Bella did gain sexual satisfaction from watching others perform, maybe she would get him to do it right in front of her. Justin was convinced that if he were put into that position he wouldn't be able to get it up and his humiliation would be total. So as the limousine swung into the familiar driveway Justin was conscious of a sick hollowness in his stomach, a nervousness he'd only previously felt before taking exams.

The singer greeted him effusively, with a kiss on each cheek. She was wearing a new perfume, something spicy and sultry, that immediately overwhelmed his senses, disorientating him. Equally unnerving was the top she was wearing, of fine turquoise lawn with a low V-neck that revealed far too much of her cleavage for that time of day. Justin couldn't keep his eyes off it.

But her next statement disconcerted him even more. 'After coffee we'll work on your duet. I shall sing Mimi to your Rodolfo.'

All the terror he'd felt when called on to perform with her in front of the class now returned. He gaped at her, only just managing to stammer, 'Th . . . that'll be very nice.'

'Don't worry, I shan't eat you!' she grinned, obviously enjoying his discomfiture. 'It won't be like before. After all, I think we know each other pretty well by now, don't we?'

Justin could only stare at her, wondering what was going on behind those dark, inscrutable eyes. It was part of Bella's appeal that she remained essentially a mystery. But suppose what Marina had said about her being some kind of narcissistic voyeur were true? Then he was privy to inside information about one of the greatest *divas* in the world. It was a scary thought.

Coffee was over far too soon, plunging Justin back into a state of panic. Bella did her best to make him relax through the breathing exercises and this time she tried to make him visualise his voice coming out loud and strong with the sound filling the room like sunshine, growing brighter and brighter. But Justin couldn't help remembering how she'd told him to fantasise, too. What if he substituted *her* as his leading lady, instead of Marina? Was that what she'd intended him to do all along? He scrutinised her face as she sat at the piano but she was giving nothing away.

When the warm-up was completed to Bella's satisfaction she rang for Olga to take over the piano part and came to stand at an angle to Justin, as if they were together on stage. She ran through the dramatic scenario briefly, emphasising the fact that Rodolfo had been smitten by Mimi at first sight.

'If that has ever happened to you, Justin, you must try to recall it in every detail. Have you ever been thoroughly infatuated with a woman?'

He nodded, feeling his throat constrict with emotion. Did she know that his greatest obsession was herself? From the astute way she was regarding him he had a feeling that she did. So was she playing games with him once more, leading him on only to make a fool of him? The irony was that, for Justin, it was all part of her charm.

Seeing Bella draw herself up into a stately posture, her generous breasts thrust out as her lungs filled to capacity and her eyes gleaming with anticipation of the joy of singing, it wasn't difficult to imagine that he was madly in love with her. Justin felt his chest swell and their voices melded into harmony, the notes coming out of Bella's open mouth with as much natural fluidity as from a blackbird's beak.

They sang the duet straight through without a break, rising effortlessly together at the end to make the final held chord. Olga stopped playing and there was a hiatus, with only the sound of breathing. Justin didn't know what to think, he was so overcome by having completed the ordeal. But when the normally restrained Olga rose from the stool and rushed up to congratulate him with a kiss on each cheek, he knew that something rather special had happened.

'*Stupendo!*' she grinned. 'Wasn't he great, Bella?'

'Not bad for a beginner!' she said, with wry understatement. 'You certainly rose to the occasion, Justin. Well done. Now let's get back to work, shall we?'

He was deflated, but knew she was right. There was always more that could be got out of a part, another few steps towards perfection. They worked through it bar by bar, analysing, repeating, until he felt utterly exhausted but still she wouldn't let it rest.

'Sing through Rodolfo's part again,' she urged him. 'I'll just hum Mimi's part. That way I can concentrate on what you are doing without distraction.'

The session was the most arduous Justin had ever experienced. It went on and on without respite, and when Bella finally called a halt he was horrified to find they'd been at it for four hours non-stop.

Bella placed a finger beneath his chin, lifting his face. 'Are you hungry?' she asked, teasingly.

'Starving!'

'Good. Cook has made a wonderful dish *Coda alla Vaccinara*. Speciality of the region. Now off to refresh yourself. We shall meet in the dining-room at two-thirty.'

Justin knew that the *Villa Gandolfini* ran to its own timetable, so he didn't complain that lunch seemed a little late. It was worth waiting for, too. The stew was delicious – oxtail with celery – and Justin was delighted to find that he had Bella's sole company as Olga had to go into town to shop that afternoon. She seemed in a sweetly capricious mood, teasing him about English food which she pretended to despise.

'And your famous fish and chips – ugh! Soggy batter and greasy potatoes all wrapped in newspaper! How could that ever be considered a culinary masterpiece?'

Justin laughed. 'There's no accounting for taste.'

'Yes.' Bella looked thoughtful, adding, 'That goes for sex too. One man's meat is another's *poisson*, isn't that what you English say?'

He laughed harder. Then, emboldened by their hilarious mood, he said, 'And what is your particular *poisson*, Bella? I have a feeling you're not into meat.'

She gave him a look he found hard to interpret. 'What exactly do you mean by that, young man?'

Justin sensed he'd gone too far. Trying desperately to backtrack he said, 'Oh, just . . . well, hunky types. You know. I thought you'd fancy . . . er . . . people with more brain than brawn.'

'I see. What gave you that idea?'

'Oh, just a feeling.'

He was out of his depth, and she knew it. Her lovely eyes turned hard and there was a deep furrow between her brows. 'Has Olga been talking about me?'

'Olga? No . . .'

'Who, then – Marina?'

Justin felt his cheeks grow hot. 'N . . . no, not particularly.'

'You're lying. I can always tell. What has she been saying about me?'

'Nothing much.'

'But she has said something. Come on, out with it. If you don't tell me I shall wring it out of you and I don't think you'd like that very much.'

Despite his misgivings, Justin decided to confront her. He was just curious enough to know if there was any truth in the rumour. He took a deep breath. 'Well, she said you'd rather watch other people than do it yourself. A weird thing to say, I thought. I don't know where she got that idea . . .'

'Olga!' Bella punched her fist into her palm, making Justin wince. 'The bitch! Any chance she gets . . .' Suddenly she turned on Justin as if she'd only just realised he was there. 'Well? And did you believe her? Did you believe I was . . . what you call a "Peeping Tom"? That I spy on people making love?'

He shrugged. 'I didn't know what to believe.'

'Hah!'

The earlier pleasant mood was shattered and an ugly, threatening one had taken its place. He could tell that Bella was extremely annoyed. Her impressive bosom was shaking like a jelly beneath its turquoise covering. Justin cursed himself for his lack of judgement. He should have known that Bella would have been furious to know that she was being talked about behind her back, whether or not the rumours were true. He wished, fervently, that he could turn the clock back five minutes and start again.

She rose from the table, a study in outraged dignity, and left the room without a word. Justin was at a loss to know what to do. He sat at the table picking idly at some grapes and watching the play of light on the water through the window until he heard raised voices somewhere in the villa. In a few minutes Olga entered. She, too, had a face like thunder and he guessed that he had managed to upset both women at once. What horrible punishment would they devise for him now?

'You are to go to your room and wait until you are sent for,' she told him, coldly.

He obeyed at once, but the intervening hour and a half crawled by and with each passing minute Justin grew more apprehensive. At last he heard the door open and Olga came in wearing a pair of black boots and a calf-length dress in black rubber. It had the style of a Russian general's greatcoat, with buttons that fastened diagonally across the front and a standup collar. Her hair was slicked back with gel and she wore a pair of gold-rimmed spectacles that gave her the air of an SS officer.

'Strip!' she commanded him. 'Then get into this!'

She tossed a kind of harness onto the bed. It was made of black leather and studded with silver. Once he'd removed his clothes it took Justin a while to work out how it went on, but at last he got into it and found that the straps ran around his sides while the pouch fitted snugly around his genitalia. As usual his buttocks were left bare, but tonight that seemed more ominous than usual.

'You will not be blindfolded tonight,' Olga informed him. 'It is important that you see. Down on your knees now, and follow me.'

Justin knelt on the carpet and began to shuffle along behind her as she went out onto the landing and down the stairs. She led him into the lounge, where Bella was already waiting clad in a see-through negligée in pink silk, trimmed with swansdown. It was reminiscent of the costume of a Thirties' movie star and seemed somehow appropriate. Through its diaphanous folds Justin could see the dark vee of Bella's pubic hair and the equally dark areolae of her nipples. She was Erotica, Goddess of Sexual Love. It excited him terribly. He could feel his cock harden as he sat back on his haunches.

Olga stepped forward, the rubber of her costume creaking slightly. He noticed that she had tucked a pair of handcuffs and a businesslike whip into the belt of her dress. The leather thong was plaited and looped while the handle was thick and shaped like a dildo. She detached the instrument and used it to point at Justin's groin. 'Shall I remove the pouch, mistress?'

'Yes. I want to see his arousal.'

With a deft movement Olga pulled off the modesty shield. Instinctively Justin put both hands over his growing erection. The whip snaked out and caught him on the upper arm, stinging horribly and making him cry out.

'Foolish creature! Do you think we care about the state of your pathetic phallus? It is of no interest to us except as a barometer of your libido. Shall I immobilise his hands, mistress?'

'Yes. Tie them behind his head. I want him to be uncomfortable.'

Olga wrenched his arms up and secured them with cuffs behind his neck so that his elbows stuck up in the air. It was certainly uncomfortable, and Justin had the feeling that after only a few minutes it would be pretty painful. Worse, though, was his suspicion that the women had some particularly sadistic game to play with him that evening. He'd managed to offend both of them, and they were working in concert to achieve their revenge.

Bella came up close and looked him straight in the eye. He saw a deep contempt lurking there, which confused him. Only a few hours ago they had been singing in sweet harmony and now she seemed to loathe him. What was he supposed to make of it all? Was there any part of this extraordinary woman that was genuine, sincere?

'You accused me of being a voyeur,' she snarled.

'Not accused. I don't mind if . . .'

Without any warning the whip fell across his buttocks, making him yelp more with surprise than pain. He realised that Olga was standing by ready to administer punishment the instant he stepped out of line.

'Are you telling me you don't like to watch such things too?' Bella went on, smoothly, following her own agenda. 'Surely not. Don't tell me you never looked at a dirty magazine or a porno video. Every man does those things. It's in the nature of the beast, isn't that right, Olga?'

'Yes. They are all filthy, vile creatures. They can't help themselves. It's their disgusting cocks. Look at his, even as we speak. It's halfway to erect already.'

'Hm. I wonder why. Do you think it's my state of *déshabille* that's getting him going, Olga?'

The rubber-clad woman smiled. 'I should imagine so. It's certainly doing a lot for me.'

'Well let's see if he can overcome his nature and control his urges, shall we?' Bella walked over to a velvet-covered chaise longue and arranged herself on it fetchingly, her long legs spread out in front of her. She casually undid the three satin bows that held the front of the flimsy garment together and the two sides fell apart, revealing her naked body.

Justin gasped, a surge of adrenalin rushing through him at the amazing sight. Although she was very well-covered, Bella's flesh was firm and smooth, her breasts as round and shapely as footballs despite their large size. The gentle swell of her stomach between her broad hips led Justin's eyes inexorably down to the dark bush between her thighs. He gasped again as her legs parted and her hand crept down to toy provocatively with her pubic hair.

It was impossible to prevent his excitement from becoming obvious. His cock instantly swelled to its fullest extent and his balls weighed heavy. But just as he was transfixed by the sight of Bella starting to caress her own breast Olga gave him another painful flick on the buttocks.

'Wretched creature! How dare you point that impudent thing at my mistress. Stop it!' Justin looked down at his rampant erection. 'I . . . I can't!' he moaned. Another crack of the whip caught him across the back of his thighs, making him call out. 'No, please!'

'Then behave yourself.'

'I can't. Not while she's . . . like that.'

He glanced towards Bella again. Her thighs were parted and her fingers were pulling open her labia, displaying her sex. The pussy lips were pink and swollen, deliciously moist and tender. Justin didn't want to look. He wanted to look anywhere but there, where the sight of her voluptuous nudity would feed his cock and earn him more chastisement. But it was impossible not to stare at her blatant sexuality. His mind was focused on one thing, and he could not distract himself no matter how hard he tried, no matter how dire the penalty.

'Leave him,' Bella's soothing voice came. 'Let him enjoy it a little. Maybe his organ will subside in time.'

'I doubt it,' Olga snarled. 'He's feeding it with vile thoughts, I can tell. He's thinking about what he'd like to do to you if I let him loose. He's like a ravening beast: you can chain him up, but you can never tame him.'

But she kept her distance all the same, perching on the edge of a chair with a disapproving air. The whip was in her hand, ready to be used at a moment's notice. Justin could almost feel the waves of contemptuous hatred that were emanating from her. Did she hate him because she was jealous of his relationship with Bella, or simply because he was a man? Either way, he knew that her antagonism was extreme and could be unleashed on him at any moment.

He should have hated her in return yet he felt a weird kind of admiration for her, even a sneaking attraction. He remembered what Marina had said about her massage and wondered if she only ever administered pain to men and pleasure to women, or whether she was in the habit of physically punishing women too.

Justin's eyes returned to Bella, the sight of her stroking her vulva instantly reviving his lustful feelings. He saw her fingers move up to find the sensitive button of her clitoris. She sighed loudly, leaning back and continuing to rub with the tip of one finger while she used her other hand to play with her nipples. He could see her bosom swelling visibly, as it did on stage, the dark nipples growing huge as she scratched at them with her nails, one after the other. He'd never watched a woman masturbating before, and the fact that it was *her* doing it, the woman who'd dominated his dreams for years, gave the spectacle a surreal kind of power.

There was no chance of his erection subsiding, of course, and he could hear Olga muttering vengefully in the wings as his eyes remained fixed on Bella. The *diva* was moaning loudly now as her ascent towards orgasm accelerated. Her throat was flushed and there was a small rivulet of sweat running between the generous curves of her breasts. Justin could even smell the unmistakable musk from her over-heated pussy as she worked it towards a climax. His cock

137

was straining at the leash and he craved the physical stimulation that would bring him release, but with his hands locked painfully behind his head there was nothing he could do but suffer the sweet torment along with the horrible anticipation.

'He's filthy, disgusting! Just look at him now!' he heard Olga say as his prick jerked in frustration, the purplish head taut and shiny, the shaft stretched thick and tight.

Bella smiled. 'What a naughty thing it is between his legs.' She sighed, pausing to push her finger right inside herself. She then proceeded to move it languidly in and out, making Justin groan with frustration.

'It wants to do what your finger's doing,' Olga continued, her tone full of loathing. 'It wants to get right inside you, to violate your sanctuary. Shall I punish it for its presumption?'

Vaguely Bella nodded, making Justin cringe with dread. He felt the bite of the whip on his still-smarting behind, this time carefully aimed at both cheeks in succession until the whole of his rear end was aflame. His aching arms and shoulders only added to his misery as he stood there helpless, but although his erection subsided a little it would not go down completely.

'That's enough,' Bella said, her voice a guttural murmur as she approached the summit of her arousal. 'If he misbehaves you may punish him afterwards. I don't want any distractions from now on.'

'Of course not, mistress.'

Olga retreated respectfully to her chair but this time she turned towards Bella, watching her avidly and with a strange smile on her face. Justin was also transfixed by the sight of her as she squeezed her tumid breasts with one hand, making the nipples stand out stiffly, while she increased the friction down below. Through the wide open labia he could see the liquid centre of her pussy and the huge, distended pleasure-knob that she was frotting wildly. His cock jerked and strained into the empty air, desperate for some relief, and the rest of him was a mass of torrid, aching flesh.

Then, in a series of noisy convulsions, she came. It proved too much for Justin. His system was dangerously overloaded, and when all restraint was lifted from the object of his desire and she gave herself up to the extremity of pleasure, he just had to do the same. Out from his glans spurted the proof of his dissipation, a fierce jet that arced in the air and spilt onto the carpet with reckless abandon.

For a split second he was filled with profound relief, but it was quickly replaced by fear when he heard Olga give a horrified cry and saw her leap from her seat brandishing the whip.

'Look what the beast has done!' she squealed, pointing to the sticky white trail on the carpet. 'Shall we make him lick up his own excrescence, the filthy thing?'

Bella turned her languid, sated eyes towards him and waved her hand. 'No, no! Let the maid clean up, that's what we pay her for. But he should have had more control. You may administer a penalty if you wish.'

Justin secretly wished they'd gone for the first option, but he steeled himself wearily for the onslaught. This time his bum cheeks were not the target. Olga stood behind him and began to thrust the handle of the whip into his anus, hurting him as she stretched it.

'Is this how you like it?' she murmured, in his ear. 'Are you one of those "bottom up" boys?' She gave the handle a vicious twist, making him squirm and yell.

'That's enough!' Bella called sharply, pulling the negligée around her as she stood. 'Don't torture him, you sadistic creature. If he goes on yelling like that he'll ruin his throat.'

'Yes, mistress. Of course you are right.'

The plug was abruptly pulled out of his arse, but it still hurt horribly. Justin hoped Bella might suggest a little soothing cream, but it seemed he was out of luck this time. She merely unclasped his handcuffs then, as he rubbed his chafed wrists, stood before him impassively. His senses were overpowered with the sight and smell of her, the afterglow of her orgasm giving her skin a rosy sheen while in the air hung the heady mix of perfumes from her body, both artificial and natural.

Justin was acutely aware of his drooping dick, his smarting behind and his aching limbs. All he wanted was to soak in a hot bath and then to fall into a deep, blissful sleep. But Bella hadn't quite finished with him. An ironic smile lifted her lips and her eyes surveyed him with wry disdain as she said, 'Well, young man, which one of us is the *voyeur* now?'

Chapter Ten

Marina had a miserable weekend. It wasn't for want of trying. She went out to a restaurant with Laurie and another couple, then on to a disco, but her heart wasn't in it. She couldn't help wondering what was going on at the *Villa Gandolfini*, and it preyed on her mind all evening so that she hardly took part in the conversation. Eventually, in the disco, Laurie tried to kiss her but she put him off.

'What's up, Marina?' he asked, crossly. 'You've been acting weird all night.'

'I'm sorry. I'm not feeling too good. I think I'd better go back to my hotel.' He called a cab for her with bad grace and she felt mean, but she was relieved to be alone. On the way back she attempted to examine her feelings but they were a confused mess. All week she'd been trying to convince herself that she didn't give a damn about what Justin got up to with Bella, but it was no use pretending. She was becoming as obsessed with him as he was with the opera singer. And ever since Olga had told her a bit about what went on at the villa she'd been feeling uneasy about Justin going there again.

It had even crossed her mind to go there tomorrow and sniff around a bit. She pictured herself turning up at the villa pretending she had lost something: an item of jewellery, perhaps. But it would cost the earth to hire a cab and she didn't think she could make her excuse seem at all convincing. Bella, Olga and Justin would all realise that she had come to the villa simply because she was jealous.

There, she'd admitted it! She was desperately jealous of Bella and the hold she had over Justin. Why? Because she wanted him all to herself. That was the only possible explanation. The truth hit Marina with devastating force.

Despite her casual behaviour during the past week she'd been secretly longing for him to throw himself at her feet, to declare he was no longer interested in Bella, only in her. It hadn't happened, of course.

If only she could find some distraction, but her mind kept imagining the goings-on at the villa. She also wondered why she hadn't been invited back. After that glorious singing lesson, when both she and Justin had excelled themselves, it seemed odd that another invitation was not forthcoming. Had Olga had anything to do with it? Maybe the woman had wanted the 'massage' to turn into a lesbian encounter and Marina had disappointed her.

Her mind was striving to make sense of it, exploring theories and explanations that were probably quite wrong, but she couldn't let it alone. Even after a soothing bath in the hotel Marina couldn't sleep but stared listlessly at the soft porn film on late-night Italian TV until she grew too aroused to bear any more. While the nubile couple went through their paces on screen she moaned out her desire for Justin, caressing her breasts and rubbing her clitoris with her vibrator until the spasms of a brief orgasm gave her some temporary relief.

Marina was not satisfied, however. Now she realised that only making love with Justin could fulfil her completely. She had tried to deny it to herself but her need was overwhelming. She couldn't wait to see him again on Monday. This time, she vowed, she wouldn't play it cool. She would seduce him through her singing, make him understand that she wanted him.

His response when she saw him was not encouraging. They met in the corridor of the academy just before the first class and she asked, with forced brightness, if he'd enjoyed his weekend at the villa.

'It was okay,' he said, grumpily.

'Just "okay"?'

He glared at her, shrugged and moved on. Marina's heart slumped in her chest. After anticipating how she would coax a smile out of him his surliness was a big let-down. Later that day, though, they had a private rehearsal booked and she was pinning all her hopes on that.

The day dragged, with a lecture from a famous tenor about the life and works of Verdi followed by voice exercises with Renata Bellini. In the afternoon Marina had a movement class with a dictatorial female called 'Madame Stephanie'. The men and women were separated in a way that Marina thought sexist. While the women were prancing around like ballet dancers the men were in the gym, developing their pectorals and biceps.

At four Marina and Justin met in the practice room they usually used, this time without the benefit of a *répétiteur* as they'd forgotten to book one. Although this would make the work more tedious, since they'd have to keep re-setting the backing tape, Marina was glad of the privacy. At first she was nervous, unsure what mood he would be in, but he greeted her with a big smile and a hug that reassured her.

'Sorry I was a bit offhand this morning,' he said. 'It was kind of a weird weekend and I just wanted to forget it.'

'That's okay.' Marina knew better than to question him right then, despite the fact that she was dying to know what it was all about. 'Shall we get straight down to work then?'

A mood of harmony was soon established once they'd done their warm-up exercises. This time the duet went well. Not quite as well as it had at the villa, under Bella's expert tuition, but as the session progressed they remembered more and more of what she'd told them and strove to put it into practice.

'Let's record ourselves, shall we?' Justin suggested. 'Then we can be more objectively critical.'

As Marina listened to the recording of their blended voices she felt a shiver down her spine. Although it was obviously not the work of great professionals, there was a delicate poignancy about their singing that brought tears to her eyes. The duet was meant to be a passionate declaration of love at first sight, but somehow their voices had managed to hint at the tragic end of the affair. When the last chord died away she turned to Justin and saw that he had been affected too.

'Not bad!' he grinned, blinking at her with a wry grin. 'We may not win this festival, but I reckon we stand a jolly good chance.'

'It's not really about winning, is it? More about exploring our potential.'

'That's it. I don't think I've ever felt more at home with another singing partner, Marina. Renata must have had some kind of sixth sense when she paired us up.'

Marina said nothing, but she felt secretly gratified. If their voices were so compatible maybe their bodies would be too. She glanced at Justin's sturdy figure, his well-muscled arms displayed in a short-sleeved T-shirt. He had a nice bum and he was good-looking too. Clear greyish eyes, that turned blue when they lit up with a smile the way they did now, when he caught her looking at him.

She remembered how good it had felt to caress his glossy, dark hair as he licked her pussy and a sharp pang of desire hit her. But on that occasion she had encouraged him to think of Bella as he mouthed her. Next time she wanted him all to herself, mind and body. The surging tide of her lust was making it difficult for her to be alone with Justin without throwing herself at him, but she knew she had to remain in control if she didn't want to frighten him off.

'Shall we call it a day?' he said at last. 'I'm starving. Let's go back to that place we went to before.' He paused, his eyes suddenly darkening. 'Unless you're . . . unless you have other plans.'

'Oh no,' she replied happily. It was good that he'd had a momentary doubt, though. He was probably remembering how he'd seen her flirting with Laurie. Well, that was all over now. She knew that Laurie wasn't her type. He was too predictable, too straightforward. Justin had far more depth to him, even though she suspected that something murky lurked within his soul. As they left the academy and walked towards the *trattoria* she linked her arm in his.

The meal was tasty and filling, the wine basic but satisfying, and by the end of it they were both in good spirits. Justin suggested they should stroll around for a while, seeing Rome by Night, and for an hour or so they wandered contentedly from bar to bar, observing the smartly-dressed Roman couples and sampling a variety of drinks. They studiously avoided talking about Bella, or even about Opera, choosing instead to share life-histories.

'I almost got engaged once,' Marina confessed. She hardly ever talked about her broken love-affair but now it seemed right to do so. 'He was only my third boyfriend and I was besotted. It was just sex, really. He gave me my first orgasm. But fortunately I came to my senses in time.'

'And you've been playing the field ever since, is that it?'

Justin sounded just a bit peeved. Marina frowned. 'If I have, what's it to you?'

He shrugged. 'Nothing, of course. It's just that I saw the way you were flirting with that other guy . . .'

'You mean Laurie? There's nothing in it. I was super-ficially attracted to him but I soon found out he wasn't my type.'

She was gratified to see the relief in Justin's face. He took her hand, squeezed it. 'That's good. I thought you'd gone off me, you see. I couldn't have blamed you, not with me going on about Bella all the time. But still . . .'

His voice tailed off as their gazes locked, direct and intense, their expression far more eloquent than words. With a twinge of excitement in her belly, Marina realised that he was itching for her too. They were in a small crowded bar and she wished they were somewhere else, somewhere more private.

Justin seemed to read her thoughts. 'Shall we go?' he murmured. 'I think you and I have some unfinished business. My hotel's nearer: let's go there.'

She appreciated his blunt approach. There was no point in beating about the bush since they both knew what they wanted. It was one of the things she admired about Justin that, when it came to the crunch, he knew how to get what he wanted, and this time she would give him his head. The time for playing games was over.

As they hurried through the dark streets Marina found the strong grip of his hand reassuring. His warmth flooded through her, filling her spirit with optimism and gearing up her body for the joys to come. Between her thighs she could feel the hot pulse of her sex and her breasts strained beneath the cotton top, nipples bulging visibly. It was good to know that Justin wanted her at last. Whatever had happened at the villa that weekend seemed to have cleared away the fog of uncertainty that used to surround him revealing a new, more focused Justin.

Once they were in the privacy of the hotel bedroom, Marina stripped off her top and skirt without more ado and pulled him onto the bed, wearing only her white lace panties. She stretched and purred like a cat as he unzipped his jeans and soon he was similarly clad, the sun-browned flesh of his torso filmed with sweat. She stroked his dark chest hairs and looked up at him coquettishly. 'Well? Aren't you going to ravish me?'

His response was instant and overwhelming. Fierce lips crushed hers with relentless force while his fingers squeezed her breast and pulled at the erect nipples until she was squirming with appetite. Their tongues duelled in her mouth, fresh saliva sweetening their kiss, and Marina moaned languidly as one of his hands began to caress her stomach in lazy circles. Her pants were damp and sticking to the tingling crevice of her vulva.

Justin put his hand down the front of her panties and his fingers tangled in her damp curls. She moaned and thrust her hips up towards him, trying to gain contact with her clitoris. The tip of one finger found it, gave it gentle pressure until she moaned encouragingly. Then he began to rub it softly while she felt herself opening to him just below.

Soon Marina wanted him inside her. She reached down and felt the solid bulk of his penis. Carefully she pulled the cotton waistband down over his tumid glans. She rubbed her finger softly across it, feeling its smooth viscosity. Her hand moved down to clasp his shaft, which was satisfyingly long and thick. But it was not enough just to feel him, she wanted to see as well. Wrenching her mouth away from his she sat up and surveyed his rampant cock.

'Oh!' she breathed, thrilled at the length and girth, the sculpted perfection of it. 'Do you mind if I kiss it?'

'Do I *mind*!' he laughed, whipping off his pants. 'Turn around, let me kiss you at the same time. I don't like to do things by halves.'

Delightedly she obeyed. This was a new Justin she was experiencing and he was filling her with joyous expectation. Eagerly she took the bulbous end of his penis into her mouth, licking around the groove where it joined to the shaft, tasting the fresh essence of him. He thrust into her uncontrollably, the glans sliding along the roof of her mouth while her tongue laved the underside. She loved the feeling of her mouth being filled up. It was a foretaste of things to come. Her hand found the heavy sac beneath the root of his penis and began to play with it, scratching and squeezing lightly until he was groaning out his bliss.

But it was her bliss too, not only the pleasure she felt in dealing with such a fine specimen of the male organ but also the pleasure he was giving her, slowly and insistently, his tongue moving around her outer lips with delicate precision until she was longing for him to penetrate her further. At last she felt him enter the hot well of her sex, lapping at her juices and then moving up to bathe her aching clitoris with them. His agile tongue knew exactly how to arouse her, flicking back and forth over the trigger of her orgasm until the moment she craved was upon her and she cried out in abandon.

Her coming was prolonged and sweet, rising slowly to a peak and then subsiding equally slowly so that Marina had a sense of time, as well as her own climax, being spread out in one long voluptuous wave. When it was over she flopped back onto the bed, noting briefly that Justin's erection was still solid. The prospect of more to come was extremely pleasing.

He didn't hang about. While she was recovering, Justin reached into his wallet for a condom and was soon rubber-clad and ready to enter her. He slid into her molten quim like a hot knife through butter, pushing his impatient cock right up to her cervix which gave her a sensual, tickling feeling. She moaned and wriggled, making him smile down at her and slowly he retreated until his prick was poised at her entrance again.

'Want it fast or slow?'

'Both!'

He obliged, kicking into a wonderful rhythm of 'quick, quick, slow' that soon had her gasping her way towards a second orgasm. The thick base of his shaft was pressing hard against her clitoris to good effect and the constant friction was taking her quickly back to the place she had just been, making her nipples rear and tingle and her vaginal walls clench at the stiff intruder as he came and went, in and out, growing more reckless as the end was in sight for him, too.

'Oh, Justin!' she cried as the first delicious spasms hit her. Dimly she felt him pulsating inside her, the hot shaft pushing in to its fullest extent and thrusting against the inner core of her sex. She clutched at his perspiring shoulders, feeling the barriers between them break down in a welter of blissful sensation that left her full of breathless wonder.

'Oh, Justin!' she repeated, more quietly, as the afterglow enveloped them both.

They lay there inert, arms around each other, her head on his shoulder, with their breathing and heartbeats synchronised, a symbol of their closeness. Marina felt they were at some still centre of the world where nothing could touch them. The distant bustle of the street sounded as if it were a million miles away. Her body was humming with a new kind of energy. She imagined it would be glowing in the dark if she opened her eyes, only it was too magical to risk breaking the spell.

When she drifted back from her slumber Marina felt sad. *Post coitum triste,* she supposed it was. The experience had been overwhelming for her, but what about him? Self-doubts came to torture her. Justin was besotted with Bella, he could never love another woman.

Love, was that what she wanted from him? Earlier that night she had presumed that all she was hungry for was his body, but now she wasn't so sure. Seeing him lying beside her in the dim lamplight, his dark hair tousled over his brow and his lips still red and swollen from their kisses, Marina felt a profound longing that she could not remember feeling before. Always the 'love 'em and leave 'em' type up to now, the notion that she might actually want their affair to have a degree of permanence came as a shock to her.

Justin's eyes opened slowly and surveyed her solemnly. For several long seconds they regarded each other, then he reached up and brushed her cheek with the back of his knuckles.

'That was some session, eh, Marina?'

'You make it sound like singing practice.'

He grinned. 'Maybe it was, in a way. I mean, we're bound to sing even better together after this, aren't we?'

'Are we?'

She stared at him uncertainly not knowing how to take him now that he was awake and reacting to her with a will of his own. He reached up and pulled her head down towards his, giving her a sensual kiss on the lips. Marina felt herself being pulled back into his orbit like a stray planet. She sank against him and his hand toyed with her breast, pulling her nipple back into prominence. Insistent flurries in her stomach told her that she was ready for more, despite her previous sense of utter fulfilment. How extraordinary the sex urge is, she thought, as he rolled her over onto her side and prepared to penetrate her once again.

This time their love-making was lazy and relaxed, his cock probing beneath her loose thighs time after time while his hand reached over and caressed her tender clitoris with careful strokes. She climaxed tenderly, full of the most exquisite feelings, and he came soon afterwards in a flurry of rapid spurts. They remained like that for some time, her back to his belly, the erotic impulse fighting with the urge to sleep until the latter overwhelmed it and they both sank into oblivion again.

Marina was astonished to find it was dawn when she awoke, the lamp still burning and Justin's penis, with its early-morning erection, still clamped between her thighs. She opened her legs and turned over, unable to resist the temptation to caress that jaunty, irrepressible organ. As soon as she began Justin gave a sleepy moan but he didn't open his eyes. She grew bolder, sliding the skin of his foreskin up and down over the glans until he was completely hard and ready

149

for her again. This time it was she who found the small packet in his wallet, unrolled the pink latex and fitted it. Feeling wide awake now she straddled him and lifted her hips, tilting her pelvis so that she could make contact between his glans and her hard little clitoris. She began to rub him on herself and soon his hands crept up to her breasts, stimulating her even more as she rode him with increasing ferocity.

This time her climax was incredibly strong and satisfying. She almost tumbled from her perch as the racking waves overtook her and filled her whole being with intense pleasure. When she had finished he was still going so she let him stay inside her, riding him like a cowgirl on a bucking bronco until he, too, was sated.

'God, that was good!' he exclaimed as she slid off him. 'I don't know where you find the energy, first thing in the morning.'

'I think you re-charged my battery last night!'

They both chortled with glee and he pulled her into the crook of his arm beneath the sheets. Marina sighed. 'Why did we take so long to get it together? We've wasted three whole weeks and now there's only a little time left.'

Justin put a finger across her lips. 'Don't! Let's not spoil whatever time we have. Anyway, I was too blinded by glamour to see what was under my nose. I don't have to tell you whose glamour, do I?'

Marina shook her head. 'What happened at the villa this time? You needn't tell me if you don't want to. Only after what Olga told me . . .'

'I think Olga may have been right. Except that Bella turned the tables on me, so to speak. Made me watch while she . . . displayed herself before me. She's definitely one hell of an exhibitionist, but I suppose that goes without saying if you're in the opera business.'

'Exhibitionist? What did she do, a strip-tease?'

'Something like that. She certainly enjoyed seeing me get into a lather over her. She's one hell of a weird woman, and I think there's definitely something going on between her and Olga. But that doesn't alter the fact that she's a heavenly singer, does it?'

150

'Of course not, that goes without saying. But her weirdness must surely fuel her performances in some way. You know, I've always felt there was something a bit manic about the way she is on stage. All that histrionic eye-rolling and bosom-beating. Her acting style owes more to the silent film era than anything.'

'Yes, she's definitely way over the top. But that's exactly what her fans love about her.'

Suddenly Marina sat up, filled with impatience. 'Just listen to us! She's won again, hasn't she? Here we are, after having made the most glorious love, and all we can find to talk about is Bella-bloody-Conti! Well, I'm going for a shower.'

Marina stalked off into the bathroom, anger filling her veins like hot poison. She turned on the shower full blast and let the tepid water cascade over her, washing away her excess adrenaline. Afterwards, as she soaped her breasts and stomach, she felt sad. Justin was still unable to carry on a conversation for more than a few minutes without bringing up the subject of 'that woman' in some shape or form. She was sick of it. What hope was there for their budding relationship if the shadow of *La Bellissima* lay between them at every turn?

When she came out of the shower, however, Justin looked contrite. He opened his arms and, reluctantly, she gave in to his embrace. He kissed her softly, murmuring, 'I'm sorry for going on about *her*. It's just a habit of mind, really. I don't *want* to be so obsessed with that woman, I want to be free of her. Will you help me, Marina?'

She looked up at him. His grey eyes were regarding her sincerely. Slowly she placed her lips on his then drew back. 'Okay, I'll give it a go.' She grinned. 'Maybe we should try aversion therapy. Every time you mention her I'll give you one of these!'

She delivered a sharp pinch to his arm, making him cry out. He grinned back, ruefully. But then, realising that if she didn't sort herself out soon she'd be late for her first class, Marina started to dress. It was hard to tear herself away from Justin but all her books and papers for the course were back at her hotel, so she had to go. As she left, however, a superstitious fear took hold that the wonderful rapport they'd developed through their love-making would not last. Later, when she arrived at the academy, she looked around apprehensively but her fears redoubled when she couldn't see him anywhere.

The morning went by in a haze of uncertainty. They were booked in for another rehearsal at two that afternoon, but Marina began to wonder if Justin would turn up for it. All her old insecurities about men returned to plague her as she ran through a mental list of possible reasons for his absence, not one of them comforting.

Then, just as she was coming out of the voice class, she saw him waiting in the corridor outside. His face lit up when he saw her and he approached eagerly. 'Shall we go to lunch? We've got an hour and a half before our rehearsal.'

Relief enveloped her like a warm blanket. 'What happened to you?'

He looked endearingly sheepish. 'I fell asleep again.'

They giggled, in the close-conspiratorial way of lovers, and Marina felt much better. When they returned to their favourite restaurant the waiter recognised them and greeted them like old friends. He already sees us as a couple, Marina thought, delighted.

Their rehearsal that afternoon was something special. Whatever barriers there had been between them had completely vanished and they seemed to know intuitively how to sing in harmony, when to speed up and when to slow down. This time they'd engaged the services of a *répétiteur*, and even he was impressed.

'If you sing as well as that you should stand a good chance on Friday,' he told them.

Knowing that he'd played for most of the other students on the course, Marina felt very encouraged. But they only had three more days to fine-tune their performance. Instinctively she knew that if they could improve their performance in bed at the same time they would excel themselves. But it would be difficult to improve on last night . . .

It was very hot that afternoon and the air was thick with dust and petrol fumes. Justin suggested they should go back to his hotel which had a rooftop swimming pool surrounded by orange and bay trees in pots. Marina went back to pick up her swimming gear then met him up there, above the traffic and below the sapphire sky. It was half past five, and they had the place to themselves. Quickly Marina changed into her bikini and plunged into the tepid water, revelling in the cool caress that her skin received from the waves she made.

'Oh, this is glorious!' she exclaimed as Justin made a bigger splash then struck out towards her. He caught her round the waist and they exchanged a wet, slightly chlorinated, kiss.

They swam in tandem around the small pool, Justin caressing her bottom as they went. Marina's relaxed mood subtly altered to one of sensuality as they swam like seals and bobbed beneath the water, play-fighting. She relished the slippery feel of his skin against hers and began to fantasise about making love at the poolside, where sunbeds were invitingly arranged.

He saw her eyeing them. 'Want to get out?'

'Mm.'

'Shall we sunbathe, or be a bit more . . . active?'

'What if someone came?'

'Then they'd get a bit of a shock, I imagine.'

'Justin, you just don't care, do you?'

'Not where you're concerned. I'd dare anything, to please you.'

'Is that so?' She stared at him, trying in vain to read his blue-grey eyes. He took her hand and led her over to one of the beds.

She lay down obediently and he knelt astride her. 'Do you think this thing will take our combined weight?'

'I'm not sure. It won't be very easy to relax if we're worried about it breaking all the time, will it? Why don't we just go back to your room and do it in comfort?'

'I've got a better idea.'

He pulled her up off the bed and they went to where the air-conditioning unit jutted on top of the flat roof. It was concealed from the lift shaft by a protruding wall. Justin spread their towels over the top of it and told her to strip off her pants and sit up with her feet dangling over the edge. She obeyed, smiling quizzically and he said, 'That's good. Just the right height.'

He pulled down his shorts and put his hands around her buttocks, dragging her closer to the edge. The unit was warm beneath the towels, making her bum feel nice. Justin reached for his jeans and found a condom in his pocket: he'd evidently come prepared. He slipped it on his cock then looked up at her with a grin. His hands pulled at the straps of her bikini top until one breast was exposed. Hungrily he took as much of it into his mouth as he could, licking at the nipple. Marina moaned and wriggled her mound against his stomach impatiently.

Within a few seconds he was plunging directly into her, without further preliminaries. Marina gasped as the long, thick shaft struck home sending wild spirals of sensation up throughout her body. The position was ideal for stimulating her clitoris and she relished the hard thrusting that was making full contact with that throbbing button of flesh. His hands were kneading her buttocks, his lips working around her nipples by turns, and she felt the unmistakable rise towards orgasm kick in.

But just as she was pressing Justin's head to her breast in the first flush of her climax, there came the sound of voices. Abruptly he pulled out of her, leaving her dazed and breathless. She opened her eyes to see two middle-aged ladies appear from the entrance to the lift shaft, clad in bathrobes and flip-flops with towels and beach-bags over their arms. Justin immediately darted down behind the bulk of the air-conditioning unit leaving Marina fully exposed on top. In a few seconds the ladies would be able to see her. She hurriedly pulled the towel up around her lower half and threw her head back, breasts lifted to the sun, then she closed her eyes again as if oblivious of their presence.

When she heard idle chatter beside the pool, Marina opened her eyes again as if for the first time. One of the women was looking towards her, so she waved and called brightly, 'Isn't it lovely up here!'

Marina heard a spluttering giggle from behind her and it was all she could do to keep a straight face. The woman gave an uncertain smile and called, '*Buona sera!*' She was evidently slightly embarrassed by discovering that someone else was there before them. Both women took off their robes and lowered themselves into the pool then began to swim around slowly.

Aware of the rogue male presence behind her, Marina managed to replace her pants surreptitiously under the towel and then get down from her perch. Casually she replaced her bra then walked around until she could see Justin, crouched down on his haunches stark naked and with his fist in his mouth, trying not to laugh.

'What the hell are we going to do?' Marina whispered. She was still aroused and buzzing, dying to resume their love-making but unwilling to cause a scene. Although they were only about ten metres from the lift shaft the journey would be a dangerously exposed one.

'Get me my clothes, for a start.'

They were in a heap in front of the unit. Still trying to look casual, Marina picked up the jeans and T-shirt, hiding the pants within them, and sauntered back round to Justin. He struggled to put them on without showing himself, then crawled round to the front of the unit to see if the coast was clear.

The two Italian women were still swimming in a sedate circuit around the pool so there was no way they could hide from them. Marina decided they would just have to put on a bold front. She picked up her remaining things and began to walk towards the lift. When Justin suddenly bobbed up and began to follow her she could see the look of astonishment on both the women's faces.

A spirit of devilment seized her. She turned and gestured towards him, saying, 'He's the air-conditioning engineer. If you want your air well and truly conditioned, he's your man!' Then, giggling and spluttering, the pair of them made a dash for the lift and were swooping down to the third floor before the uncomprehending women could catch their breath. Still laughing, they tumbled into Justin's room the minute he opened the door and rolled together in a heap on the carpet in helpless hysterics.

Chapter Eleven

The atmosphere in the small concert hall attached to the *Accademia del Voce* was electric, with every seat taken. The front row of the audience was occupied by the panel of judges. Justin recognised the stately figure of Bella Conti amongst them and wondered how she could possibly be objective about the performances when she knew most of the students – some more intimately than others, he reminded himself wryly. His palms felt clammy as he stared at the stage, draped with curtains of midnight blue velvet edged with a gold laurel motif. He and Marina had been drawn fourth, around halfway through the programme, but he had no idea whether that was good or bad.

Was it really almost a month since he'd first arrived at the summer school? He remembered how nervous he'd felt then too, and how he'd made an utter fool of himself in front of Bella and the others. Was he about to repeat the experience? Terror had his throat in a tight grip and he didn't know how he would be able to sing a note, but somehow he had to give of his best.

He glanced at Marina, sitting beside him, and wondered how she could appear so calm. She smiled and gripped his hand, squeezing it reassuringly. A buzz of expectation suddenly went through the audience as the curtains parted to reveal the figure of Luigi Postoni, looking very smart in a dress suit. 'Ladies and Gentlemen, welcome to our end-of-course festival . . .'

Justin stared at the man with dull hatred. Marina had told him all about their little seduction scene, and although she'd laughed it off he could tell how humiliated she'd been when the bastard snubbed her afterwards. He knew exactly how *that* felt. Staring at the back of Bella's elegant head he wondered what the other students would think if they knew the truth about the way she and her lesbian partner treated men. Last time she'd gone too far, leaving him feeling disgusted with himself, as well as her.

But then he thought of how he and Marina were now, their love-making growing better and better, and his mood softened. After all, he reminded himself, she had even more cause to be upset about his relationship with Bella. Not that even she knew the full story. He hadn't been able to bring himself to reveal everything about the goings-on at the *Villa Gandolfini*.

The introductions were over and the first couple, Mack and Gabrielle, were taking to the stage. Justin listened attentively to their singing, trying to assess their potential as rivals. They were no competition, he decided by the end. Gabrielle's vibrato was far too tight and her cadenza very ragged, while Mack sounded a quarter tone out of tune all through. It was only nerves, he knew, yet part of the test was to see how they could conquer stage fright. The question was, would he fare any better?

Although Luigi was supposed to be the chairman of the judges, he couldn't resist making slightly scathing comments on the performances. Justin was outraged: so much for impartiality! The second couple sang better, executing the Puccini piece with dash and confidence. Afterwards Luigi commented on the fact that they had shown no trace of the 'slobbering erotics' with which one critic had charged the composer.

'A pleasing rendering,' he commented. 'Any other performers of Puccini will do well to follow their example. But the next piece is the enchanting flower duet from *Lakmé* sung by two delightful young ladies.'

The girls performed sweetly but without much real feeling, their obvious nervousness expressing itself in doubtful glances and pained expressions, which Luigi didn't fail to mention. Then, suddenly, it was Justin and Marina's turn. As they walked up to the stage the *répétiteur* played the introductory music and Justin felt his knees shake uncontrollably.

They took up their positions and he tried to psych himself into the part of Rodolfo, smitten by the lovely Mimi. Looking at Marina, that wasn't difficult. She looked wonderful in a simple, but well-cut dress that accentuated her bust and slim waist. The cornflower blue of the material brought out the colour of her eyes and highlighted her hair with gold.

Justin took several deep breaths and then came in on cue. His first notes were faltering but he pressed on regardless, feeling his voice gain in strength as his confidence grew. Marina was smiling at him, giving him the support he needed to soar up in his first glorious crescendo, where he was joined by her sweet feminine tones. Once they were singing together he lost himself in the drama and music, forgetting that he was supposed to be in a competition, oblivious of the audience even. All that mattered were the feelings of love that exhilarated his soul, not just the love of Rodolfo for Mimi, but the love of Justin for Marina.

'Yes, I do love her!' he thought, and from that point on a new conviction came into his singing. She seemed to sense it, her gaze adoring when their eyes met. He longed to sweep her off to some private place and pour out his heart to her. Instead he strove to tell her by proxy, through the medium of Puccini's glorious melody. By the time he put his arm around her waist and led her slowly to the back of the stage where they were to make their exit their voices were perfectly blended in passion and harmony.

He was so caught up in the wonderful romance of it all that for a few seconds afterwards he stood there quite dazed, only vaguely aware of the enthusiastic applause that was billowing up from the audience. Marina drew him into the wings so they were hidden from view for a few seconds, and planted a passionate kiss on his lips.

'You were *marvellous*!' she told him. 'I've never heard you sing so beautifully.'

'Ditto. It was a joy to sing with you, love.'

She beamed at the endearment and kissed him again before they took a bow then descended the steps to take their place in the audience again.

Justin scarcely noticed the remaining performances, his

mind full of his own newly-acknowledged feelings for Marina. There was an adjournment of half an hour for the judges to compare notes. Champagne was being served in the *Sala Caruso* and as Justin and Marina mingled with the others they were constantly congratulated on their performance.

'You two are bound to win,' Laurie said, scarcely disguising his envy. 'You were far and away the best.'

Marina sounded quite genuine when she replied, 'Nonsense! You and Delicia were very good too. It's bound to be a close-run thing. Not that the competition matters, of course. We're here to improve our singing, that's the main thing.'

Laurie leaned close to Marina, far too close for Justin's liking, and added conspiratorially, 'You'll never guess what the prize is. Rumour has it that the lucky winners will be spending a weekend with Bella Conti, at her villa!'

Justin felt Marina freeze and his own heart seemed to stop beating for an unfeasibly long time. He struggled not to let his dismay show on his face, but Marina could scarcely conceal hers. She gasped, 'Oh no!'

Laurie, of course, looked puzzled. He knew nothing about what had been going on for the past few weekends. 'Aren't you excited? What a fabulous prize! And I'd lay money on it that you two will be winning. God, it's the chance of a lifetime! I'd give my right arm, etcetera . . .'

Justin heard him babbling on while Marina covered up her initial expression of horror, but he was still in a state of shock. He'd never wanted more fervently to lose a competition in his life! At the beginning he'd feared that both Luigi and Bella might be prejudiced against them because of their dubious sexual involvement, but now he was hoping they would be.

His apprehension grew as the time to return for the verdict approached. At first he didn't dare say anything to Marina, afraid that would only make matters worse. There was certainly nothing he could say that would make things better. Just as he and Marina were making a new start together they were in danger of being sucked back into the unhealthy atmosphere of the *Villa Gandolfini*. What would they do if they did win? They could hardly turn down such a 'wonderful' prize.

He badly needed to discuss it with Marina before they were put on the spot, but there were too many other people around. As they followed the crowd downstairs he tried to broach the subject in a whisper. 'What on earth are we going to do if we win?'

She shrugged, looking miserable. 'I've no idea. I suppose we'll have to accept publicly, then think of an excuse not to go later.'

Justin was relieved. At least Marina was of the same mind as him.

Everyone was excited as they re-assembled in the theatre. The hubbub died down when Luigi appeared on stage, clipboard in hand. He called for silence then began mouthing the usual platitudes: 'Very high standard . . . all worked extremely hard . . . difficult choice to make.' He announced the results in reverse order, with Laurie and Delicia coming third, Paolo and Vera second.

'And now, the moment you've all been waiting for!' Luigi smiled, surveying the audience over the top of his gold-rimmed spectacles. 'May I remind you that the lucky couple will be spending the weekend at Bella Conti's villa where, I believe, there will also be a very special house-guest. Isn't that right, Bella?'

Justin saw her confirming with a nod and a smile. His imagination started to work overtime: who on earth could this 'house guest' be? Fervently he prayed that he and Marina weren't the winners. It sounded as if it was going to be extremely embarrassing to turn down such a prize.

'So . . .' Luigi continued, taking off his glasses with a smile. 'The winners of the first *Accademia del Voce* summer school festival competition are . . . our very own "Rodolfo" and "Mimi" – Justin and Marina!'

With applause and congratulations buzzing in his ears, Justin staggered to his feet and, urged by Marina, made his way unsteadily up to the stage. There was a fixed grin on his face, a kind of reflex rictus that made him feel idiotic but was some defence against the horrible sinking feeling deep inside. Marina, too, was putting a brave face on it. He knew how much she disliked the idea of having anything more to do with Bella. His mind raced to try and think of some plausible excuse for backing out but he drew a blank. Well, he would go through the motions for now and think again later, when he was less confused.

Luigi's smile was false as he kissed Marina on the cheek, and Justin found his hand limp when he clasped it briefly. That bastard's putting on a front too, he thought. Then Bella was called up onto the stage and went through the same charade. The situation had a nightmarish quality. Justin couldn't help thinking about his own involvement with the *diva*, and Marina's with the director. Was their victory in the competition a fix? But Justin concluded that as there were four other panellists, none of whom knew the winning couple personally, perhaps it was just an ironic quirk of fate.

'So, Bella, let's make everyone even more envious than they are already!' Luigi said. 'Who is this famous house-guest that Justin and Marina are going to meet this weekend?'

Bella positively simpered. 'Well, it's my old friend Lodovico Buonarotti, actually.'

Gasps and squeals rose from the audience, but Justin felt the blood drain from his cheeks. Marina looked shocked and tense too but recovered quickly enough to force a smile. Justin was torn in two. If he turned down the prize now he would be throwing away the chance to meet one of the four most celebrated tenors in the world.

There was no way he could pass up such an opportunity. But he was terribly afraid that Marina would force him to make a choice. What if she put her foot down and refused to go to the villa with him, forbade him to go by himself on pain of losing her. Could he make that terrible sacrifice for the sake of his new-born love?

Dazed and full of foreboding he left the stage with Bella and Marina, leaving Luigi to wind up the proceedings. Bella led the way out of a side door and Marina followed, so Justin felt he had to join them. In the small room opposite Bella faced them both with a bright smile.

'Congratulations once again! I'm sure you will enjoy your weekend with me. I promise not to make you work, though! You have done enough work. This weekend shall be all for your pleasure. Enrico will call for you both at your hotels. Will six o'clock this evening be convenient?'

'My flight back to England is on Sunday, at seven p.m.,' Justin said, desperately playing for time.

'And mine's at three,' Marina said.

'That's perfectly okay. We'll make sure you get to the airport on time.' Justin was waiting for Marina to say something, anything, that would give him a clue as to how she was feeling but she said nothing more. If she was accepting the arrangement he didn't see how he could back out himself. There was no way he would let her go to the villa without him. She needed protecting from that monstrous Olga.

'Well then, I'll see you for dinner at the villa,' Bella smiled, before taking her leave of them.

Justin faced Marina in the silent room, wondering what she was thinking. Her pretty face was grave, pondering. He reached out for her and she came slowly into his arms.

'Well this is a bizarre situation to be in, isn't it?' he said. 'Here we are with the prospect of spending a weekend with two of the most famous singers in the world, and we look as glum as a wet bank holiday!'

Marina gave a relieved laugh, breaking the ice. 'I didn't know what to do. I was sure you wouldn't want to lose the chance of meeting Buonarotti.'

'Too right. But the thought of spending one more weekend with that woman and her spooky friend isn't exactly appealing.'

'Never mind, we'll have each other.' She gave his cheek a butterfly kiss. 'As long as I make sure you're never out of my sight she can't do anything to you, can she?'

'I suppose not.'

'Well then, let's go and enjoy it. I'm sure it won't be nearly as bad as you're fearing. After all, it's a lovely place. Good food, good wine, good music . . . imagine, if we can persuade

Lodovico and Bella to give us a private concert. Wouldn't that be fabulous?'

He had to agree it would be.

They only had just over two hours to pack and check out of their hotels, so there was no time to linger. As Justin hurried back to his room his optimism was fully restored. After all, what harm could possibly come to him and Marina in the next couple of days? They were secure in their love for each other, and if they asked to share a room at the villa that message would get through to Bella. He smiled to think that she might actually be jealous – of both of them!

The journey to Albano was fun this time, with Marina to cuddle in the luxurious back seat. Enrico kept his eyes discreetly on the road ahead while his passengers billed and cooed, thrilled to be going off to what they hoped would be a fabulous weekend. When they arrived Olga met them at the door and Justin was surprised to find he was almost pleased to see her. Marina had put him in such a good mood that he felt prepared to forgive her anything.

'How nice to see you both again,' Olga said with an attempt at a smile, but her eyes were steely. 'Follow me and I'll show you to your rooms. Enrico will bring your luggage.'

'Er . . . would it be possible for Marina and I to share a room?' Justin asked. He was surprised at how bold he sounded.

Olga looked at them with just a hint of a raised brow. 'A double? I think that can be arranged. I'll have a word with the housekeeper if you'd like to wait in the lounge. You know your way, I think.'

Alone in the splendour of the lounge, with the sun beginning to set beyond the terrace outside, Justin began to relax. 'I wonder if Lodovico will be here for dinner tonight?' he smiled.

'I hope so. But maybe he can't get here until tomorrow. We'll ask Bella. I wonder where she is, by the way.'

'Here I am!' They both turned round with a start. Bella had entered silently. She looked magnificent in a floor-length, flame-coloured dress with a low sweetheart neckline and a gold belt hung with tassels. 'Welcome, both of you.

But hasn't Olga offered you a drink? What will you have . . . I know, how about champagne? I'll give Lena a ring.'

She pressed the bell and came to sit opposite them, arranging the folds of her long skirt decorously around her. 'That's a lovely gown,' Marina smiled with genuine admiration. 'I'm afraid I've nothing nearly so grand to wear. Are you expecting Lodovico tonight?'

'Alas, no. He's indisposed and can't make it after all.'

She spoke smoothly, averting her gaze, and Justin was convinced that she was lying. The sudden conviction hit him that the promise of Lodovico had been mere bait, to lure them there. He was convinced that the tenor had never even been invited. The feeling that they'd walked into a trap made him furious, but he didn't dare say anything just in case he was wrong.

Lena entered with champagne and Bella popped the cork with a trilling laugh and poured the foaming liquid into three glasses. While her back was turned Justin tried to communicate with Marina, frowning and shaking his head, but she just shrugged. They sipped champagne until Olga entered with the news that a room had been prepared for them.

'Just *one* room?' Bella said archly, wagging her finger at them. 'Ooh, we have two lovebirds amongst us, do we? How sweet!'

Justin didn't like the way she was speaking, the surreptitious smiles that passed between her and Olga as if this was all part of their plan. He seized Marina by the arm, saying, 'Come along, love, we'd better go up and get ready.'

'Dinner is at nine tonight,' Bella said, as they slipped from the room.

It was such a relief to be alone. As soon as he'd closed the door of the guest room he pulled Marina into his arms and kissed her passionately. 'I want you!' he growled. 'And I want you NOW!'

'Oh, Justin! You're so forceful!'

They collapsed, giggling onto the king-sized bed and began to strip off. Suddenly Marina started looking around they room. 'Hey!' she whispered. 'Do you think we're being watched?'

'What the hell if we are! Do you care?'

'Nope!'

'Neither do I! It'll only make them jealous. Get your knickers off, woman, and let me get at your pussy!'

He was inside her in seconds. Marina enjoyed the occasional 'quickie', he already knew that, and it was just what he needed to give vent to his feelings. He thrust into the soft heart of her, feeling the comforting walls around his shaft and the fleshy nub of her cervix against his glans. Soon all the tensions of the day were bursting out of him in one long, rapturous orgasm.

After he'd sunk down, with his head between Marina's pneumatic breasts, he heard her say, 'Well that's you sorted, lover boy, but what about me?'

'Didn't you come too?'

'The hell I did! You pulled out just as it was getting interesting.'

'Sorry. Give me a few minutes.'

'No, give *me* a few minutes. Just your finger will do fine. I don't expect miracles. Only I'm so hot and ready it won't take me long if you do it now.'

Justin loved the way she was able to talk so frankly about sex, to tell him what she needed and how to please her. He readily obliged, stroking her swollen clitoris with his finger and dipping into the hot honey pot of her pussy from time to time to keep her lubricated. She was right, it didn't take long. With a long moan of pleasure she thrust her hips hard against his invading finger and he felt the sharp contractions of her vagina as she climaxed over and over.

'Oh, wow, that was so good!' she sighed, sinking back into the cradle of his arms.

They dozed awhile, then showered. Marina let him use the shower gel on her, working her up into a lather once again until she shuddered against him as the water cascaded down.

'Oh God, I love it when you come!' he breathed into her ear. Then, on impulse, he added, 'God, I love *you* too! Honestly, Marina. I know we met less than a month ago, but it feels so damn *right*!'

She turned, lifting her smiling face to his, 'It does, doesn't it?'

They kissed tenderly, with new feeling, and then she went to dry herself in the other room leaving him to rub gel into his hair. He began to sing in the shower, 'O sweet girl . . .'

He wanted to stay in that room with her all weekend, to treat it like a honeymoon, but he knew Bella wouldn't stand for that. At a quarter to nine, when he and Marina were still lying naked on the bed, dozing in each others' arms, there came a discreet tap on the door and Lena's voice called, 'Dinner is in fifteen minutes. Pre-dinner drinks are being served in the lounge.'

'Oh God!' Marina leapt up and rushed into the bathroom, leaving Justin to get himself ready. Somehow they managed to be downstairs in the lounge by five to nine, but neither Bella nor Olga looked pleased. They were not offered drinks but ushered straight into the dining-room where the table was set for four.

'No other guests?' Marina said, unable to conceal the disappointment in her voice.

Bella's reply was sugary. '*You* are our honoured guests, remember? Lena, pour them some wine. We hope you will enjoy your stay with us. It will be a pleasant memory to take home to England with you.'

While Bella and Olga ate heartily and drank champagne throughout the meal, Justin found he could only manage to consume a fraction of what was put in front of him. His stomach was tied in knots as he kept remembering the way those two women had treated him before. Would they act the same again, making him look ridiculous in front of Marina? Her good opinion of him mattered more than anything in the world now, and that gave those harpies a frightening power over him.

As the courses progressed, Bella and Olga kept lapsing into Italian and making jokes that elicited gales of laughter from each other. Justin kept raising his eyebrows at Marina, who looked most uncomfortable. After dessert Bella suddenly turned to Olga and said, 'I know, we'll have those crackers left from Christmas. They should make things go with a bang!'

'Christmas crackers?' Marina frowned. 'In the middle of July?'

While Olga rose to fetch them from another room Bella explained. 'These are not ordinary crackers. Olga brought them back specially from a shop in London. You'll just love them, wait and see!'

The crackers were big and gaudy, decorated with pictures of scantily dressed women. Justin eyed them suspiciously. Bella handed him one and they pulled it. She giggled at the sharp snap of the cracker and then began to unravel the contents. Giggling again she drew out what was obviously a green condom studded with rubbery black points.

'This one's for you, Justin!' she smiled, snapping it between her fingers then blowing it up like a balloon until the thing looked like an obscene green porcupine. She let it go and the air spluttered out of it, propelling it towards Marina.

'You keep it, dear,' Bella smiled. 'Slip it on him sometime and give yourself an extra thrill!' Olga was demanding that Bella pull a cracker with her. The two women tussled briefly and then the paper fell apart and something heavy fell onto the table. It was a small dildo, shaped and coloured to look exactly like a penis.

'Oh, look!' Bella squealed in delight. 'More toys!' She picked it up and flicked the switch, making it hum and vibrate. Justin watched in disgust as she stroked it between her breasts and left a gleaming smear. 'So lifelike!' she grinned, her eyes on Marina who was looking extremely embarrassed. 'It's even got some sticky stuff inside, just like the real thing! You have it too, Marina. You never know when it might come in handy.'

She tossed it across the table and Marina was obliged to catch it to avoid breaking any of the expensive china. The evening was taking an uncomfortable turn for Justin, however, and he'd had enough. He knew the signs of Bella getting into a manic mood and he also knew what the consequences were likely to be. There was no way he wanted Marina exposed to that sort of lewd behaviour. He pushed back his chair and got to his feet.

168

'I think Marina and I would like to go up to our room now, if you don't mind. It's been a long day, what with the strain of the festival and everything . . .'

Bella looked dismayed. 'Oh, you can't leave us yet! We've planned all kinds of fun, haven't we, Olga?'

The other woman nodded, her expression grim. She left the room abruptly. Bella asked Marina if she wanted to leave.

'Well, I am rather tired,' she began hesitantly.

Bella gave a pout. 'I hoped you might sing for Olga. She wasn't able to be there this afternoon, and I know she'd love to hear the winning duet.'

'Maybe tomorrow,' Justin offered, pulling back Marina's chair. She got to her feet and he put his hand in hers. He was about to say goodnight when he heard Olga enter behind them. By the time he'd started to take his leave it was too late: the lesbian had grabbed both their wrists and clipped handcuffs around them.

'Oh, Olga, you are a terrible woman!' Bella tittered, her large breasts shaking beneath the flame-coloured chiffon of her robe.

Olga smiled, just a little. 'I don't think they will be leaving us just yet, *cara*. Not until they've seen the floor show, at least.'

Bella picked up the discarded dildo and switched it on. She let the vibrating shaft caress her throat then make its way down her cleavage, looking at Marina all the while. Then she said, very quietly, 'Did you know your boyfriend likes to watch people pleasuring themselves, Marina? You might let him watch you sometime.'

'Bella, you're out of order!' Justin snapped. He'd scarcely finished speaking when Olga bent down behind them and secured a chain around both their ankles, effectively shackling them together.

'Well I don't think you two are going anywhere!' Bella laughed. 'Not until we've finished with you, anyway. Don't worry, Marina. this is just our little joke. We love playing silly games, don't we, Olga? You're going to enjoy this!'

'I don't think so, actually,' Marina said frostily. 'I really think we would prefer to leave now, if you don't mind.'

'Ah, but we do mind. We mind very much. Now you can either make yourselves comfortable on the settee in the other room and enjoy what we have in store for you, or you can submit to even more of Olga's restraints. The choice is yours.'

'What do you mean, "restraints"?' Marina asked, nervously.

'Justin can tell you. He knows all about it, don't you, Justin?'

'Tell me!' Marina faced him, her complexion pale.

'I suppose they might gag or blindfold us.'

'Or both!' Olga said with glee.

'We have the double harness too, don't we?' Bella added. 'We could turn them into pretty little ponies and make them trot up and down the hall. Shall we do that, just for fun?'

'Maybe later. Let's take them into the other room first. And bring the rest of the crackers.'

Olga led the way through the door into the lounge. Justin and Marina shuffled along with painful slowness, with Marina muttering, 'Ridiculous party games!' Justin wanted to warn her that the two women together made a dangerous combination but he didn't want to alarm her too much so he contented himself with kissing the nape of her neck when he thought neither of the women was looking. He hoped it would reassure her.

The lounge was lit by candles. The soft glow might have seemed welcoming, romantic even, in other circumstances but now it gave the room an eerily decadent atmosphere that chilled Justin's spine. He moved his lips close to Marina's ear and whispered, 'Just play along with them for the time being. If they turn nasty there's no telling what they'll do.'

She made no reply but just stared, pale and tense, at the portrait of Bella as 'Queen of the Night' that hung over the marble fireplace.

Bella invited them to make themselves comfortable on the pink velvet settee.

'Some chance of that!' Marina grumbled as they gingerly sat down, taking care not to pull away from each other. Their joined legs were stuck out straight in front of them, as if in splints. 'My wrists and ankles are aching,' she complained, loud enough for Bella to hear.

'Oh dear!' she came up to them, full of false concern. 'Would you like Olga to massage your poor chafed skin? You know what an excellent masseuse she is, don't you, Marina?'

'No thank you!'

'Let's pull another cracker!' Bella said, prancing over to the table where Olga had deposited them. 'Isn't this fun? Just like Christmas.'

She brought one over to Marina who reluctantly took one end with her free hand. It gave a bang and two crumpled balls of red and black nylon fell to the floor. Bella held them up and it was obvious that the garment was a see-through bikini.

'A bit small for me,' she commented. 'But I think it would be perfect on you, Marina!'

For a moment Justin was afraid Marina might be stripped and forced to wear the vulgar bikini, but Bella laughingly draped the bra over her head and the pants over his.

'Party hats! Don't you adore them? They seem to be missing from these crackers, but who cares? We'll improvise! I know what we need to get us all into the party spirit, Olga – more champagne! Ring for Lena.'

Justin had no intention of consuming more alcohol and neither had Marina, but when they were both accused of being party poopers and threatened with more restraint they each took a few mouthfuls. Olga put a recording of Lodovico Buonarotti on the CD player and Bella said that was as near as they were going to get to the great man that weekend.

'You knew all along he wasn't going to be here, didn't you?' Justin said, sourly, unable to prevent himself. 'You got us here under false pretences.'

Bella's smile was dazzling. 'My dear Justin, do you think that I have no faith in my own power to draw you here? There are thousands, possibly millions, of opera lovers who would give their right arm for a weekend at the private villa of *La Bellissima*.'

Yes, but they don't know what you're really like, Justin thought sourly.

She went on, 'Don't you think you could try to appear a little more . . . grateful?'

'Shall I see if I can get some gratitude out of him?' Olga asked.

Justin felt his stomach churn at the ominous note in her voice. She went over to a drawer and took out a short-handled whip. Marina gasped to see it, and he knew it was probably too late to protect his love from knowing about what went on at the *Villa Gandolfini*. Nevertheless he had to do something. His buttocks were clenched and his throat constricted as he turned to Bella and said, even though the words choked him, 'I am grateful to you, Bella. Really I am.'

She came up close and twirled a strand of his hair around her finger with a self-satisfied smile. 'Then shall we see just *how* grateful you are, *caro Justino*?'

Chapter Twelve

Marina stared in horror at the way Justin was cringing before Bella. It looked as if the woman had some weird hold over him – but what, and why? The fact that she and Justin were chained up made it seem all the more sinister. She'd heard about people who got their kicks from torturing others: was that the kind of woman Bella was? She could believe it of Olga. But Bella was an international star, a legend almost. Surely she couldn't be into that kind of thing?

'Olga, detach this young man from his lady friend,' Bella said. 'I want Marina to see how we treat him. It might be useful to her if she intends to continue their relationship.'

Swiftly Olga moved to free their hands and feet. Marina felt as if she were in a nightmare, the kind where you want to move or cry out but your body is no longer under the control of your will. Had she been hypnotised? The idea would have seemed ludicrous an hour or so earlier, but now she couldn't be sure of anything.

Bella commanded Justin to kneel before her. As he did so he glanced briefly over his shoulder at Marina. Olga was at his side in seconds, gripping a bunch of his hair and wrenching his head back. 'How dare you look round like that! Keep your eyes downcast at all times, unless specifically instructed otherwise. You know the rules.'

'Yes, mistress. Sorry, mistress.'

'I'll make you sorry.' She turned to Bella. 'Shall we strip him, ready for punishment?'

'Not yet, he may redeem himself.'

'You are too kind!' Olga pouted.

Bella smiled, stretching out languidly on the chaise longue

opposite. 'I'm in a good mood tonight. Fetch the dildo that came out of the cracker, slave!'

Marina remembered she'd left it on the table in the other room. She was astonished to see Justin get down on all fours and crawl from the room. As soon as he'd gone she turned on Bella. 'This is disgusting! Justin's a human being, not an animal. How dare you treat him like this!'

Bella gave a fond smile. 'Believe it or not it's exactly what he wants, my dear. You saw how he obeyed me. He's the sort who loves a strong woman to take control over him, and there are many more like him I can assure you. Be grateful, Marina. I'm giving you an object lesson in how to treat your man.'

Before she could reply there came a sudden shrill noise. A look of irritation came over Bella's face. '*Mamma mia, che cosa c'è?*' A torrent of Italian passed between her and Olga before she explained, 'It's the fire alarm. They made me put them in when I had this place renovated. It's probably a false alarm but we can't be sure. Come, Olga, through the patio door. Marina, go and fetch Justin from the dining-room. He'll be wondering what's going on. Bring him back in here – this is the quickest exit route.'

She rushed to open the sliding doors and Marina hurried into the dining-room. Justin was nowhere to be seen and she began to panic. She went into the hall and he suddenly appeared, struggling with both their suitcases.

'Quick, there might be a fire!' she began, agitatedly.

He shook his head. 'No, it was me. I set the alarm off to create a diversion. I've had about enough of their nonsense, and I'm sure you have too. Take your case, love, and follow me.' She did as she was told, following him down the back stairs and out of a side door into the kitchen garden. Bella and Olga had gone round to the front of the house, so Justin suggested they should make their way towards the beach. No-one would think of looking for them there.

As if to add dramatic urgency to the situation, while they were running across the lawn there was a crack of thunder and the heavens opened. Justin led the way to the small summer house that stood in the grounds. They rushed in, shaking the droplets from their clothes and hair. Once they were inside the shelter they broke into helpless giggles.

Soon Justin tossed her a towel and a travel rug and they sat down on the bamboo sofa to dry their hair. It had turned chilly with the storm and Marina was glad of the rug around her shoulders. Outside the sky was still being rent by flashes of summer lightning.

'Oh God!' Justin said. 'I feel like an escaped prisoner.'

'Me too! Those dreadful women! I don't care if Bella is an international star, she's really weird. She told me you were into being bossed around. Tell me it's not true!'

'It's not how I want to be with you, Marina. But with her it all seemed to fit, somehow. I mean, I already held her in such awe that she had a lot of power over me. I was fascinated by their games at first, but then she just seemed to go further and further. So when she started to make me do things in front of you I just had to do something to get out of the situation. I was afraid she'd go too far.'

'What did she make you do then, Justin?'

He stopped towelling his hair and looked around him, peering into the semi-darkness. 'Just a minute.' He began to prowl around the room, searching high and low.

'What is it, Justin? What are you looking for?'

'A closed-circuit TV camera. I just remembered she's got this place under surveillance, for her kinky pleasure. Well we're not putting on any show for her benefit, that's for sure!'

Marina shivered, pulling the rug around her shoulders. Justin found the camera, hidden behind a plant on a shelf with the lens poking through its leaves. He pulled out the wires savagely, then returned to sit beside her. 'That's better, we can relax now.'

'What if they come looking for us? What are we going to do?'

'We're going to stay put until it stops raining, at least, then we'll go to the village just along the shore and phone for a taxi. It'll be expensive, but I reckon it's worth it. There's no point trying to get a hotel for the night. We'll get the driver to take us straight to the airport and grab whatever kip we can there.'

'I'd rather stay here,' Marina said. 'There's a fire, stuff for making coffee. Can't we barricade the door, or something? Then if they come looking for us we can make a bolt for it through the window.'

'I suppose we might be all right here,' Justin said, doubt-fully. 'They'll probably expect us to have taken to the road by now. Okay, we'll stay put until dawn, at least.'

They bolted the door on the inside and pulled a heavy sideboard across it. There was no way anyone could catch them unawares now. Justin put the oil fire on low just to take the damp chill out of the atmosphere and, for the first time that evening, Marina began to relax. They had found themselves a cosy little love-nest, so they may as well take advantage of it. She snuggled up to Justin and kissed his neck.

'I don't know, it's never far from your mind, is it?' he grinned.

'What?'

'Sex, of course.'

'Are you suggesting that your mind is different from mine, then?'

'Nope!'

'So it's a case of "two minds but with a single thought", is it?'

'Whadda you think?'

They kissed, long and deep, until Marina felt her insides curling up with longing for him. It didn't take long for them to get each other out of their wet clothes and onto the thick peasant-style rug in front of the fire. They threw down cushions for extra comfort, then Justin made his way down between her legs and she opened her thighs to his questing lips. The shudder she gave as his mouth touched her pussy-lips turned into a long sigh as his tongue slid between them, licking up until it found the small, stiffly protruding clitoris.

Warmth from the fire bathed her skin but the heat inside her was even greater. When Justin caught her nipples be-tween his fingers and began to twirl them simultaneously she arched her back in sheer delight and felt the hot current of energy run straight from nipple to clitoris. He continued to rouse her with his lips and tongue, his hands stroking her breasts until they strained beneath his touch, yearning for more, always more. Her hunger for him tasted sweeter the keener it grew, with Marina revelling in the certain knowledge that it would soon be satisfied. She could feel her orgasm coiling like a dormant creature in the pit of her stomach, ready to explode into bliss.

Justin's hands moved beneath her, caressing the smooth globes of her buttocks and lifting her pelvis so that his mouth could make better contact with her vulva. His tongue thrust into her and became the trigger for her release. She arched back again, gasping in her abandon as the flutterings within became stronger and her body pulsated with extreme pleasure.

Marina was barely aware that, seconds later, he was poised at her entrance ready to plunge his cock into her. Only when she felt the length of his shaft fill her up did she open her eyes and smile at him. Her vagina still felt slightly numb, the aftershocks of her orgasm still rippling quietly away, and he took it easy for a while. But then his fingers found her nipples and pinched them back into active life, kick-starting her libido once again.

'Oh, Justin!' she sighed, wriggling comfortably against the cushions. 'We've won, haven't we? We've beaten them at their own game. Wouldn't Bella be furious if she knew we were making love in her summer house?'

But he didn't smile. On the contrary a cloud darkened his brow. 'We're not out of the wood yet!' he warned her.

Marina felt cross with herself. Why had she gone and spoilt it, just when everything seemed so lovely? She'd once accused Justin of bringing Bella into every conversation but now she'd done exactly the same, and at a time like this! Would they ever be able to exorcise that woman's ghost?

His thrustings became more urgent and Marina soon succumbed to the delicious waves of sensation that were building up inside her again. The velvet-smooth motion of his shaft was making the walls of her vagina feel fantastic, and she could also feel the hard base of it rubbing against her vulva, making the clitoris swell and throb. She thrust against him with her hips, enjoying the closer contact this produced, and he bent his head to suck at her nipples, rasping them softly with his front teeth while licking around the areolas. The feelings were exquisite and she caught her breath, silently willing him to continue.

'Oh, your cunt is so incredibly beautiful!' he groaned, 'I don't think I can keep going much longer like this.'

'Then slow down.'

'It's torture not to be able to thrust really hard, but if I do I know I'll come too soon. What a dilemma!'

'Slow down then and I'll give you a squeeze, how's that?'

When he was drifting lazily in and out she was able to get a grip on him with her vaginal walls. The action of clenching his cock was very good for her own arousal, making her clitoris throb hotly every time. Marina imagined his prick was a delicious spoonful that she could hardly bear to let go out of her mouth. She hung onto every last inch of it, lovingly.

'Mm!' she murmured, as the friction took her nearer the edge. Soon her climax was unstoppable and she surrendered to the explosion of pure bliss with a joyful cry. Justin was unable to hold back any longer and his rapid shafting redoubled her pleasure, making the spasms very intense as he reached his own peak of pleasure. They seemed almost to struggle for a while, each vying with the other to wrest the maximum sensation out of the moment, until they sank back into harmonious peace.

'My wonderful love!' Justin said tenderly, kissing her face several times.

Marina lay contentedly on their makeshift bed. If this was true love, she wanted more of it. Justin seemed sure of his feelings, but this was neither the time nor the place to examine her own. She was used to complications in her love life. Up to now her men had been, variously, married and unwilling to leave their wives; single, but not wanting to settle down; unsure whether they were straight or gay; divorced, and wary of women; encumbered by offspring. The list went on. Marina had despaired of ever finding someone she could love and be loved by without any excess baggage.

But now, suddenly, everything seemed very simple and straightforward. It made a nice change. Compared to the twisted sexuality of the two women at the *Villa Gandolfini* their love was positively innocent.

'There I go again, thinking of *her*!' Marina chastised herself. But it was difficult to put Bella completely out of her mind when they were surrounded by her things. Although the place was done out in a kind of Italian rustic style it was evident that all the furnishings were of the best quality and impeccable taste. A collection of fans was pinned to a screen, a signed photograph of Lodovico Buonarotti hung on one wall and next to it were programmes from several productions in which Bella had starred, mounted and framed behind glass. There was even a collection of her recordings next to a CD player and a book of her press cuttings casually placed on a coffee table.

Marina felt a jealous hatred seize her. She sat up abruptly, causing Justin's eyes to flick open. 'Let's not stay here,' she said. 'This place gives me the willies. It's full of *her*!'

'Okay, I agree. I think the storm's over, by the sound of it.'

They got dressed, putting on more appropriate clothes from their suitcases. Then they pushed back the sideboard and unbolted the door. Outside the night was calm again, everywhere washed and fresh. The lights were still burning in the villa, however, making Marina feel nervous.

'Which way do we go?' she asked Justin.

He pointed along the lakeside. 'That way. But I don't know if there's an exit on that side of the garden. We may have to go back round the house.'

Marina prayed fervently that they would find a way through, but a tall hedge barred their exit on one side and a wall topped with barbed wire on the other.

'It's no good,' Justin concluded. 'We'll have to go round the side of the house. But they're most unlikely to see or hear us, as long as we're careful. Come on.'

She followed him over the sodden lawn, carrying her

travel bag. A weariness came over her which wasn't surprising when she thought of all she'd been through that day and how late it must be. The thought of spending the rest of the night in an airport lounge wasn't appealing, but although the summer house would have been physically more comfortable it would have been most disturbing emotionally. The sooner they got right away from this creepy place the better. They were very near the house now, and although the lights were still on it was silent.

But not for long. Suddenly there came a tremendous barking and through the French windows bounded two large hounds.

'Damn!' Justin muttered. 'I forgot about the dogs.'

They came straight towards them but then began to frolic around, wanting to play. A voice that Marina recognised as Olga's called from the house, '*Bravo! Viene giù, cara. Eccoli!*'

The two women appeared, framed in the open window. Olga was dressed in an all-leather black suit but Bella was wearing a long, midnight blue dressing gown. When Justin tried to make a bolt for it the dogs bounded up and knocked him down, growling. Marina, petrified, stayed just where she was. Olga came out into the garden with a smile on her face.

'You didn't manage to get very far, did you?' She gave a shrill whistle and the two dogs immediately rushed to her side. She snapped leashes onto their collars and held them fast.

'They look like two drowned rats,' Bella commented. 'Come in, my poor dears, and have a glass of brandy to warm you up. There's no fire raging in here, I can assure you.'

Marina didn't trust them for one minute, but with the dogs still straining at the leash she wasn't going to argue. Justin picked himself up and gave her a rueful look. 'Nice try!' he whispered as they reluctantly entered the villa once more in the wake of the two dogs, now enthusiastically wagging their tails.

Marina felt cold and depressed. She was beginning to wonder whether she would make her flight. Before she knew it, Olga had slipped on the handcuffs again and tethered her like an animal to an iron ring at the side of the fireplace.

Marina cursed and spat at the woman, but she gave her a stinging slap on the cheek that made her eyes water. When she protested, Olga just laughed, saying, 'Now where were we, before we were so rudely interrupted? Ah yes, the slave was about to perform an intimate service for his mistress. On your knees, slave!'

Bella lay back on the sofa with a nauseating smile on her face. She parted her dressing gown to reveal the plump, hairy mound of her vulva, and Olga pushed Justin towards her, making him kneel on the carpet by her thighs. Marina felt sickened but, with her wrists secured, she could do nothing and she was afraid to speak in case Olga turned on her again. She was beginning to understand the ruthless nature of the beast who had her in thrall.

'Here!' Olga handed Justin the dildo. 'Use this with care. If you harm my mistress, or displease her in any way, you will answer to me!'

Justin looked cowed, and Marina could only guess at how he was feeling. Bella had said he actually enjoyed this kind of thing, but how could he? She shuddered in horror as he switched on the sex toy and moved it towards the couch, then she closed her eyes. She didn't have to watch. She wouldn't watch, it was too disgusting.

But suddenly her head was being wrenched back by the hair and Olga's voice hissed in her ear, 'My mistress wants you to see this, sweetie! It's for your instruction. Make sure your eyes stay open or you'll suffer the consequences!'

Marina gave a choking sob as she saw her lover plunge the dildo right inside Bella's cunt. The *diva* began giving Justin instructions: 'Slowly, more slowly! Make sure you touch my love-button on the way in and out . . . Ah! That's better!' She talked as if she owned him, as if he truly were her love-slave, and Marina felt humiliated. How dare he obey that arrogant cow!

Olga went over to stand behind the couch and soon she was kissing her mistress full on the mouth, her hands parting the folds of her gown to fasten onto her large breasts, Marina felt even more disgusted, but she daren't look away. Every so often Olga's beady eyes would swivel in her direction, just to make sure she was still watching.

In and out went the humming dildo with Bella writhing and moaning loudly on the couch. Olga was stimulating her nipples with her fingers while Justin concentrated on making sure the dildo brushed against the clitoris as it moved in and out. He seemed completely oblivious of Marina and she wondered what was going through his mind. She was also afraid of what might happen afterwards. Once Bella was satisfied would Olga find something even more unpleasant for them to take part in? She felt a cold dread seize her. What a monster she was!

So why did Bella put up with her? And how did the pair of them have such power over Justin? Marina had thought she was getting to know him but this was a dark side of his personality, a kind of addiction, that she could not begin to comprehend. Was he enjoying what he was doing? She remembered how he had made love to her, so sweetly and with no complications, and her heart felt choked up with misery. How stupid she had been to think they could have a simple, straightforward relationship after this!

Bella was obviously close to orgasm now, her hips thrusting and guttural moans escaping from her swollen, open lips. Olga had put one nipple in her mouth and was kneeling beside Justin on the carpet, her hand pinching his left buttock in a kind of reflex action as she became totally involved in what she was doing. As Marina watched the display a weird kind of detachment came over her, as if she were watching a film, and it no longer seemed to have anything to do with reality.

The climax came, loud and long, then everyone subsided into relaxation and the room went quiet. Marina suddenly realised that tears were streaming down her cheeks, quite involuntarily. A part of her saw Bella, Olga and Justin as some grotesque *ménage à trois* from which she was completely excluded. She had never felt quite so alone in her life.

Sinking to the floor, Marina slumped beside the fireplace. After a few minutes Olga came over and unlocked her handcuffs. 'I think it's time for you to leave,' she said.

'What?' Marina looked up at her with scared-rabbit eyes. Her gaze turned to Justin, lying with his head on the couch where Bella was ranged in exhaustion.

'It's all right,' Olga said, with a wry grin. 'He can go upstairs with you. Lena will wake you with coffee at eight then Enrico will drive you to the airport in plenty of time for your flight.' Justin looked utterly spent. He gave Marina a weary, dissipated look and rose slowly to his feet. Staggering a little, he put his arm around her shoulders and together they made for the door. Behind them they could hear Olga talking to Bella in Italian.

'I'm sorry, Marina,' Justin said as they made their way upstairs to the guest room. 'I truly am. I never meant this to happen, but as soon as we arrived in the villa I was afraid it might.'

Marina didn't know what she felt, so she said nothing. Could she forgive his complicity? She didn't know. All she wanted right now was the blissful oblivion of sleep.

Yet once they were lying naked together in the double bed she was amazed to find she really wanted him. Despite everything, the image of her lover pleasuring another woman had insinuated itself into her mind and was now driving her wild with hunger for him. She began to caress his warm body, pressing hers against him, and soon his cock began to stir.

'What are you doing to me?' he murmured, sleepily.

'You've serviced that bitch, now it's my turn!'

Justin gave an incredulous laugh. 'You mean you still want me?'

'More than ever!'

It was the truth, Marina realised. She flung back the covers so that they were both exposed to the warm air, and straddled his chest, pushing a pillow beneath her buttocks so that her pussy was within reach of his lips. 'Now, lick me, suck me, and don't stop till I come!' she commanded him.

He gave an odd little chuckle and set to work with enthusiasm. Marina flung her head back and let the keen sensations flood through her, relishing the soft wet touch of his tongue on her fevered clitoris. She was well aroused, her juices streaming out and her whole vulva swollen with longing. One hand crept up to her breasts and the other stroked her buttocks, feeling down the crack between to her sensitive anus. She began to rock back and forth on her haunches, wriggling to wrest the maximum pleasure from his touch.

Marina was exulting in the power she had over him, making him do to her whatever she desired. When she was ready to be penetrated she told him to finger-fuck her and he obeyed at once, plunging four of his fingers into her gaping pussy and turning them round and round to gave her an internal massage. She squealed in delight and began to ride up and down on his fist, faster and faster, awakening the fire deep within her.

Fiercely she squeezed his fingers, closing over them like a vice then letting go in rapid succession until her orgasm burst inside her like a rocket. It spread throughout her whole body, turning her into an incandescent being, invoking a sensory overload that was almost unbearably intense. The spasms of pure lust that overwhelmed her were delicious, but over and above it all was the heady sense of power she gained over her lover. She had grown more like Bella, she had absorbed something of that woman's hold over him, and from now on Justin would worship her as he had once worshipped the *diva*. The thought excited her immensely.

Even the way he held onto her afterwards, like a little boy, made her feel good. She caressed his damp hair and kissed his brow tenderly, fully in charge, while he drifted into sleep. For a good hour or so she lay awake, with his head cradled against her breast, pondering the mystery of human sexuality and its strange byways. Never before had she dared to tell a man what to do to her in that way. She had sometimes made suggestions, given out hints, but the idea of ordering a man to give her pleasure had never occurred to her. Of course, it wouldn't work on everyone. But Justin seemed to like it, there was no doubt about that. Had she found the secret to making him exclusively hers, at last?

Marina was in the middle of a dream where she, Bella and Olga danced around the kneeling figure of Justin, bound and blindfolded, when she was suddenly awakened by a shaft of light. She moaned and rubbed her eyes, finding Lena placing a tray of coffee on the bedside table. Justin was stirring beside her, so she thanked the maid and poured herself a cup.

'You have half an hour,' Lena told her as she left the room.

After an infusion of hot, sweet coffee Marina felt more human. The events of the night were hazy in her mind, and there was no time to reflect on anything. She kissed Justin and relayed the message to him, telling him there was coffee poured, then went to shower.

Before they left the *Villa Gandolfini*, Justin and Marina had to face Bella and Olga. The two women appeared perfectly rested and composed, Bella looking particularly grand in a quilted turquoise housecoat trimmed with gold. Her face was subtly made up and she wore her dark hair piled up on her head with just a few loose tendrils. Olga was severely dressed in a plain grey trouser suit with a mandarin collar.

'Well, my dears, I hope you enjoyed your last visit here, after all,' Bella smiled, ever the gracious hostess.

Marina was reminded of just who this woman was, how famous, and how important in the world of opera. Yet that was still quite a narrow world, she reminded herself as she shook the *diva*'s elegantly ringed hand. The cool brown eyes surveyed her implacably as she added, in a low voice meant for her ears alone, 'You ruled him splendidly last night, my dear. Congratulations!'

Marina mumbled a farewell and frowned, wondering what she meant. She was still wondering as she and Justin left the grand portal and walked towards the limousine with Enrico holding the rear door open. As she slid onto the back seat, however, she recalled what Olga had told her about her mistress being something of a *voyeur*. Of course! She must have had the guest room rigged up with a camera, just like the summer house. That appalling woman must have seen everything that she and Justin did last night, once they were alone. A flush spread over her cheeks, caused more by anger than shame, and as the long car pulled away from the house she stared determinedly at the back of the chauffeur's head, ignoring the couple who stood waving in the porch.

Justin was ignoring them too. He squeezed her hand as they started down the long drive, silently reaffirming his sympathy. Of course he didn't know exactly why she was so upset, but Marina knew he could sense her mood and she was sure it mirrored his own.

Neither of them wanted to talk in Enrico's presence so they endured the ride to the airport in silence, arriving with several hours to spare before Marina's mid-afternoon flight. Then it was all she could do to make small talk. A weary despair had settled on her, the aftermath of last night's euphoria, and she just wanted to be winging her way back to normality. They had a couple of drinks at the bar, a snack lunch, but the tension between them remained.

At last the time came for her to go through the barrier into the departure lounge. Looking at Justin's handsome, sad face she wanted to throw her arms around him and tell him everything would be all right, but something was stopping her. The shadow of Bella Conti was still between them, like a malevolent ghost, and they seemed like strangers.

They'd already exchanged addresses so there seemed to be no more to be said. Yet Marina lingered uncertainly at the barrier, waiting for him to say something to break the ice. But her cue to open up her heart never came. Instead he kissed her on the cheek and patted her arm, wishing her a good flight, then stood back as she hurried past the official at the desk clutching her flight bag. She turned and waved to him, forcing a smile, but her eyes were wet and blurry. All she had to remember him by was a face whose expression was blank and foreign, a figure that seemed shrunk and awkward. She gave a half-hearted little wave then went off to await her flight, the insistent thudding of her pulses in her ears being the only indication of the turmoil within.

Chapter Thirteen

Four bloody hours! Justin stared gloomily at himself in the mirror over the washbasin in the men's room, wondering what to do with himself while he waited for his flight. He'd just seen Marina off and he was feeling really let down. She'd been acting weird ever since they left the villa, behaving as if she never wanted to see him again. Which, presumably, she didn't. He fished in his wallet for her address: 14 Harper Street, Reading. Not far from London, where he lived. Near enough to make the continuance of their affair possible, at least. If only she'd lived in Newcastle, or somewhere, he might have felt better. The idea that they *could* go on seeing each other, yet almost certainly wouldn't, was just too galling.

He put the card away and flicked a comb through his hair. After leaving the men's he strolled across to the news-agents and began to browse the magazines. It seemed ironic that *Oggi* had a picture of Bella Conti on the cover. He read the headline, which he translated as best he could: 'The Divine Bella is to star in a new opera, Jacob Puggi's *Canton*, with Lodovico Buonarotti . . .' He threw the paper down in disgust, remembering how she'd lured him and Marina to her villa by promising they would meet the tenor. Maybe he had turned up that very afternoon, after they'd left, and the pair of them were laughing at those foolish students with stars in their eyes. She might be telling him about her English 'slave' at that very moment, embellishing the story to make him laugh. Justin would put nothing past her, nothing!

He went to the bar, ordering a *caffè correto* and knocking it back. His mind was fixed on Marina, longing to see her already. The thought that he might never see her again was eating into him, corroding his soul, and not even the warm

187

caress of the brandy could comfort him.

Suddenly he had an idea. Pulling her card out from his wallet he checked that there was a phone number. Hurriedly he paid his bill and rushed to the nearest phone, slotting in his credit card then dialling her number. As he'd hoped, there was an answer phone. He cleared his throat, suddenly stage-struck, but then found the inspiration to continue.

'Er . . . Marina, it's Justin here. I'm still at the airport, actually. I thought I'd ring just to leave a welcome home message. We parted without saying good-bye properly and . . . well, I wanted to say how much I . . . God, what I wanted to say was, is this going to be just a holiday romance, or can we make a go of it? It's up to you, of course. But if you want to see me again you've got my number. Only . . . don't wait too long, okay? I'd better go. My flight's being called. Look, give me a ring, eh? I should get home around midnight tonight, with a bit of luck. I've left my answer phone on too, so . . . well, it's been great, Marina. Hope you had a good flight home. There's a lot more I could say but it's not the same, talking into a machine. 'Bye, now. Love ya.'

He almost whispered the last two words before replacing the receiver with a clatter and hurrying towards the departure lounge. He felt a fool, convinced that she would only listen to his message and laugh contemptuously – if she bothered to listen at all. He couldn't blame her. After what had happened at the villa he wouldn't blame her if she never wanted to see him again. Oh, why had he gone along with that dreadful woman's games last night? Why hadn't he stood up to her, tried to gain Marina's respect?

He knew why. He'd been afraid that if he didn't do as he was told Marina would suffer the consequences. Justin gave a deep sigh. At least she'd been spared the worst excesses of Olga's temper. The thought of that monster treating Marina as she'd treated him was horrifying, but he knew she wouldn't have hesitated to get her whip out if Justin had disobeyed her. The trouble was, he might never have another chance to explain to Marina what a beast that woman was.

The journey home was tedious. His case was heavy and he couldn't get a trolley. He missed the train by minutes at

Gatwick and had to wait around. Eventually, at half past midnight, the taxi dropped him at his door and he entered as fast as he could, going straight to the phone. There were several messages, and he listened impatiently to them all until the very last one, which turned out to be from Marina. He held his breath, hearing her sweetly familiar voice say, 'Hi, Justin!'

She'd got home safely, although the flight was delayed by twenty minutes. What a good job she hadn't asked her brother to meet her . . . Justin listened impatiently to the chatty stuff, waiting for her to say something meaningful, but it never came. At the end all she said was, 'Well, I'll be in touch. Right now I can't wait to have a nice warm bath and get into bed. 'Bye for now, Justin.'

Bath and bed. He pictured her delightful body surrounded by foam, then curled up under a duvet all alone, and his heart ached. The urge to see her again was so strong it formed a frustrated knot of pain around his heart. To be there in England together, yet not together, was unbearable. He thought of phoning her but she would probably be asleep by now. He switched on the TV, seeking distraction, but the images moved unseen before his eyes. God, how he wanted her! And now he must wait, wait! What if she never phoned him again? How long must he wait before phoning her? He lifted his receiver, wanting to do it now, but then thought better of it.

There was little sleep for Justin that night. He dozed fitfully while Marina raced in and out of his mind, playing hide-and-seek in his dreams. At six he felt wide awake and got up. He had several cups of black coffee, re-examining the idea that had come to him just before dawn. Why not go to her? She was only half an hour or so down the M4. Okay, so he might get a cool reception, but that would be no worse than tormenting himself as he was now. At least he would know, one way or the other, and not be living in this dreadful state of uncertainty.

By seven he was on the road in his VW Polo, crossing the network of South London streets as he sped towards the Hammersmith Flyover. He reached Reading too early and found a café where he perused a newspaper without taking in a thing. Then he looked at the map he'd bought and found her street, tucked away in the midst of a dozen similar streets in an area called Newtown. Although tempted to go there at once, he ordered another coffee and prepared to stick it out. Probably she wouldn't be up before ten, he reasoned. It had been a stressful weekend. Now, on this bustling Monday morning, everyone else seemed caught up in the normal daily round. He felt as if he'd just landed from Venus.

Justin managed to spin it out until ten-thirty but then he couldn't bear to wait around any longer. He studied the map again and set off in his car, finding the place without too much difficulty and jolting over the speed bumps. There was no parking space outside her door so he had to move on down the street, and by the time he walked back he could hear someone playing the piano inside. Could that be Marina herself playing? Then he remembered that she shared the house with two music students and his heart sank. He wasn't in the mood to be polite to strangers.

The curtains upstairs were closed and he guessed that might be her room, that she was still asleep, but he wasn't going to wait any longer. He rang the bell and nothing happened, so he banged on the window next to the door. The piano music stopped abruptly and soon he was staring at a long-haired man with very blue eyes who gave him a friendly smile.

'Hi!' he said. 'How can I help you?'

The empty longing that had possessed Justin's soul ever since he and Marina had parted now changed to something else: jealousy and suspicion. She hadn't mentioned that she shared the house with a man. Was she living with him? The ache in his balls intensified as he imagined the pair of them in bed together. He saw her scornful face, heard her mocking laugh, and wanted to flee, but something persuaded him to stay.

'I . . . er . . . came to see Marina.'

'Want to come in? She's still asleep. Just got back from Italy . . .'

'I know.'

190

'Coffee? I could do with some myself.'

The sweet reasonableness of the man was making it all the more difficult. Justin wanted to take him by the throat and wrest the truth from him, but knew he couldn't. It occurred to him that he was being ridiculous, but he couldn't help it.

'My name's Ed, by the way.'

They shook hands. Justin looked around the kitchen, searching for clues. He saw a postcard from Rome on the wall and knew it was hers. A burning desire to read it came over him. 'Don't let me disturb your playing, Ed,' he said.

'That's okay. Sugar?'

Once the coffee was made, Ed went back to his practice leaving Justin alone in the kitchen. He tore the card off the wall and read it swiftly but he was disappointed. No mention of him. She'd sent it within a couple of days of her arrival, before they'd got together. Yet it was good to see her hand-writing, careful and artistic, unlike his own. The sound of the piano came floating out from the other room, Chopin.

'God, Marina, I want you so much!' he murmured, kissing the signature on the postcard. Something told him he was being a prat, that he was riding for a fall, but he didn't care.

Just as he was finishing his coffee there came sounds of stirring upstairs, doors closing, toilet flushing. It was all he could do to stay put. He paced around the small kitchen, looking out into the yard where flowering plants stood in tubs. Marina's work? Who else lived here? The feeling of looking in through a window at her life, a life he knew little about, was overwhelming him. Then he heard footsteps descending the stairs and he braced himself for her entrance.

She came in bleary-eyed, wearing a pink dressing-gown that she hadn't had in Italy. It took her a few seconds to recognise him and, when she did, her blue eyes opened wide with astonishment. 'Justin! What on earth are you doing here?'

It was an inauspicious beginning. 'I came to see you, of course,' he said, lamely.

'Oh.'

His heart stopped in that pregnant pause. Then her eyes

met his again, frank and searching. She came forward and, slowly and deliberately, put her arms around him. Her body felt soft and squashy against his, and he relaxed for the first time in ages. His lips brushed her hair as he murmured, 'How are you?'

She pulled away from him, matter-of-fact again. 'Not sure yet. Have you made coffee?'

'Ed made some, but it's finished now.'

'Oh, you've met him then.'

Uncertainty returned. Without the warm reassurance of her body Justin felt bleak. He watched her put on the kettle, light the gas. She stretched and yawned, unself-consciously. This wasn't what he'd imagined, this cosy domesticity. He wanted passion, but perhaps it was expecting too much at this time in the morning after she'd had a late night. On the other hand, if she really cared for him . . . His thoughts see-sawed as he watched her neat bum move beneath the pink gown, teasing him.

'I hope you don't mind me just turning up like this,' he began.

'Well I am surprised. I thought you'd be feeling as zonked as I am this morning.'

Still that infuriatingly blasé tone. He didn't know what to make of her, and it was killing him. 'I got your phone message,' he said.

'It was nice of you to leave one for me. Did you have a good flight?'

Justin couldn't stand this pussy-footing around any longer. He balled his fist beneath the table then found the courage to cut through it in a sentence, 'Let's stop all this, shall we?'

She turned around, spoonful of coffee in her hand, eyebrows raised. 'All what?'

'You know. I came here to find out if you want to go on seeing me, and you're not making it easy for me. I want to know . . . I want to know if you still feel the same about me as I feel about you.'

She emptied the spoon into the cafetière and came over to him, letting him encircle her waist with his arms. His head rested on her midriff, just beneath her breasts. 'Marina, I couldn't stop thinking about you, wanting you. I had to come. If you don't want me just let me know now and I'll try to forget you, but don't keep me hanging on . . .'

Soft fingers invaded his hair, lifting and stroking. Her fingertips moved over his scalp and down his neck, where the skin was sensitive. She whispered, 'I didn't want to say or do anything until I knew how *you* felt!'

He laughed. 'You mean, we'd have gone on waiting for the other one to make a move?'

He looked up to see her eyes laughing down at him. 'Mm. Stalemate!'

'Then thank God I came.'

'Yes. Thank God you did!'

The kettle whistled. Marina detached herself and made a pot of coffee. She put it on a tray with the milk and two mugs. 'Shall we take this lot up to my room?'

She lived at the front of the house, just as he'd guessed. Her room was cosy and comfortable: opera posters on the walls, a big CD collection, books on opera. The bed was in one corner, sheets rumpled, duvet flung back casually. She saw him glance at it and chuckled.

'I didn't sleep much last night either, if you want to know!'

'I'm shattered!' he confessed, flopping into the one armchair. She poured the coffee. 'Maybe this will revive you.'

'No, only *you* can do that. I feel like I've been sleep-walking since yesterday. Why were you so distant with me on the way back from the villa? Didn't you know how much you were hurting me?'

She shrugged, handing him his drink. 'I'd had a shock, Justin. Bella and Olga – I'd never met people like that before. And when they made me watch you . . .'

'I'm sorry!' Putting down the mug he reached out for her hand and drew her onto his lap. 'I know how much you must have hated it, but I also knew that if I didn't play along they would do something to you. Actually you got off lightly, you know.'

Marina shook her head, her eyes sad. 'Do you honestly believe that physical pain would have hurt me more than the emotional torment they put me through? To see you making love to that woman as if you were enjoying it. To watch you doing things to her that you'd done to me . . . it was pure hell, Justin!'

'But it meant nothing, love. You must believe that. I didn't even want to be there, but you insisted – remember? We both thought Buonarotti would be there. What fools we were!'

'So you're over her, are you? Your obsession with *La Bellissima* – it's finished?'

He nodded, pulling her closer. Reaching up with his mouth he placed a soft kiss on her lips. 'Completely. I can't understand what she ever meant to me. Of course, it was all an illusion. She touched some chord in me . . .'

Marina's expression hardened. 'I'll never forget the way you were with her. So . . . abject.'

'I know. I wanted to make her my goddess, but I discovered she had feet of clay and then it was too late. She had me in her power.'

'Just as Olga has Bella in her power. It's weird, isn't it? Makes us all seem like puppets. And how do I know it's going to be any different with you and me?'

Justin sighed. He took her hand and played lightly with her fingers, struggling to find the right words. 'All we can do is have faith, Marina. It was good between us in Italy, but it may not last now we're back in England. I know that. All I ask is that we give it a try. Are you willing?'

Her eyes were the blue of an Italian sky as she smiled back at him. 'Yes, I'll give it a try.'

They kissed then, with all the fervour that they'd shared under those same Italian skies. Justin felt his soul expand and rouse itself from torpor, sending new wake-up signals throughout his body. His hand passed through the gap in her dressing gown and found the smooth, warm flesh of her thighs to caress. With a soft moan he explored the upper reaches, feeling the wiry mat of hair already wet with her love-dew, and knew that soon his pent-up desire for her would be satisfied. That wonderful prospect cheered him as he lifted her out of the chair and pulled her over to the bed, confident that she was experiencing the same heartfelt delight as he was.

Their tongues mingled in mutual passion, furling and licking, sending his libido soaring. Justin could feel the hard proof of his need for her nudging at her body, seeking admittance. He wanted to spear straight into her, and his fingers found her already wet and ready for him. She made no protest as he raised himself into position and found the way through her swollen labia to the door of her pussy, wide open to him.

Marina gave a little moan of assent as he lodged his glans in the humid entrance to her pussy. Then, as he pushed in, she clung to him tightly and squeezed his shaft all the way down. He nibbled at her ear lovingly, acknowledging her response, and they began to move together with instinctive rhythm. However he moved she was with him, fast or slow, like a part of his own body. She found new ways to pleasure them both, circling and bucking her hips in a wild horizontal dance, urging him on towards the inevitable cataclysm.

Justin felt the blind rush towards a climax begin but he didn't want it to happen, not yet. He opened his eyes and looked down at her in the dim morning light. Her face was rapt, beautiful. He kissed her closed eyelids tenderly and slowed his thrusting until he was barely moving at all. They remained locked together in bliss, absorbed in each other, content to let their bodies float adrift for a while.

Then Marina began to run her hands down the taut backs of his thighs. She felt between them and found his balls, scratching them softly with her nails and sending exquisite shudders through him. The urge to possess her returned, making him push his way deep into her, feeling the thick velvety walls swallow him up as he gave his cock its head. Now it was a rampant thing, full of demented energy as it shuttled in and out like a piston rod, making her squirm and cry out in joy. His whole shaft felt on fire, the glans like molten glass, buffeting her cervix.

After a while Justin was no longer conscious of what he was doing. His movements had become automatic and he was riding waves of pure erotic energy, pulsing towards a climax. Somewhere on the fringes of his awareness he knew that Marina was with him, that she would always be with him, that this was what they meant by love, and the knowledge spurred him on to greater heights. He knew that his pleasure would be hers, that they would meet at the peak, and that was all he cared about.

So when his orgasm burst from him like golden rain he knew that she was coming too, her vagina clasping his cock in great throbbing ripples, making his gratification all the more intense. He buried himself in her lush, hot body and let her take him completely into herself, using him for her pleasure, giving him back new knowledge of himself. 'I am a man in love,' he thought, and it no longer seemed strange but the most natural state to be in.

His lips formed the words soon afterwards. 'God, Marina, I love you!' he groaned as he rolled off her stomach and into the crook of her arm.

'I love you too,' she murmured, kissing his sweaty brow.

It was enough for now. Justin knew there were more things to talk about, but his body was satiated and that was all he wanted. The tensions and doubts of the past twenty-four hours were fading into dreamtime and a deeply contented glow was taking their place. The odd thing was, it was all so familiar as if he'd always known it would be like this if only he could meet the right woman. Well, now he had.

They stayed together all day. Neither of them had any commitments that week, although Justin's front-of-house job at a West End Theatre resumed the following Monday and Marina was planning to visit her sister in Reigate before starting her college course in September. They had a whole week for each other, and it became a wonderful journey of discovery. Justin took Marina out for a meal to celebrate their reunion then they returned to her flat for more love-making. This time, since Ed and Julie were out for the evening, they put on some Wagner and rode with the Valkyries.

Marina sat on top of him, magnificent in the light of a dozen candles with her golden hair flying out as she fucked him vigorously, and Justin knew that he had found a new goddess to worship, one whose intent towards him was pure. He had put away the dark goddess, the Queen of the Night, whose desire was only to feed her own lust for power. Equally splendid in her own way, she nevertheless required male sacrifice, and he wasn't going to play her game.

Instead Justin revelled in the subtler power of the Queen of the Light, all incandescent above him as she empowered his magic wand within her body. When he thrust it was upward, up to the heavens from where his bliss came, and as the glorious music swelled to a climax he felt the fountain of his love gush up within her and they were both lost in the exquisite communion that followed.

Afterwards they lay together happily, talking of their hopes and dreams. In September Marina was taking a full-time course in Operatic Studies at a London college, and she was very excited about it. She leapt out of bed to show him the syllabus and then confessed that she hoped it would lead to some kind of job with a professional company.

'I don't mind what I do at first. Of course I don't expect to get prima donna rôles straight away. But if I could only sing in the chorus it would be a start. How about you, Justin? What do you want out of life?'

'I'm joining the Norwood Operatic Society in September. That's as far ahead as I can look right now. Of course I'll go on having lessons, and since I'm already working in the theatre I'm getting good experience. But as for singing professionally . . . well, I don't know.'

'Why have doubts? You've got a good voice, you know that. And the fact that we won the festival competition . . .'

Justin made an angry noise. 'What does that mean? You know very well why we won. She just wanted to lure us back into her clutches, both of us.'

Marina sat up, perturbed. 'You don't really think that, do you?'

'Yes, I do. It had little to do with merit. Oh, we sang pretty well but so did several others.'

Marina looked ready to burst into tears. 'I don't know

197

how you can be so mean, Justin! I felt really proud of having won, and I thought you did too.'

He took her into his arms and said soothingly, 'Think about it, Marina. Do you really feel happy about the way the course went? When I arrived I had high hopes of catching Bella's eye. I thought if I impressed her she might recommend me, help me get somewhere. I never imagined things would turn out the way they did. I'm as disappointed as you, can't you see?'

'So the whole thing was pointless, is that what you're saying?'

He laughed. 'Silly girl! How could it possibly be pointless if it brought us together? Besides, I've learnt a great deal over the past few weeks. Not only about opera and singing, but about myself. And I suspect you have too.'

'Mm,' she said, doubtfully. 'But I'd hate to think that woman has put you off opera altogether.'

'She hasn't. But now I've seen at close quarters how big stars like her behave I'm not sure I want to mix with them.'

'They're not all like her, surely?'

'No. But it's still a strange world, Marina. The power of opera is special. It makes use of words, music, drama – three powerful elements in themselves. Combined, they work a special kind of magic and it takes a special kind of person to handle it. Those who do often seem to pay a fearful price in their private life, and now I've got you I'm not sure I want to pay that price.'

Marina said nothing, evidently brooding on his words, but he kissed and caressed her until she became a sensual animal again and feeling took over from thinking. This time, when they made love, it was with a special kind of confidence – in each other, and in their joint future. Justin felt sure of her but, even more important, he felt sure of himself. He was a man who had faced his demons and, somehow, come to terms with them.

Chapter Fourteen

Marina was in the kitchen when Justin produced the tickets from his wallet with a flourish. She had just finished ironing some costumes for the *Beggars Opera* that a local operatic society were putting on, and her back was aching. She stared at the two tickets incredulously at first, then with increasing delight.

'*Magic Flute* at Covent Garden! Oh, you are wonderful!'

'Look at the date,' he smiled.

'The twelfth – our anniversary!'

'So all you have to do is make sure your mother can baby-sit. I did have a word with her a while back, hinting that we wanted to do something special on our fifth wedding anniversary, so I think you'll find she kept the date free.'

Marina flung her arms around his neck and kissed him. 'You think of everything, don't you?'

'When it's important, yes.'

He left the room and she read the tickets again, just to make sure. The production was a daringly modern one that had earned great critical acclaim. Front row of the circle, perfect. It was ages since she'd been to Covent Garden. And *the Magic Flute,* too! Usually she had to make do with whatever production the local players were putting on. Sometimes she had a small part, the most she could manage now she had Toby and Jake. But generally she just acted as assistant wardrobe mistress, which tended to mean washing and ironing and mending.

Not that she minded too much. The boys were worth giving up her ambitions for and, anyway, she kept up with the world of opera through Justin. His post as touring manager for a small professional company meant he was away from home a lot, but at least he was working in the field he'd always loved.

Sometimes Marina wondered if he'd regretted giving up his singing, but once the boys came along the uncertainties of a singing career had to be ditched in favour of a regular income. If he had regrets he never showed them. And they were a happy family, Marina told herself proudly, hearing the boys' shouts of laughter as Justin played with them in the lounge.

Not only that, but after five years of marriage Justin could still make her toes curl. She gave a catlike smile of satisfaction as she recalled their love-making of the previous night, when he had taken her from behind with his hands roving all over her breasts, eager fingers pulling at her nipples, stroking her clitoris while he banged away inside her until she came with remarkable force and pleasure.

Then they'd collapsed sideways with him still erect inside her, only to start up again after a brief rest. This time they'd taken it easy, revelling in their mutual sensuality, feeling the slow build-up towards a mutual orgasm that had them gently vibrating in harmony. Marina never ceased to wonder at the variety of their love-making. It was the cornerstone of their marriage.

Some of her married girlfriends complained that their sex-life had grown boring, but with her and Justin it was always exciting. Perhaps because he was away such a lot. Whenever he came back from a tour they practically tore the clothes off each other in their eagerness to make love.

Carefully hanging the gaudy costumes in three portable wardrobes, Marina began to reminisce about their early days together. They'd seemed so young then, returning from Italy in a state of confusion before realising that they were truly in love and prepared to make a go of it. Those first months had been difficult for both of them, meeting at weekends and trying to sort out the emotional mess that their time at the *Villa Gandolfini* had produced.

Sometimes, even now, she really hated Bella and that vile Olga. She had the idea, probably false, that Justin might have been less complicated in his approach to sex if he hadn't been subject to their bizarre whims. Not that it seemed to have had any long-term effect. Sometimes, just for fun, she played at being the dominatrix, but it was all for their mutual pleasure and she would never dream of going as far as those women had. To this day she didn't know in detail how they'd treated him, and she didn't want to know, either.

That ill-fated summer school had scarcely been mentioned since, but Marina couldn't help following *La Bellissima*'s subsequent career. She was often mentioned in the operatic press, sometimes in the Sunday papers. There had even been a documentary about her on television. But after her triumphant rôle in *Canton* she had mysteriously faded from the scene. Some said her voice was spent. She was, after all, forty-three.

On the morning of their wedding anniversary Justin couldn't wait to give Marina the present he'd bought for her. She unwrapped the bright package eagerly and found a complete set of Buonarotti's finest performances. She was overjoyed. But, in the midst of her happiness she couldn't help remembering how she'd once expected to meet him. The memory of Bella's perfidy still stung, even now.

Justin had given her money to buy a new dress for the occasion and she spent the afternoon getting ready while her mother amused the children. It was lovely to soak in a sensual bath of her favourite perfume, to make herself up at leisure and coil her shoulder-length fair hair up on her head, secured by combs of fake tortoiseshell and diamanté. She didn't get much of a chance to dress up these days, but tonight she was pulling out all the stops.

The dress, which she'd chosen from a designer collection in a 'nearly new' boutique, was a wonderful creation by a fashion student who was starting to make her name on the catwalks. Not one of her more flamboyant efforts, but an inspired blend of royal blue velvet shot with purple and a matching purple devoré jacket. The dress had a low sweetheart neckline and made Marina feel very feminine, and she added the crystal drop earrings that Justin had given her on their last anniversary and which gave her eyes extra sparkle.

For a few seconds, there in the bedroom, a moment of self-doubt assailed her. What if, five years down the line, their marriage wasn't as rock solid as it appeared? Already several of her friends were divorced and, in a couple of cases, they'd had no inkling that anything was wrong until their husbands confessed to having serious affairs. Had she let herself go, become boring or unattractive? The face that regarded her wistfully from the mirror was still pretty. She shouldn't worry. Yet, as she went downstairs, there was a nagging doubt in the back of her mind about the evening ahead. What if something went wrong with their celebration? What if cracks they'd been ignoring up to now began to show?

'You look wonderful, dear!' her mother smiled in approval when she appeared. Justin said nothing, but the light in his eyes expressed it all, restoring her confidence. Everything was fine, and they were going to have a lovely time. Her little wobbly had been nerves, that was all. The kind of nerves that singers had before a performance. She did so want everything to be perfect for their anniversary night out.

Glowing with excitement, Marina enjoyed the ride through London. It was going to be an evening of fairy tale romance and she was looking forward to it tremendously. Two of her favourite singers were billed to appear, with Eloise Cartier playing the Queen of the Night rôle that Bella had once made her own. Well, a new generation of singers was taking over now, Marina thought with satisfaction. They were strong on dedication and teamwork, not like the old prima donnas of which Bella was the prime example. Eloise was known for her sweet nature and intelligent interpretation of any rôle she was called upon to perform.

The foyer of Covent Garden was thronging with people by the time they arrived. For once Marina felt at home amongst the *glitterati*. She smiled to think of all the performances she'd attended there as a student, queuing for returns at the box office and, more often than not, ending up in the 'Gods'. She took Justin's arm as they ascended the staircase, proud to be there with him in one of the great opera houses of the world.

In his dress suit, with his dark hair impeccably groomed, he was still gorgeous to her eyes. Although his face and body had filled out since they first met he had retained much of his boyish charm and Marina knew they made a good-looking couple. People were giving them more than a passing glance, liking what they saw. They held themselves well, moving amongst the crowd with graceful ease, and she knew that Justin was feeling equally proud of her.

They found their seats and Justin produced a small box of the exquisite hand-made chocolates which she adored. She settled back in her seat, picking up the opera glasses and preparing for the delights to come. Slowly the auditorium filled and the orchestra tuned up, the air of expectation reaching a crescendo as the appointed time for the performance to begin approached. Marina put her arm through Justin's and whispered in his ear, 'This is going to be great. Thank you, darling!'

'My pleasure,' he smiled back. 'And my thanks, for five wonderful years.'

It did cross Marina's mind, momentarily, that this was all a bit too good to be true, but she didn't give it a second thought. Only when the curtains parted to reveal a worried-looking man in a dress suit instead of the expected stage-set, did her suspicion that something was going to go wrong intensify. He put up his hand for silence and Marina sat, tense and apprehensive, while he addressed the audience.

'Good evening, Ladies and Gentleman. Before this evening's performance begins I have an announcement to make. Unfortunately, Miss Cartier has become suddenly indisposed and is unable to appear tonight.' A murmur of disappointment went round the theatre, which he weathered bravely. 'We were planning to cancel, but by a happy co-incidence another great singer has offered to step in at the last minute, for which we are extremely grateful. I know that you will all be delighted to hear that the part of Queen of the Night will be sung, for tonight's performance only, by that supreme interpreter of the rôle, Bella Conti.'

The buzz of surprise that rippled through the audience was followed swiftly by applause. Marina and Justin were like an island of stunned silence in the midst of it all, unable to believe what they had just heard. To Marina, it seemed horribly ominous. Here they were, celebrating five years of marriage, and now that ghost from the past had resurrected herself in the most dramatic way. It was easy to believe, superstitiously, that the substitution had been arranged by a malevolent fate, purposely to taunt them.

A man in the row behind murmured, 'This should be interesting!' Marina knew what his wry tone implied. Tonight would be the perfect proof of whether Bella really was 'past it' or not. Once she could have sung the part practically in her sleep, but now? It was extremely brave of her to step into a new production at the last minute, without much chance to rehearse. Marina couldn't help feeling a grudging admiration for the star, knowing what a risk she was taking. But her main concern, right now, was Justin.

She turned to look at her husband. He was staring straight ahead at the empty space in the curtains where the manager had stood, his face dark and unreadable. Squeezing his arm with hers she murmured, trying to sound casual, 'What a weird coincidence! On our anniversary, of all nights!'

His gaze was frightening in its haunted intensity. 'Coincidence?'

'Of course. What else could it be?'

'I wouldn't put anything past that woman!' he muttered, darkly.

Marina was instantly transported back where she didn't want to be, into the past. His old obsession with that woman had been a thorn in her side during the first year or so of their relationship but she had believed it to be well and truly over. Seeing him react like this now, she wasn't so sure.

The overture began, reminiscent of a world reassuringly ordered and familiar, then the stage came to life, a panoply of baroque splendour and strong, confident voices. Marina found herself sitting tensely, almost holding her breath and quite unable to relax and enjoy the performance. She was filled with suppressed anger that what should have been a delightful evening was turning into a nightmare. As the cue for Bella's appearance approached she could hardly bear the suspense.

Pamina was alone on the stage and the lights dimmed. Suddenly, against a backdrop of a dark, starry sky, the Queen of the Night was lowered in a silvery cage. She looked magnificent in a shimmering blue-black gown sewn with silver stars and with a crescent moon head-dress. A halo of shimmering light surrounded her, and at first Marina found it hard to believe it was really Bella. As soon as she began to sing, however, the familiar timbre of her voice sent shivers down her spine.

As the aria proceeded there was an eerie difference in her voice, a kind of ethereal wavering that at first Marina thought was being used for deliberate effect but, after a few bars, she wasn't so sure. There was a restlessness amongst the audience that told her they were uneasy about it too. She looked at Justin. He was staring at the stage as if mesmerised, an expression of incredulity on his face. The trilling solo proceeded to its incredible height and the uncertainty in the prima donna's voice increased so that, by the time she was faced with her top F it was obvious to everyone that she wasn't going to make it. The note cracked and died, the orchestra carried on but there was an embarrassing hiatus in the singing.

Marina felt incredibly tense, unsure of what she felt. The mixture of emotions was intense and it was making her want to get out of there, to flee from the scene of the great *diva*'s public humiliation. Even now she was willing her to recover, to carry on as if nothing had happened, but Bella was clearly in distress. The woman playing Pamina didn't know what to do. She was wringing her hands in a genuine display of distress while Bella floated there in weird suspension, her face a pale mask. The man in the row behind said, gruffly, 'They should bring down the curtain. Put the poor cow out of her misery.'

Despite everything she'd felt about Bella Conti, all the grudges she bore her, Marina couldn't help feeling deeply sorry for the woman as the cage, bearing its crumpled, defeated cargo, swung off into the wings and the curtain was belatedly pulled down. No-one in the audience knew how to react. A few unfeeling individuals uttered catcalls, but they were emphatically 'shushed' by those of finer sensibilities.

The manager came on stage, a model of solicitous apology. 'Ladies and Gentlemen, I'm sure you will want to join me in applauding Signora Conti's brave effort this evening. It was not her fault that she could not sustain her performance. Due to technical reasons she was forced to sing under conditions that her vocal range could not sustain. Please join me in expressing our gratitude for her valiant effort in attempting to stand in for Miss Cartier who will, we hope, be able to resume her performances next week. Miss Bella Conti, Ladies and Gentlemen.'

The applause rang to the rafters, but Bella did not appear. Neither Marina nor Justin felt able to join in, but sat in mortified silence imagining what the *diva* must be feeling. Despite everything she had been a great star, and it was distressing to see her unable to shine as she used to.

The scene was scrapped and the opera continued as best it could, limping through to its conclusion with a mediocre singer performing as Queen of the Night an octave lower. It made a farce of Mozart's work but at least it enabled the other singers to pursue their rôles as best they could. At the end, the man in the row behind – whom Marina had come to hate – announced to his companion that he would be demanding a refund at the box office.

'A travesty, that's all it was!' he pronounced. 'I mean, we don't come here expecting a charity performance by has-beens, do we? Disgraceful, I call it.'

'She did her best, dear,' soothed his companion.

'Well it wasn't good enough, was it? I never did see why people raved about her, anyhow. Grossly overrated, that's what I've always thought of her.'

Marina and Justin got to their feet and began shuffling to the end of the row. She felt utterly deflated. The evening that she'd been so looking forward to had been a disaster, and now she had no desire to join Justin in the supper he'd booked for them. All she wanted to do was get home and forget about the evening, as soon as possible. She imagined that was what Bella would want to do, too.

But it was not what Justin wanted. When they reached the end of the row he turned back towards the stage, his face tense and resolute. 'I have to see her, Marina.'

'What?'

'I have to go to her. She must be feeling terrible.'

'No! Justin, you can't! Please, for my sake . . .'

But he was already battling against the crowd that was streaming up the aisle, making for the backstage door. Marina knew she couldn't let him go alone. If he was going to confront that woman she must be there with him. She was his wife, after all, and this was their wedding anniversary. That must count for something, surely?

As she struggled to follow in his wake her heart felt heavy and there was a sick dread in her stomach. All the old insecurity was returning, the feeling that Bella held him in thrall and there was nothing she could do to break the spell. The years in between seemed to count for nothing when she surveyed his dark, obsessed face and the determined set of his jaw.

The musicians were packing up their instruments in the pit, the ushers attending to the crowd, and no-one seemed to notice the pair who slipped through the door marked 'No Exit' and into the passage that led to the dressing rooms. They found Bella's more by luck than judgement. The door was ajar and they could hear the unmistakable sound of Olga's voice murmuring what sounded like comforting phrases in Italian.

Justin only hesitated for a moment, then marched straight in. The two women gasped to see him. Bella was wearing a green silk dressing-gown, her face still painted with exaggerated stage make-up that had become grotesquely smeared. The gown that had looked so glamorous on stage was hanging up behind her, but now it looked piecemeal and tawdry, its spangles obviously re-positioned and the seams held together with tacking where it had been hastily let out to make it fit.

'You!' she said, her eyes glittering with anger. 'How dare you appear like this, after all this time, unannounced and unwelcome!'

'I'm sorry, Bella . . .'

'If you've come to gloat you can leave right now!' Olga snapped. 'If you are not gone by the time I count to three I shall call the porters and have you thrown out, the pair of you!'

'No, we are here as friends,' he said placatingly. Marina felt strangely guilty, since she had little in the way of friendly feeling. Yet she knew she had to be there, for Justin's sake.

'I never counted you amongst my friends,' Bella said, wearily. 'Fans, yes. There is a difference, you know.'

'I know. All I meant was, I came to say I thought you were incredibly brave tonight. I know you'll probably get a slating from the critics, but that's not how your true fans will regard you. We all admire you. We all wish . . . you . . . well . . .'

To Marina's horror, he burst into tears. She felt as if she were in the middle of some strange opera herself, one where she didn't know the libretto. At first she stood there gaping, then made ineffectual efforts to put her arms around him while Olga poured out a stream of Italian invective.

At last Marina found her tongue. She stared at Bella crossly. 'What is she saying?' she demanded.

'She says tears and sympathy are the last thing I need right now.' Bella gave a weary smile. 'I think a stiff drink would be more helpful, don't you, Olga? Let's all toast times gone by. Go and fetch four large brandies from the bar.'

'Are you sure? You might not sleep . . .'

Bella's hooded eyes regarded her friend with barely disguised contempt. 'If I sleep or not it hardly matters now, does it? Hurry, Olga, before the bar closes. I don't think I have the clout to get a drink after hours these days, do I? Not like the old days, when there was always a crate of champagne in my room after the show.'

Olga muttered something that made Bella frown and then, suddenly, the three of them were alone in the cluttered dressing room. An awkward silence fell. Then Bella said, 'So, the two of you are still together. I must say I'm surprised.'

Marina felt compelled to say, 'We've been married five years. Tonight is our wedding anniversary.'

Bella's full, sensual mouth twisted into a bitter smile. 'Congratulations!'

'We have two sons, aged three and eighteen months,' Marina continued. Although she was well aware that she was rubbing salt into the wound she just couldn't help it.

Bella shrugged. 'Your domestic life does not interest me. Obviously neither of you profited from your tuition at the *Accademia del Voce*. What a waste of two fine voices!'

'We're still connected to opera,' Justin said, too eagerly for Marina's liking. 'I work as manager for a small touring company. And Marina helps make costumes for an amateur group. We could never give up opera entirely, you see. We love it too much.'

'You cannot love opera too much,' Bella said. 'If you do, she destroys you. You give her everything, the Muse, and still she demands more. You sing like a trapped bird, you make your swan song for her, and still she demands your humiliation. Tonight I made my sacrifice to the Muse and still it is not enough, still she wants more.'

Marina stared into her wild, rolling eyes and listened to her histrionic ramblings with contempt, only just tinged with pity. That woman's whole life was lived like an opera – a soap opera – she now realised. The grand passions, bizarre fantasies and larger-than-life rôles that she lived out on stage she attempted to equal in her private life, with disastrous results. Well, tonight public and private lives had met in one. She was playing the tragic heroine for all she was worth, the fallen Goddess, the noble failure.

Justin was listening to her in rapt silence, which irritated Marina all the more. Surely he wasn't being taken in by that woman's ravings? The door opened abruptly and Olga entered with a tray of drinks. Marina didn't want to take one, but she found herself going along with it. She took a sip of the raw, caramel-flavoured spirit and felt it sear its way down to her stomach.

'These two,' Bella said, turning to Olga. 'They're married, two kids. What a waste!'

Olga gave a sneering laugh. 'They'd never have made it anyway. You have to have balls to get where you are, Bella.'

'Where I've *been*, you mean.' Bella's tone had become threatening. 'Why pretend any more, Olga? I'm a has-been. You've been suspecting it for the past two years, I've secretly known it. Well tonight I've proved it, to the whole, wide world. And I hope everyone is satisfied. Now I can retire gracefully!'

'Why did you do it?' Justin asked. 'Why did you take the risk? You didn't have to.' Bella put down her glass. Her face looked weary, heavily-lined and clownish under the streaky make-up, and Marina felt a cruel desire to see it cleaned off, revealing her naked, ageing skin. She watched as the *diva* reached for Justin's hand and, holding it between her own, patting it in a way that at first seemed condescending.

'My dear boy, I *did* have to, don't you see? I was in London, and Monty came to me. He said they needed a stand-in for the Queen. Of course, he gave me a get-out clause. "I know you are resting, not rehearsed in the part," he said. But he knew I was never one to turn down a challenge. He persuaded me I could still do it. In my sleep, he said. I thought so too. But after a while the voice becomes . . . unreliable. It is hard to accept, you see. For years you have trained and trained, you know the strengths and weaknesses of your voice so well. You know the effect of the weather, of certain foods, of medicines. You know how you are affected by your own hormones, your own moods. It is all under your control, you see. And then, one day, you sing a certain note – a top C perhaps – one that you have sung effortlessly so many times before, and suddenly it is not your note. It is a weak, cracked sound, not your sound at all. You try again: it works a little better. But something has begun, a process of doubt, of unreliability. You over-compensate with your breathing. You try a different diet. You seek expert advice. Yet all the time you know there is no ultimate remedy. It is the slow death of the voice that you are hearing. And, for a singer, that is also the voice of death.'

There was silence in the room. Marina felt choked, her own voice dead in her throat. She could see that the tears were streaming down Justin's cheeks but she could do nothing, say nothing. Olga was staring glassily into space and Bella was looked perfectly composed, as if she had at last accepted the inevitable. She picked up her glass and swallowed the rest of her brandy, then turned in her swivel chair and began, methodically, to remove her make-up with cotton wool balls of cold cream.

'I'm sorry,' Justin said, his voice faraway. 'I shouldn't . . . I mean, I should have known you'd be feeling bad. I . . . we'll go now.'

Bella gave him a radiant smile. 'Thank you, all the same.' She held up her arms to him and he gave himself up to her embrace. Marina felt embarrassed, but then it was her turn. She felt a slick cheek being pressed to hers, smelt the faint odour of sweat and greasepaint. The air seemed sweeter once she was released.

Olga merely nodded abruptly at them as they left. Evidently she couldn't wait to get them out of the room and have Bella all to herself again. As they walked back through the corridor towards the exit Marina clung to Justin's arm, needing the warm reassurance of his bulk. She was filled with contradictory emotions and didn't know what to do about it.

'I think we should go for that meal regardless,' he said, as they emerged into the night air.

'I don't feel very hungry.'

'You will, once you smell the food,' he grinned. 'Come on. It's not far. They specialise in tempting late-night meals for opera-goers.'

He was right, once they were ensconced in the corner of the restaurant with a delicious array of dishes being wafted past their noses Marina felt her appetite return with a vengeance. While they ate they discussed the performance, omitting all mention of Bella and concentrating on the other singers who had all given of their best in obviously difficult circumstances. Only when they were in the taxi on the way home did Justin bring up the subject of Bella.

'I had to go to her tonight, you know,' he began. 'She meant so much to me at one time. But I'm over her, you needn't worry about that. I just see her as a pathetic woman facing a lonely middle age without the thing she loves the most.'

'I think that's a bit unfair. She's got Olga, at least. I'm sure she won't be abandoned by Luigi either. And she can always teach.'

'But she'll miss the adulation, the glory. I know she will.' Justin sighed, squeezing her hand. 'You know, love, I used to think I'd give anything to be a great star, like her. But now I've seen another side to it, had a glimpse of the pressures she's under. I think she's been driven more than a little crazy by it all.'

'I'm with you there!' Marina laughed.

He leaned close, his breath warm against her ear. 'And I tell you another thing, I wouldn't trade what we have – you, me and the boys – for anything in the world!'

He kissed her gently, sending slow swirls of desire curling through her, making her long to arrive back home so they could go straight to bed. For the rest of the journey they kissed intermittently, keeping the flame alive until they could give it full rein. Once indoors they found the house quiet, Marina's mother and the boys all asleep. Justin put his finger on his lips and led her into the lounge. He lit the gas fire and the two candles on the mantelpiece then pulled out the sofa bed.

Marina knew just what he was doing, and why. They had made love in that room, on that bed, on their wedding night. The bedroom was being decorated at the time and they didn't even have a proper bed so they'd had to make do, but neither of them had cared. Even at the end of their long, tiring wedding day they were still eager to fall into each others' arms.

The same was true now. Watching him make the bed ready Marina felt an aching need for him, despite her earlier upset. It had been a very emotional evening, not unlike their wedding day in that respect, and she needed the reassurance of his warm body close to hers. When he had made up the bed he hesitated, then moved towards the cabinet that held their CD collection. He took out his favourite: The Best of La Bellissima. The picture on the front showed her in the midnight blue gown studded with silver stars that had become her trademark.

'That was Bella at the height of her power,' Justin said, his voice sad.

He didn't have to spell out the rest. Putting the CD on at low volume, he came over to where Marina was sitting and took her in his arms. 'You don't think we'll wake them, do you?'

'I doubt it. They all sleep like logs.'

'We didn't have them to worry about on our wedding night, did we?' Justin grinned, taking off her shoes. His hands caressed her feet through her tights, making her legs tingle and glow. They moved to the bed and the strains of *O Soave Fanciulla* lifted their spirits until they were kissing passionately, remembering how they had felt singing the same poignant refrain.

The exquisite singing roused Justin urgently so that he didn't even wait for them to undress. He lifted up Marina's crumpled dress until he was able to pull down her tights then his mouth kissed her pussy through the thin, damp layer of silk, making her moan with frustration. His finger found its way in through one leg and when he touched the overheated bud of her clitoris she sighed contentedly.

'I want you to come straight into me,' she told him. 'I'm more than ready for you.'

His finger slipped down into the liquid entrance to her quim. 'Oh yes you are, aren't you!' he grinned, full of pride in his ability to arouse his wife. Impatiently Marina pulled the dress up over her head and unhitched her bra so that her breasts flopped out. They weren't quite as firm as on their wedding night, but she was still proud of them. Justin's mouth nuzzled against her nipple, filling her with increased desire, and she reached down towards his fly to feel the solid meat of his prick pushing against her hand.

'Quick, let me undo you!' she begged.

There was a quick scramble while she unzipped his fly and pulled the rampant cock out of his pants. Now it was her turn to feel pride in her ability to arouse her husband. A brief tussle followed, both of them wanting to be on top, but Marina won. She pulled off her bra and pants then plunged herself down onto his erection, feeling the warm, hard shaft of him fill her up inside with satisfying completeness.

The music reached a crescendo and she worked towards hers, confident in her ability to give and receive pleasure. Her hips swivelled and bucked to maximise their joint friction and soon she was speeding helplessly towards an orgasm, the keen sensations ripping through her like electric shocks. Justin groaned when he felt her pulsating pussy clench his organ, but somehow he managed to hold out, knowing that his services would be required again soon.

While they lay in each others' arms, listening to the supremely beautiful aria from *Madame Butterfly*, tears sprang into Marina's eyes. 'She was so great, wasn't she?'

'Mm. But we mustn't confuse art and life. I thought what I felt for her was love, but it was only obsession, infatuation. Only when I met you did I discover what love really means.'

'Yet she sings as if she really means it.'

'That's great art. Sometimes it's hard to live up to in real life, and I guess that's the price Bella has paid. I'm so glad I've got you, my love. I'd be a lost soul, otherwise.'

Justin turned to her, letting her see the warmth in his eyes that was far more than reflected candlelight, and found the same glow in hers. She was his Queen of the Night and Day, she lit up his darkness. And together they soared effortlessly to the heights, time and time again.

A Message from the Publisher

Headline Liaison is a new concept in erotic fiction: a list of books designed for the reading pleasure of both men and women, to be read alone – or together with your lover. As such, we would be most interested to hear from our readers.

Did you read the book with your partner? Did it fire your imagination? Did it turn you on – or off? Did you like the story, the characters, the setting? What did you think of the cover presentation? In short, what's your opinion? If you care to offer it, please write to:

> The Editor
> Headline Liaison
> 338 Euston Road
> London NW1 3BH

Or maybe you think you could do better if you wrote an erotic novel yourself. We are always on the look-out for new authors. If you'd like to try your hand at writing a book for possible inclusion in the Liaison list, here are our basic guidelines: We are looking for novels of approximately 80,000 words in which the erotic content should aim to please both men and women and should not describe illegal sexual activity (pedophilia, for example). The novel should contain sympathetic and interesting characters, pace, atmosphere and an intriguing plotline.

If you'd like to have a go, please submit to the Editor a sample of at least 10,000 words, clearly typed on one side of the paper only, together with a short resume of the storyline. Should you wish your material returned to you please include a stamped addressed envelope. If we like it sufficiently, we will offer you a contract for publication.

Adult Fiction for Lovers from Headline LIAISON

PLEASE TEASE ME	Rebecca Ambrose	£5.99
A PRIVATE EDUCATION	Carol Anderson	£5.99
IMPULSE	Kay Cavendish	£5.99
TRUE COLOURS	Lucinda Chester	£5.99
CHANGE PARTNERS	Cathryn Cooper	£5.99
SEDUCTION	Cathryn Cooper	£5.99
THE WAYS OF A WOMAN	J J Duke	£5.99
FORTUNE'S TIDE	Cheryl Mildenhall	£5.99
INTIMATE DISCLOSURES	Cheryl Mildenhall	£5.99
ISLAND IN THE SUN	Susan Sebastian	£5.99

All Headline Liaison books are available at your local bookshop or newsagent, or can be ordered direct from the publisher. Just tick the titles you want and fill in the form below. Prices and availability subject to change without notice.

Headline Book Publishing, Cash Sales Department, Bookpoint, 39 Milton Park, Abingdon, OXON, OX14 4TD, UK. If you have a credit card you may order by telephone – 01235 400400.

Please enclose a cheque or postal order made payable to Bookpoint Ltd to the value of the cover price and allow the following for postage and packing: UK & BFPO: £1.00 for the first book, 50p for the second book and 30p for each additional book ordered up to a maximum charge of £3.00. OVERSEAS & EIRE: £2.00 for the first book, £1.00 for the second book and 50p for each additional book.

Name ....

Address ....

....

....

If you would prefer to pay by credit card, please complete:
Please debit my Visa/Access/Diner's Card/American Express
(Delete as applicable) card no:

Signature .... Expiry Date ....